William Henry Giles Kingston

The south sea whaler

A story of the loss

William Henry Giles Kingston

The south sea whaler
A story of the loss

ISBN/EAN: 9783337192785

Printed in Europe, USA, Canada, Australia, Japan

Cover: Foto ©Andreas Hilbeck / pixelio.de

More available books at **www.hansebooks.com**

THE SOUTH SEA WHALER:

A STORY OF THE LOSS OF THE "CHAMPION," AND THE ADVENTURES OF HER CREW.

WRECK OF THE PRIZE.

Page 360

Thomas Nelson and Sons,

LONDON, EDINBURGH, AND NEW YORK

THE SOUTH SEA WHALER:

A STORY OF THE LOSS OF THE "CHAMPION," AND THE ADVENTURES OF HER CREW.

BY

W. H. G. KINGSTON,

AUTHOR OF "OLD JACK," "IN THE EASTERN SEAS," "ON THE BANKS
OF THE AMAZON," "IN THE WILDS OF AFRICA," ETC.

" 'Twas theirs to mourn misfortune's rudest shock,
Scourged by the waves and cradled on the rock."

CAMPBELL

LONDON:
T. NELSON AND SONS, PATERNOSTER ROW;
EDINBURGH; AND NEW YORK.

1879.

Contents.

CHAPTER I.

CHAPTER II.

CHAPTER III.

CHAPTER IV.

CHAPTER V.

CONTENTS.

CHAPTER XIII.

CHAPTER XIV.

CHAPTER XV.

THE SOUTH SEA WHALER.

CHAPTER I.

"A PROSPEROUS voyage, and a quick return, Captain Tredcagle," said the old pilot as he bade farewell to the commander of the *Champion*, which ship he had piloted down the Mersey on her voyage to the Pacific.

"Thank you, pilot. I suppose it will be pretty nearly three years before we are back again,—with a full cargo, I hope, and plenty of dollars to keep the pot boiling at home. It's the last voyage I intend to make; for thirty years knocking about at sea is enough for any man."

"Many say that, captain; but when the time comes they generally find a reason for making one voyage more, to help them to start with a better capital. But as you have got your young ones aboard, you will have their company to cheer you."

As the old pilot stepped along the deck he shook hands with two young people, a boy and a girl, who were standing near the gangway.

"Good-bye, Walter; good-bye, Miss Alice; look after father, and obey him, and God will bless you. If we are all spared, I hope to see you, Walter, grown into a tall young man; and you, Miss Alice, I suppose I shan't know you again. Good-bye; Heaven protect you." Saying this, the old pilot lowered himself into his boat alongside, and pulled away for his cutter, which lay hove-to at a little distance.

The *Champion* was a South Sea whaler of about four hundred tons burden; with a crew, including Mr. Andrew Lawrie, the surgeon, of fifty officers and men. The chief object of the voyage was the capture of the sperm whale,—which creature is found in various parts of the Pacific Ocean; but as the war in which England had been engaged since the commencement of the century was not over, she carried eight guns, which would serve to defend her both against civilized enemies and the savage inhabitants of the islands she was likely to visit. The usual license for carrying guns, or "Letters of Marque," had been obtained for her by the owners; she was thus able not only to defend herself, but to attack and capture, if she could, any vessels of the enemy she might meet with. Captain

Tredeagle, being a peace-loving man, had no intention of exercising this privilege,—his only wish being to dispose of the ventures he carried, and to obtain by honest exertions a full cargo of sperm oil.

Walter and Alice waved their hands to the old pilot as his little vessel, close-hauled, stood away towards the mouth of the river. It seemed to them that in parting from him the last link which bound them to their native land was severed. They left many friends behind them; but it was their father's wish that they should accompany him, and they eagerly looked forward to the pleasure of seeing the beautiful islands they were likely to visit, and witnessing the strange sights they expected to meet with during the voyage.

While the pilot vessel was standing away, the head-yards of the *Champion* were swung round, the sails sheeted home; with a brisk northerly wind, and under all the canvas she could carry, she ran quickly down the Irish Channel.

"Here we are away at last," said Captain Tredeagle, as his children stood by his side; "and now, Walter, we must make a sailor of you as fast as possible. Don't be ashamed to ask questions, and get information from any one who is ready to give it. Our old mate, Jacob Shobbrok, who has sailed with me pretty nearly since I came to sea, is as anxious to teach you as you can be to get instruction; but remember,

Walter, you must begin at the beginning, and learn how to knot and splice, and reef, and steer, and box the compass, before you begin on the higher branches of seamanship. You will learn fast enough, however, if you keep your eyes and ears open and your wits about you, and try to get at the why and wherefore of everything. Many fail to be worth much at sea as well as on shore, because they are too proud to learn their A B C. Just think of that, my son."

"I will do my best, father, to follow your advice," answered Walter, a fine lad between fourteen and fifteen years of age. His sister Alice was two years younger,—a fair, pretty-looking girl, with the hue of health on her cheeks, which showed that she was well able to endure the vicissitudes of climate, or any hardships to which she might possibly be subjected at sea.

When Captain Tredeagle resolved to take his children with him, he had no expectation of exposing them to dangers or hardships. He had been thirty years afloat, and had never been wrecked, and he did not suppose that such an occurrence was ever likely to happen to him. He forgot the old adage, that "the pitcher which goes often to the well is liable to be broken at last." He had lost his wife during his previous voyage, and had no one on whom he could rely to take care of his motherless children while he was absent from home. Walter had expressed a strong wish to go to sea, so he naturally took him; and with regard to Alice, of two evils he chose that which he considered the least. He had seen the dangers to which girls deprived of a mother's watchful care are exposed on shore, and he knew that on board his ship, at all events, Alice would be safe from them. Having no great respect for the ordinary female accomplishments of music and dancing, he felt himself fully competent to instruct her in most other matters, while he rightly believed that her mind would be expanded by visiting the strange and interesting scenes to which during the voyage he hoped to introduce her. " As for needle-work and embroidery, why, Jacob and I can teach you as well as can most women ; and our black fellow Nub will cut out your dresses with all the skill and taste of a practised mantua-maker," he had said when talking to Alice on the subject of her going.

Alice was delighted to accompany her father, and hoped to be a real comfort to him. She would take charge of his cabin and keep it in beautiful order, and repair his clothes, and take care that a button was never wanting ; and would pour out his coffee and tea, and write out his journal and keep his accounts, she hoped. And should he fall sick, how carefully she would watch over him ; indeed, she flattered herself that she could be of no slight use. Then, she might be a companion to Walter, who might otherwise become as rough and rude as some ship-boys she had seen ; not that it was his nature to be rough, she thought, but she had often written in her copy-book, "Evil communications corrupt good manners," and Walter's truly good manners might deteriorate among the rough crew of the whaler. Alice also intended to be very diligent with her books, and she could learn geography in a practical way few young ladies are able to enjoy. And, lastly, she had a sketch-book and a colour-box, by means of which she hoped to make numberless drawings of the scenery and people she was to visit. Altogether, she was not likely to find the time hang heavy on her hands.

In many respects she was not disappointed in her expectations. As soon as the ship was clear of the Channel and fairly at sea, her father began the course of instruction he intended to pursue during the voyage. Mr. Jacob Shobbrok the mate, and Nub, delighted to impart such feminine accomplishments as they possessed; and it amused her to see how deftly their strong hands plied their needles.

Nub, as the black steward was generally called, had been for the best part of his life at sea with her father. He had been christened Nubia, which name was abridged into Nub; and sometimes she and Walter, when they were little children, had been accustomed, as a term of endearment, to call him "Nubby," and even now they frequently so called him. He was truly devoted to his captain's children, but more especially were the affections of the big warm heart which beat in his black bosom bestowed upon Alice.

It is no exaggeration to say that he would gladly have died to save her from harm.

Alice, indeed, was perfectly happy, not feeling the slightest regret at having left England. The weather was fine, the sea generally smooth, and the ship glided so rapidly on her course that Alice persuaded herself she was not likely to encounter the storms and dangers she had heard of. She carried out her intentions with exemplary perseverance. Never had the captain's cabin been in such good order. She learned all the lessons he set her, and read whenever she had time; she plied her needle diligently; and Mr. Shobbrok took especial delight in teaching her embroidery, in which, notwithstanding the roughness of his hands, he was an adept. Indeed, not a moment of her time was idly spent. She took her, walks regularly on deck during the day, with her father or Walter: and when they were engaged, Nub followed her about like her shadow; not that he often spoke to her, but he seemed to think that it was his duty ever to be on the watch to shield her from harm.

Walter, in the meantime, was picking up a large amount of nautical knowledge: for he, like his sister, was always diligent, and, following his father's advice, never hesitated to ask for information from those about him; and as he was always good-natured and good-tempered, and grateful for help received, it was willingly given. He was as active and daring as any of the crew, and he could soon lay out on the yards and assist in reefing topsails as well as anybody on board. He could soon, also, take his trick at the helm in fine weather; indeed, it was generally acknowledged that he gave good promise of becoming a prime seaman. The crew were constantly exercised at their guns; and Walter, though not strong enough to work at them himself, soon thoroughly understood their management, and could have commanded them as well as any of the officers. He also studied navigation under his father in the cabin, and could take an observation and work a day's work with perfect accuracy. He advanced thus rapidly in his professional knowledge, not because he possessed any wonderful talent except the very important one of being able to give his mind to the subject, and in being diligent in all he undertook. He was happy and contented, because he really felt that he was making progress, and every day adding to his stock of knowledge. He had also the satisfaction of being conscious that he was doing his duty in the sight of God as well as in that of man : he was obedient, loving, and attentive to his father, from the highest of motives,—because God told him to be so, not in any way from fear, or because he felt that it was his interest to obey one on whom he depended for support. Captain Tredeagle himself was a truly religious, God-fearing man ; that is to say, he feared to offend One who, he knew, loved him and had done so much for him—an all-pure and all-holy God, in whose sight he ever lived—and therefore did his best to bring up his children in the fear and nurture of the Lord; and he had reason to be thankful that his efforts were not in vain.

Had all his crew been like Captain Tredeagle, his would have been a happy ship. His good mate, Jacob Shobbrok, was in some respects like him; that is to say, he was a Christian man, though somewhat rough in his outward manner and appearance, for he had been at sea all his life. He was an old bachelor, and had never enjoyed the softening influence of female society. Still his heart was kind and gentle. Both Alice and Walter, having discernment enough to discover that, were accordingly much attached to him. There were several other worthy men on board. Andrew Lawrie, the surgeon, was in most respects like Jacob, possessing a kind, honest heart, with a rough outside. Nub has been described. He made himself generally popular with the men by his good temper and jokes, and by bearing patiently the ill-treatment to which he was often subjected by the badly disposed among them. But though kicked, rope's-ended, and made to perform tasks which it was not his duty to do, he never complained or showed any vindictive feeling. His chief friend was Dan Tidy. Dan, who had not been long at sea, and consequently was not much of a sailor, was quite as badly treated as Nub, but did not take it with nearly the same equanimity. He generally retaliated, and many a tough battle he had to fight in consequence. But though he was often beaten, his spirit had not given way. A common suffering united him and Nub, and when they could they helped each other.

A large portion of the crew were rough, ignorant, and disorderly. The war had kept all the best men employed, and even a well-known commander like Captain Tredeagle had a difficulty in getting good men ; so that the few only who had constantly sailed with him could be depended on. The rest would remain with him and do their duty only so long as they thought it their interest. And though he did his utmost to keep up strict discipline, he was obliged to humour them more than he would have been justified in doing under other circumstances. Though he might have used the lash,—very common in those days,—to flog men was repugnant to his feelings, and he preferred trying to keep them in order by kindness. Unhappily, many of them were of too brutal a nature to understand his object, so they fancied that he treated them as he did from timidity. Old Jacob Shobbrok urged stronger measures when some of the men refused to turn out to keep their watch, or went lazily about their work.

" We shall have the masts whipped out of the ship, if we don't trice up some of these fellows before long," he observed one day to the captain.

"Wait a bit, Jacob," answered Captain Tredeagle; "I will try them a little longer; but you can just let them know that if any of them again show a mutinous disposition, they will be flogged as surely as they are living men."

"They don't understand threats, captain," answered Jacob. "There's nothing like the practical teaching the cat affords with fellows of this description. I'll warn them, however, pretty clearly; and if that don't succeed, I must trust to you to show them that you will stand it no longer."

Jacob did not fail to speak to the men as he promised, and for a time they went on better; but the spirit of insubordination still existed among them, and gave the good captain much concern.

The boatswain, Jonah Capstick, who ought to have been the first to preserve discipline, was among the worst. It was the first voyage he had made with Captain Tredeagle, to whom he had been recommended as a steady man. One of his mates, Tom Hulk,—well named, for he was a big hulking ruffian,—was quite as bad, and with several others supported the boatswain.

Alice knew nothing of what was going forward, though Walter suspected that things were not quite right.

The great delight of Alice, as the ship entered the tropics, was to watch the strange fish which swam about the ship as she glided calmly on ; to observe the ocean bathed in the silvery light of the moon, or the sun as it sank into its ocean bed, suffusing a rich glow over the sky and waters.

She and Walter were one day standing on deck together, when, looking up, they saw a small black dot in the blue sky.

"What can that be ?" asked Alice. "It seems as if some one had thrown a ball up there. Surely it cannot be a balloon such as I have read of, though I never saw one."

"That is not a balloon, but a living creature," observed Jacob, who had overheard her. "It is a frigate-bird watching for its prey ; and before long we shall see it pounce down to the surface of the ocean if it observes anything to pick up, though it is a good many hundred feet above our heads just now."

"See ! see ! what are those curious creatures which have just come out of the water ? Why, they have wings ! Can they be birds ?" she exclaimed.

"No; those are flying-fish," said Walter, who knew better than his sister.

"And the frigate-bird has espied them too," exclaimed the mate. "Here he comes."

As he spoke, a large bird came swooping down like a flash of lightning from the heavens ; and before the flying-fish, with their wings dried by the air, had again fallen into the water, it had caught one of them

FRIGATE-BIRD AND FLYING-FISH.

in its mouth. Swallowing the fish, the bird rapidly ascended, to be ready for another pounce on its prey. The flying-fish had evidently other enemies below the surface, for soon afterwards they were seen to rise at a short distance ahead; and once more the bird, descending with the same rapid flight as before, seized another, which it bore off.

"Poor fish! how cruel of the bird to eat them up," cried Alice.

"It is its way of getting its dinner," said the mate, laughing. "You would not object to eat the fish were they placed before you nicely fried at breakfast. Many seamen have been thankful enough to get them, when their ship has gone down and they have been sailing in their boats across the ocean, hard pressed by hunger."

"I was foolish to make the remark," said Alice; "and yet I cannot help pitying the beautiful flying-fish, snapped up so suddenly. But how can the bird come out here, so far away from land? Where can it rest at night?"

"It can keep on the wing for days and days together," answered the mate. "It is enabled to do this by having the muscles of its breast, which work the wings, of wonderful strength, while the rest of the body is exceedingly light. Its feet are so formed that it cannot rest on the surface of the water as do most other sea-birds; which proves what I say about its powers of flying."

The bird which he was describing was of a rich black plumage, the throat being white and the beak red. Nothing could be more graceful than the way it hovered above the ship in beautiful undulations, or the rapidity with which it darted on its prey. Alice and Walter stood admiring it.

"It is a determined pirate," observed the mate. "When it cannot catch fish for itself, it watches for the gannets and sea-swallows after they have been out fishing all day, and darting down upon them, compels them in their fright to throw some of their prey out of their crops, when it is caught by the plunderer before it reaches the water. The gannets are such gluttons, they generally fly home so full of fish that they are unable to close their beaks. If the gannet does not let some of the fish fall, the frigate-bird darts rapidly down and strikes it on the back of the head; on which it never fails to give up its prey to the marauder."

"Though I cannot, I must confess, help admiring the beauty of the frigate-bird, robber as he is, my sympathy is all with the flying-fish," said Alice.

"They are certainly to be pitied," said the mate; "for they have enemies in the water and out of it. Several of those we saw just now are by this time down the throats of the albicores or bonitoes, which are following them. To try to escape from their foes, they rise out of the water, and fly fifty yards or more, till, their wings becoming dry, they cannot longer support themselves, when they fall back again into the sea, if they are not in the meantime picked up by a frigate-bird or some other winged enemy. I have known a dozen or more fly into a boat, or even on to the deck of a ship; and very delicate they are when cooked, though hungry people are glad enough to eat them raw."

Sometimes at night Alice came on deck, when the stars were shining brightly and the ship was bounding over the waves, to watch the foam as it was dashed from off the bows to pass hissing by, covered with sparks of phosphorescent light, while the summits of the dark waves in every direction shone with the utmost brilliancy. The strange light, her father told her, was produced by countless millions of minute creatures, or, as some supposed, by decomposed animal matter. She delighted most, however, in going on deck on a calm night, when the moonbeams cast their soft light upon the ocean, and the ship seemed to be gliding across a sea of burnished silver. Walter now regularly took his watch, and never failed to call her when he knew she would be interested in any of the varied beauties which the changing ocean presented.

Frequently the ship was surrounded by bonitos, moving through the waters much like porpoises; and the seamen got their harpoons ready, to strike any which might come near.

As the ship one day was gliding smoothly on, the boatswain descended to the end of the dolphin-striker, a spar which reaches from the bowsprit down almost to the water. Here he stood, ready to dart his harpoon at any unwary fish which might approach. Walter and Alice were on the forecastle watching him. They had not long to wait before a bonito came gambolling by. Quick as lightning the harpoon flew from his hand, and was buried deeply in the body of the fish. A noose was then dexterously slipped over its head and another over its tail, and it was quickly hauled up on deck by the crew. It was a beautiful creature, rather more than three feet long, with a sharp head, a small mouth, large gills, silvery eyes, and a crescent-shaped tail. Its back and sides were greenish, but below it was of a silvery white. The body was destitute of scales, except on the middle of the sides, where a line of gold ran from the head to the tail.

Alice was inclined to bemoan its death ; but Walter assured her afterwards that she need not expend her pity on it, as three flying-fish had been found in its inside. Several other bonitoes were caught which had swallowed even a greater number. Indeed, they are the chief foes of the flying-fish, which, had not the latter the power of rising out of the water to escape them, would quickly be exterminated.

Some of the officers got out lines and hooks baited

with pieces of pork; not to attract fish, however, but to catch some of the numerous birds flying astern and round the ship. Several flights of stormy petrels had long been following in the wake of the ship, with other birds,—such as albatrosses, cape-pigeons, and whale-birds. No sooner did a pigeon see the bait than it pounced down and seized it in its mouth, when a sharp tug secured the hook in its bill, and it was rapidly drawn on board. Several stormy petrels, which the sailors call " Mother Carey's chickens," were also captured. They are among the smallest of the web-footed birds, being only about six inches in length. Most of the body is black, glossed with bluish reflections; their tails are of a sooty-brown intermingled with white. In their mode of flight, Walter re-marked that they resembled swallows : rapidly as they darted here and there, now resting on the wing, now rising again in the air; uttering their clamorous, piercing cries, as they flocked together in increasing numbers.

" We shall have rough weather before long, or those birds would not shriek so loudly," observed Jacob to Walter. " I don't mind a few of them ; but when they come in numbers about a ship, it is a sure sign of a storm."

" We have had so much fine weather, that I suppose it is what we may expect," answered Walter. " We cannot hope to make a long voyage without a gale now and then!"

"It is not always the case," said the mate. "I have been round the world some voyages with scarcely a gale to speak of; and at other times we have not been many weeks together without hard weather."

Though the stormy petrel shrieked, the wind still remained moderate, and the sailors continued their bird-catching and fishing.

Among those who most eagerly followed the cruel sport was Tom Hulk, the boatswain's mate. He had got a long line and a strong hook, which he threw overboard from the end of the main-yard.

"I don't care for those small birds," he cried out. "I have made up my mind to have one of the big albatrosses. I want his wings to carry home with me, and show what sort of game we pick up at sea."

Several of his messmates, who had a superstitious dread of catching an albatross, shouted out to him not to make the attempt, declaring that he would bring ill-luck to himself, or perhaps to the ship. Though not free from superstition himself, he persevered from very bravado.

"I am not to be frightened by any such notions," he answered scornfully. "If I can catch an albatross I will, and wring his neck too."

Before long, a huge white albatross, with wide-extended wings, which had been hovering about the ship, espying the bait darted down and swallowed it at a gulp, hook and all. In an instant it was secured, and the bold seaman came running in along the yard to descend on deck; while the bird, rising in the air, endeavoured to escape. Its efforts were in vain; for several other men aiding Hulk, in spite of its struggles it was quickly drawn on board. Even then it fought bravely, though hopelessly, for victory; but its captor despatched it with a blow on the head.

"It would have been better for you if you had let that bird enjoy its liberty," said the boatswain with a growl. "I have never seen any good come from catching one of them."

"Did you ever see any harm come?" innocently asked Walter, who had come forward to look at the bird.

"As to that, youngster, it's not to every question you will get an answer," growled the boatswain, turning away. Walter, though liked by most on board, was not a favourite of the surly boatswain, who, for his own reasons, objected to have the keen eyes of the sharp-witted boy observing his proceedings.

Walter, begging Hulk to stretch out the bird's wings, went to bring Alice to look at it. He told her what the boatswain had said about the ill luck which would pursue those who killed an albatross.

"Depend on it, God would not allow what He has ordained to be interfered with by any such occurrence," observed the captain to his children. "It may be a cruel act to kill a bird without any reason; but though persons who have caught or shot albatrosses may afterwards have met with accidents, it does not at all follow that such is the result of their former acts. I have seen many albatrosses killed, and the people who killed them have returned home in safety; though possibly accidents may have occurred in other instances to those who have killed one of the birds. Still seamen have got the notion into their heads, and it is very hard to drive it out."

"I am sure of that," said Walter, "though the boatswain was quite angry with me for doubting what he asserted."

While he was speaking, another large albatross came sweeping by.

"For my part, I am not afraid of catching a second," exclaimed Hulk; "and if there is ill luck in killing one, there may be good luck in catching two." Saying this, he prepared his hook and line, and was ascending to the yard to let it tow overboard as before.

"It will be a good thing for you if you do catch two," exclaimed the boatswain. "We want good luck for the ship, for little enough of it we have had as yet." But before Hulk could get out his line the albatross was seen to swoop downwards, and immediately afterwards it rose with a huge fish in its talons, into which it plunged its powerful beak with a force which must have speedily put an end to its prey.

A WINGED FOE

Powerful, however, as were its wings, it could not rise with so great a weight, but commenced tearing away at the flesh of its victim as it floated on the surface. It thus offered a fair mark to any who might wish to shoot it. Three of the ship's muskets were brought up by some of the younger officers, who were about to fire.

"Let me have a shot," said the boatswain, taking one of them. "I seldom miss my aim."

The captain, who had been below, just then coming on deck, observing what they were about, ordered them to desist, observing,—"I don't wish to lower a boat to pick up the bird, and I consider it wanton cruelty to shoot at it."

The boatswain pretended not to hear him, and taking aim, he fired. The bird was seen to let go its prey, and, after rising a few feet, to fall back with wings extended into the water, where it lay fluttering helplessly. The ship gliding on, soon left it astern.

"I consider that a piece of wanton cruelty, Mr. Capstick," exclaimed the captain. "I must prohibit the ship's muskets being made use of for such a purpose; they are intended to be used against our enemies, not employed in slaughtering harmless birds."

The boatswain returned the musket to the rack, muttering as he did so; but what he said neither the captain nor his mates were able to understand.

The ship had now nearly reached the latitude of the Falkland Islands, and in a short time she would be round Cape Horn, and traversing the broad waters of the Pacific. Hitherto few ships had been seen, either friends or foes; a look-out had been kept for the latter, as the crew hoped that, should they fall in with an enemy's merchantman of inferior size, the captain would capture her to give them some much coveted prize-money. Two had been seen which were supposed to be small enough to attack, but the captain had declined going in chase of them, greatly to the annoyance of the crew; and the boatswain and others vowed they would not longer stand that sort of thing.

Walter was walking the deck during his middle watch the next night, when Dan Tidy came up to him.

"Hist, Mr. Walter," he said in a low voice. "Will you plaise just step to the weather-gangway, out of earshot of the man at the helm? I have got something I would like to say to you."

Walter stepped to the gangway, and, seeing no one near, asked Tidy what he had to communicate.

"I wouldn't wish to be an eavesdropper or a tale-bearer, Mr. Walter; but when the lives of you and your father and most of the officers are at stake, it's time to speak out. I happened to be awake during my watch below when the boatswain came for'ard, and I heard him and Tom Hulk and about a dozen others talking in whispers together. I lay still, pretending to be asleep, as, of course, they thought were the rest of the watch. Capstick began grumbling at the chance there was that we should take no prizes; and declared that, for his part, he was not going to submit to that sort of thing. The others agreed with him, and swore that they would stand by him and do whatever he proposed. Some said that the best thing would be to go to the captain, and insist that he should attack the first enemy's merchantman they could fall in with. 'And the captain will tell you to mind your own business, and that he intends to act as he considers is most for his own interest and that of the owners,' said Hulk, with an oath. 'I tell you, the only thing we can do is to make him and his young fry, and the old mate and some of the rest of them, prisoners; or, better still, knock them on the head and heave them overboard, and then we will make the boatswain captain, and live a life of independence, just taking as many prizes as we want, and never troubling ourselves to give an account of them to the owners.' Some agreed to this, and some didn't seem to like the thought of it; but they were talked over by the boatswain and Hulk, and agreed to what they proposed. I cannot say, however, when they intend to carry out their plan. They talked on for some time longer, and then they all turned into their hammocks. I lay as quiet as a mouse in a cheese, and when I thought they were all asleep slipped up on deck to tell you or the mate, if I could manage to speak to either of you unobserved, that you might let the captain know of their intentions towards him."

Walter, though considerably agitated at this information, acted with much discretion, telling Tidy to keep the matter to himself, and to behave towards the intended mutineers as he had always done, without letting them have a shade of suspicion that he had discovered their plot. Having no fear, from what Tidy said, that they intended carrying it out immediately, he waited till his watch was over to inform his father and the chief mate. Bidding Tidy go below and turn in again, he resumed his walk on deck.

They would probably, he thought, wait for a change of weather and a dark night to execute their project, which, it was evident, was not as yet fully matured.

The second mate had charge of the watch, but Walter was unwilling to communicate the information to him; for, though an honest man, he somewhat doubted his discretion. It was an anxious time for the young boy, but his courage did not quail, as he felt sure that his father and Mr. Shobbrok, aided by the other officers and the better-disposed part of the crew, would be able to counteract the designs of the mutineers.

CHAPTER II.

WALTER was thankful to hear eight bells strike, when Mr. Shobbrok coming on deck, sent the second mate below.

"Why don't you turn in, Walter?" asked the first mate, on seeing him still lingering on deck.

"I should like to speak a word to you," said Walter.

"If it's a short one, my lad, say it, but I don't wish to keep you out of your berth."

As several of the mutineers were on deck, Walter thought he might be observed, and therefore merely whispered to the mate, "Be on your guard. I have information that the boatswain is at the head of a conspiracy to take possession of the ship. I will go below and tell my father how matters stand. Be careful not to be taken at a disadvantage, and let none of the men come near you."

"I am not surprised. I will be on my guard," answered the mate in a low tone; adding in a higher one,—"Now go below, youngster, and turn in."

Walter, hurrying to the cabin, found his father asleep. A touch on the arm awoke him.

"I want to speak to you about something important," he said; and then told him all he had heard from Dan Tidy.

"It does not surprise me," he observed, repeating almost the words of the mate. "We of course must take precautions to counteract the designs of the misguided men without letting them suspect that we are aware of their intentions. Call Mr. Lawrie, that I may tell him what to do; and then I will go on deck and speak to the first mate."

"I have told him already. I thought it better to put him on his guard," said Walter.

"You did right," said the captain. "We must let the other officers know. Bring me two brace of pistols from the rack." The captain quickly loaded the firearms. "Now, Walter, do you go and wake up Nub; then bring all the muskets into my cabin while I am on deck."

The captain's appearance would not excite suspicion, as it is customary for a commander to go on deck at all hours of the night, especially when there is a change of weather; and the mate was heard at that moment ordering the watch on deck to shorten sail.

Captain Tredeagle did not interfere, but allowing the mate to give the necessary orders, waited till the top-gallant-sails were furled and two reefs taken in the top-sails. He then went across to where Mr. Shobbrok was standing.

" Walter has told me what the men intend doing," he said in a low voice. " Do you try and find out who are likely to prove stanch to us."

" I think we may trust nearly half the crew," answered the mate; " and I will try and speak to those on whom we can most certainly rely. Tidy will be able to point them out."

" In case they should attempt anything immediately, here are the means of defending yourself," said the captain; and finding that none of the men were observing him, he put a brace of pistols into the mate's hands.

" Who is at the helm ? " he asked.

" Tom Hulk," answered the mate.

" He is among the ringleaders," said the captain; " he will be suspicious if he sees us talking together. I'll warn Beak, that he may be on the alert, and will send him to speak with you."

The captain crossed the deck to where Mr. Beak, the fourth mate, was standing. Telling him of the conspiracy which had been discovered, he put a pistol into his hand, and desired him to go over and speak with the first mate, who would direct him what to do.

On returning below, he found that Walter and Nub had carried out his orders, and that Mr. Lawrie had awakened the other two mates, who soon made their appearance in the cabin. Two midshipmen, or rather apprentices, who slept further forward, had now to be warned. Nub undertook to do this without exciting the suspicion of the mutineers. The captain in the meantime gave the officers the information he had received, and told them the plan he proposed following,—assuring them that they had only to be on the alert and to remain firm, and that he had no doubt, should the mutineers proceed to extremities, they would soon be put down ; no one, however, felt inclined to turn in again, not knowing at what moment the mutiny might break out. Had the boatswain and his companions guessed that Tidy had overheard their conversation, they would have lost no time in carrying out their plan, and would probably have caught the captain unprepared.

The night passed quietly away, and when morning came the mutineers went about their duty as usual. Notwithstanding the threatenings of a gale on the previous evening, the wind continued fair and moderate, and the ship was standing on under all sail.

Breakfast was over, and the captain and mate, with Walter, were standing with their sextants in hand taking an observation to ascertain the ship's latitude. Mr. Lawrie having been in his surgery mixing some medicines for two men who were on the sick-list, was going forward when he observed a number of the crew with capstan-bars, boat-stretchers, and other weapons in their hands, the boatswain and Tom Hulk being among them. He at once hurried to the captain and told him what he had seen.

"Call aft the men whom we selected as a guard, Mr. Shobbrok," whispered the captain. "Let the officers arm themselves, but keep out of sight in the cabin, ready to act if necessary."

The mate had agreed on a private signal with the trustworthy men. He was to let fly the mizzen-royal, when they were to come aft on the pretence of hauling in the sheet. This would give them the start of the mutineers, and allow them time to obtain arms,—though of course the object of the device would quickly be perceived.

The captain and Walter went on taking their observation full in sight of the crew forward, as if there were nothing to trouble them. The mate made the signal agreed on. As the sail fluttered in the wind, Dan Tidy and eight others came running aft, and immediately the muskets, which had already been loaded, were handed up from below and placed in their hands. So quick had been their movements that the mutineers, who had been looking at the captain, had not observed them ; and, confiding in their numbers, and not knowing that the officers were armed or prepared for them, came rushing aft, led by the boatswain, uttering loud shouts, to intimidate their opponents. The captain stood perfectly calm, with Walter by his side.

" What does this strange conduct mean, my men ? " he asked, turning round.

" We will show you, captain," answered the boatswain. " We want a captain who understands his own interest and ours, and won't let the prizes we might have got hold of slip through our fingers as you have done."

" You are under a mistake, my friends, in more ways than one," answered the captain. " I call on all true men on board to stand by me."

As he spoke, Tidy and the men who had come aft showed themselves with muskets in their hands ; and at the same moment the officers sprang on deck, fully armed.

" Now I will speak to you," said the captain, handing his sextant to Walter, and drawing his pistols. " The first man who advances another step must take the consequences. I shall be justified in shooting him, and I intend to do so. His blood be upon his own head. Now lay down these capstan-bars and stretchers, and tell me, had you overpowered us, what you intended to do."

The mutineers were dumbfounded, and even the boldest could make no reply. Most of them, indeed, did as they were ordered and threw their weapons on the deck, hanging down their heads and looking ashamed of themselves. The boatswain and Hulk, and a few of the more daring, tried to brazen it out.

"All we want is justice," blustered out the boatswain. "We shipped aboard here to fight our enemies, like brave Englishmen, and to take as many prizes as we could fall in with; but there does not seem much chance of our doing so this voyage."

"You shipped on board to do as I ordered you, and not to act the part of sea-robbers and pirates, which is what you would wish to be," answered the captain. "Those who intend to act like honest men, and obey orders, go over to the starboard side; the rest stand on the other."

The greater number of the crew—with the exception of the boatswain and Hulk and two others—went over to starboard. The captain then ordered the remainder of the crew to be piped on deck. They quickly came up.

"Now, my lads, those who wish to obey me and do their duty, join their shipmates on the starboard side; those who are inclined the other way, stand on one side with Mr. Capstick and his mate."

Two or three cast a look at the boatswain, but one and all went over to the starboard side. The boatswain looked greatly disconcerted, for he had evidently counted on being joined by the greater part of his shipmates.

"Now," said the captain, "I am averse to putting men in irons, but as these have shown a spirit of insubordination which would have been destructive, if successful, to all on board, they must take the consequences. Mr. Shobbrok, seize the fellows and put them in confinement below."

The three mates, calling six other men, sprang on the mutineers, who, drawing their knives, attempted to defend themselves; but they were quickly disarmed, and their weapons being thrown overboard, their hands were lashed behind them, and they were carried below, to have the irons put on by the armourer, who was among those who could be trusted. None of the rest of the crew attempting to interfere, order was speedily restored on board the *Champion*.

Though the captain had quelled the mutiny, he lost the services of four of the most active of the hands; but he hoped that reflection would bring them to reason, and that, repenting of their folly, they would be willing to return to their duty.

While these events had been occurring a dark bank of clouds had been gathering to the southward; and though the ship still sailed with a fair wind, it was evident that a change was about to take place. The cloud-bank rose higher and higher in the sky.

"All hands shorten sail," cried the captain. The crew flew aloft to obey the order and lay out on the yards, each man striving to get in the sail as rapidly as possible. Sail after sail was taken in, but before the work could be completed the gale was upon them —not a soft breeze, such as they had been accustomed to, but a sharp cutting wind, with hail and sleet, which struck their faces and hands with fearful force, benumbing their bodies, dressed only in light summer clothing. It seemed as if on a sudden the ship had gone out of one climate into another.

"This is regular Cape Horn weather," observed the mate to Walter, who stood shivering on deck. "You had better go below and get on your winter clothing. It may be many a day before we are in summer again, if the wind comes from the westward."

Walter hesitated, for he thought it manly to stand the cold; but his father told him to do as the mate advised, so he hastened into the cabin. He found Alice looking very much alarmed, not having been able to make out all that had been occurring. She had seen the officers come down and arm themselves, and the muskets loaded and handed out, and had supposed that they were about to encounter an enemy. Walter quieted her fears, by assuring her that though there had been danger it was all over, and that they had now only to battle with a storm, such as all good sailors are ready to encounter and overcome.

Walter was soon equipped and ready to go on deck again, and Alice wanted to accompany him.

"Why, you will be frozen if you do, so pray don't

think about it," he answered. "I am sure father will wish you to remain in the cabin."

The gale increased, however, and the ship rolled, pitched, tossed, and tumbled about, in a way Alice had never before experienced. She sat holding on to the sofa trying to read, and wondering why neither her father nor Walter again came below. "What could have occurred?" She heard loud peals of thunder, the sea dashing against the ship's sides, the howling of the wind in the rigging, the stamp of the men's feet overhead, and other noises sounding terrific in her ears. The uproar continued to increase, and the ship seemed to tumble about more and more. At last she could endure it no longer.

"I must go on deck and see what is the matter," she said to herself, putting on her cloak and hat. She endeavoured to make her way to the companion-ladder, first being thrown on one side and then on the other, and running a great risk of hurting herself. At length, however, she managed to reach the foot of the ladder. Just at that moment Walter appeared at the top of it, looking down at her. She felt greatly relieved on seeing him.

"Oh, what has happened?" she exclaimed as he came below.

"Only a regular Cape Horn gale," he answered. "We have got the ship under close-reefed fore and main top-sails, and she is behaving nobly. It is cold, to be sure ; but the men have been sent below, as they could be spared, to put on warmer clothing, and we shall get out of it some day or other."

Walter's remarks greatly restored Alice's spirits. She had expected to see him with alarm on his countenance, bringing her the announcement that the ship was in fearful danger. The time had not been quite so long as Alice had supposed. Nub brought in dinner for her and Walter, which he advised them to take on the deck of the cabin, as there would be little use in placing it on the table, in spite of puddings and fiddles to keep the dishes in their places.

"You see, Missie Alice, if de ship gib a roll on one side den half de soup go out, and den when she gib a roll on de oder side de oder half go out, and you get none ; and de 'taties come flying ober in de same way; den de meat jump out of de dish, and before you can stop it will be on de oder side of de cabin ; and de mustard and pepper pots dey go cruising about by demselves. Now, if you sit on de deck, you put de tings in one corner and you sit round dem, and when dey jump up you catch dem and put dem back, and tell dem to stop till you want to eat dem."

Nub's graphic description of the effects likely to be produced by the storm induced Alice and Walter to agree to his proposal, and they partook of their meal in a corner of the cabin. The latter enjoyed it, for he was very hungry. Alice could eat but little ; she was, however, very anxious that her father should come down, or that he would allow her to send him up some food.

Walter laughed. "I am sure he will not do that," he answered. "He is too much occupied at present to come below."

When Walter went on deck again, Alice felt very forlorn. Nub, however, now and then looked in to cheer her up.

"It's all right, Miss Alice, only de wind it blow bery hard,—enough to shave a man in half a minute. The captain told me to keep below or I turn into one icicle." Towards the evening Nub brought in a pot of hot coffee, which he had managed to boil at the galley-fire ; and presently the captain and Walter came down. The captain had no time to eat anything, but he drank two cupfuls of the coffee scalding hot.

"Bless you, my child," he said to Alice. "We have a stormy night before us ; but God looks after us, and I wish you to turn in and try and go to sleep. We are doing our best, and the ship behaves well, so keep up a good heart and all will be right."

The mates and Mr. Lawrie came down, and Nub supplied them also with coffee. The surgeon declared he could stand it no longer, and as he was not required on deck he sat down in the cabin and tried to read ; but he had to give it up and stagger off to his berth. Walter at last came below again, saying that his father would not allow him to remain longer on deck ; though, like a gallant young sailor, he had wished to share whatever the rest had to endure. In a very few minutes, notwithstanding the tossing of the ship and the uproar of the elements, he was fast asleep.

All night long the ship stood on close-hauled, battling bravely with the gale, showers of sleet, snow, and hail driving furiously against the faces of the crew. The captain, with his mates and both watches, remained on deck, to be ready for any emergency.

The top-gallant-masts and royal-masts had been sent down ; the studding-sail-booms and gear unrove, to lighten the ship as much as possible of all top hamper.

It was still dark when Walter awoke. The ship was pitching into the seas as heavily as before, and the wind roaring as loudly. He longed to go on deck to ascertain the state of things ; but the captain had told him to remain in his berth till summoned, and he had learned the important duty of implicit obedience to his father's commands. At length the light of day came down through the bull's-eye overhead into his little berth. He quickly dressed, and entering the main cabin, found that his father had just come below. He was taking off his wet outer clothing preparatory to throwing himself on his bed.

"You go on deck now, Walter ; but don't remain long, or you will be well-nigh frozen," he said. "I ain to be called should any change in the weather take place."

Walter sprang on deck, but he had need of all his courage to stand the keen cutting south-westerly wind, which seemed sufficient to blow his teeth down his throat. The ship looked as if made of glass, for every rope and spar was coated over with ice. The men were beating their hands to keep them warm; and when they moved about the deck they had to keep close to the bulwarks, and catch hold of belaying-pins, ropes, or stanchions, to prevent themselves from slipping away to leeward. The sea, as it broke on board, froze on the deck, till it became one mass of ice. Walter, who had thought only of smooth seas and summer gales, was little prepared for this sort of weather.

"Cheer up, my lad, never mind it; we shall be in summer again, and find it pretty hot too, when we round the Horn," observed the first mate.

"I don't mind it," answered Walter, his teeth chattering. "Do you think it will last long?"

"That depends on the way the wind blows," answered the first mate.

Dark seas rose up on every side, higher than he had ever seen them before; the foam driven aft in white sheets, their combing crests shining brilliantly as the sun burst forth from the driving clouds.

"Now you have seen enough of it; you had better

go below," said the mate. "One of those seas might break aboard and sweep you off the deck. As you can do nothing now, it is useless to expose your life to danger."

Walter, who would have wished to remain had the wind been less cutting, thought the mate right, and obeyed him. He had been for some time in the cabin when the fourth mate came down.

"Come on deck, Walter," he said, "and see something you have never before set eyes on." Walter followed the mate up the companion-ladder.

As far as the eye could reach, the sea was of a dark-blue tint; the waves still high and foam-crested, sparkling in the rays of the sun, while at some distance on the larboard bow rose a vast mountain-island, its numerous pinnacles glittering in the sun like the finest alabaster, and its deep valleys thrown into the darkest shade. The summit of the mighty mass was covered with snow, and its centre of a deep indigo tint.

"What island is that?" asked Walter.

"It's an island, though it's afloat. That is an iceberg," answered the mate. "It's little less, I judge, than three miles in circumference, and is several hundred feet in height."

The vast mass rose and fell in the water with a slow motion, while its higher points seemed to reach to the sky, and often to bend towards each other as if they were about to topple over. The waves furiously dashed against its base, breaking into masses of foam; while ever and anon thundering sounds, louder than any artillery, reached the ears of the voyagers, as the mighty berg, cracking in all directions, huge pieces came tumbling down into the water. Above the thick fringe of white foam appeared an indigo tint, which grew lighter and lighter, till it shaded off from a dark blue to the pile of pure snow which rested on the summit.

Walter could not resist the temptation of bringing Alice to see the strange and beautiful sight. Hurrying below, he wrapped her up in a warm cloak, and, calling Nub to his assistance, they brought her on deck.

"That is beautiful," she exclaimed; "but how dreadful it would be to run against it in the dark!" she added, after a minute's silence.

"We hope to keep too bright a look-out for anything of that sort," said the mate; "and, happily, at night we know when we are approaching an iceberg by the peculiar coldness of the air and the white appearance which it always presents even in the darkest nights. However, there can be no doubt that many a stout ship has been cast away on such a berg as that; or on what is more dangerous still, a floating mass of sheet-ice just flush with the water."

The mate would not allow Alice to remain long on deck for fear of her suffering from the cold, and Walter and Nub hurried her below. Walter was soon again on deck. .The ship was passing the iceberg, leaving it a mile to leeward. As it drew over the quarter there was a cry from forward of "Ice ahead!" The captain was immediately called.

"Hard up with the helm!" he shouted; and the ship passed a huge mass of ice, such as the mate had before described, flush with the water. Had the ship struck against it, her fate would have been sealed. The sharpest eyes in the ship were kept on the look-out: one man on each bow, and another in the bunt of the fore-yard; the third mate forward, and one on each quarter. Two of the best hands were at the wheel; while the captain and first mate were moving about with their eyes everywhere. All knew that the slightest inattention might cause the destruction of the ship.

Hour after hour went by. No one spoke except those on the look-out or the officer in command, when the cry came from forward, "Ice on the weather bow," "Another island ahead," "Ice on the lee bow," and so on. Evening at length approached. Walter for the first time became aware of the perilous position in which the ship was placed; yet his father stood calm and unmoved, as he had ever been, and not by look or gesture did he betray what he must have felt; indeed, he had too long been inured to peril of all sorts to be moved as those are who first experience it. Gradually, however, the sea began to go down and the wind to decrease, shifting more to the southward. A clear space appearing, the captain eagerly wore ship, and then hauling up on the other tack, stood to the southward, hoping to weather the icebergs among which he had before passed. The cold was as intense as before, but it could be better borne as hopes were entertained that the gale would abate, and that at length Cape Horn would be doubled.

That night, however, was one of the greatest anxiety; for, owing to the darkness, the ice-field could not be seen at any distance, and it might be impossible to escape running on it. Captain Tredeagle could therefore only commit himself and ship to the care of Heaven, and exert his utmost vigilance to avoid the surrounding dangers.

He and all on board breathed more freely when daylight returned, and the field of ice they had just weathered was seen over the quarter, with clear water ahead. A few more icebergs were passed; some near, shining brilliantly in the sun, and others appearing like clouds floating on the surface.

In two days more there was a cry of "Land on the starboard bow!" The ship rapidly neared it. The wind coming from the eastward, the reefs were shaken out of the top-sails, the courses set, and she stood towards the west. The land became more and more distinct.

"Now," said the first mate to Walter, "if Alice would like to see Cape Horn, bring her on deck. There it is, broad on our starboard beam."

Alice quickly had on her cloak. "Is that Cape Horn?" she asked, pointing to a dark rugged headland which rose, scarcely a mile off, out of the water. "What a wild, barren spot! Can any human beings live there?"

"I have heard that some do," answered the mate; "and what is very strange, that they manage to exist with little or no clothing to shield their bodies from the piercing winds! It's a wonder they can stand it; but then they are savages who have been accustomed to the life since they were born, and know no better."

Scarcely was the ship round Cape Horn when the wind moderated, and the sea went down till it was almost calm. The order was now given to get up the top-gallant and royal masts and rig out studding-sail-booms.

The mutineers had long been kept in irons, and some of the men declared that they were better off than themselves during the bitter weather to which they had been exposed; but the boatswain and the rest had more than once petitioned to be set free, promising to be obedient in the future. The captain, willing to try them, at length liberated them, and they were now doing duty as if nothing had happened, though the captain was too wise a man not to keep a watchful eye on them.

Alice, after being so long shut up in the cabin, was glad to be on deck as much as she could during the day, watching the various operations going on. The men were aloft rigging out studding-sail-booms, when, to her horror, she saw one of them fall from the fore-yard. Her instinctive cry was, "Save him! save him!"

"A man overboard!" shouted those who saw the accident. The ship was running rapidly before the wind, and under such circumstances considerable time elapsed before sail could be shortened and the ship hove - to. Preparations had in the meantime been made to lower a boat, and willing hands jumped into her, under the command of the second mate, to go to the rescue of the drowning man. The captain had kept an eye on the spot where he had fallen, so as to direct the boat in what direction to pull. Away dashed the hardy crew, straining every muscle to go to the rescue of their fellow-creature.

A moment before not a bird had been in sight, but just then a huge albatross was seen soaring high in the air. Its keen eye had caught sight of the unfortunate man. The boat dashed on, the mate and the crew shouting loudly in the hope of scaring off the bird; but heeding not their cries, downwards it flew with a fearful swoop. In vain the wretched man, who was a strong swimmer, endeavoured to defend himself with his hands; its sharp beak pierced his head, and in another instant he floated a lifeless corpse on the surface of the water.

AN UNEQUAL CONTEST

"Who is he?" asked several voices.

"Tom Hulk," answered the mate. "I caught sight of his face just as the bird struck him, and I hope I may never again see such a look of horror in the countenance of a fellow-creature as his presented."

"It was a bad ending to a bad life," said one of the men. "A greater villain never came to sea, and it's the belief of some of us that he would have worked more mischief aboard before long."

"That he would," said another. "He was always jeering at the boatswain for his cowardice, and telling him he ought to act like a man. We knew pretty well what he meant by that." Similar remarks were made by others; for all the men in the boat were honest and true, and had been among those who had at once sided with the captain and officers. Such are always found the most ready to go to the aid of a fellow-creature, and they had been the first to spring into the boat.

By this time they were nearly up to the body of the dead man. The albatross, on seeing them coming, had flown away. Just then, either some ravenous fish had seized it from below, or the body, no longer supported by the talons of the bird, lost its buoyancy, or from some other cause, it began to sink; and before the boatman could catch it with his boat-hook it had disappeared from sight, sinking down to the depths of the ocean, there to remain till the sea gives up its dead.

When the mate returned on board, he did not fail to tell the captain what the men had said. "We must nevertheless keep a watchful eye on the boatswain and others who associated with him," was the answer. "If Hulk, however, was the chief malcontent, we have little reason to fear them."

The ship, with her lighter canvas set, was now making rapid progress towards the warm latitudes of the Pacific.

CHAPTER III.

WALTER had been rapidly gaining a knowledge of navigation and seamanship; he
had now to learn something of the business
of whale-catching. The *Champion* carried
six boats, which were so built as to possess
the greatest amount possible of buoyancy and stability
as well as to be able to move swiftly. They were
about twenty-seven feet long by four wide, and sharp
at both ends, so that they could move both ways. At
one end, considered the stern, was a strong, upright,
rounded piece of wood, called the loggerhead; at the
other, or bow, a deep groove for the purpose of allowing the harpoon-line to run through it.

The most experienced hands among the crew were
busy in preparing the boats for active work. In each
boat were stowed two lines, two hundred fathoms in
length, coiled away in their respective tubs ready for

use; four harpoons, and as many lances; a keg, containing several articles, among which were a lantern and tinder-box; three small flags, denominated whifts, for the purpose of inserting into a dead whale, when the boats might have to leave it in chase of others; and two drougues—pieces of board of a square form with a handle in the centre, so that they could be secured to the end of the harpoon-line, to check the speed of the whale when running or sounding. Six men formed the crew of each boat: four for pulling, and two being officers; one called the boat-steerer, and the other the headsman.

Hitherto not a whale had been caught; but they were in hourly expectation of falling in with some. A sharp look-out was kept for them; a man for the purpose being placed at each mast-head, while one of the officers took post on the fore-top-gallant-yard. Day after day passed by, and still no whales were seen, till the men began to grumble at their ill luck. Still they could not blame the captain, for he was doing the utmost in his power to fall in with them. The boatswain, however, took the opportunity of urging the rest of the crew that, since they could not find whales, they should go in search of an enemy, and try and pick up a prize. Tidy, as before, managed to hear what was going forward, and informed the captain. Notwithstanding this, he kept to his resolution to search for whales, and not to attack any of the enemy's merchant-vessels, unless they should fall directly in his way, or come in chase of him.   He trusted to the number of true men on board, and cared very little for the grumbling of the rest.

At length, one forenoon—the ship being only a few degrees south of the line, off the coast of Peru, as she was standing on under easy sail, the crew engaged in their various occupations, or moving listlessly about the decks overcome by the heat of the sun, which was very great, some grumbling, and nearly all out of spirits at the ill success of the voyage—the voice of one of the look-outs was heard shouting,—

" There she spouts ! "

The words acted like a talisman.   In one moment, from the extreme of apathy, the crew were aroused into the utmost activity.

" Where away ? " asked the captain in an animated tone.

" On the weather bow," was the answer.   " There again ! there again ! " came the cry from aloft, in-dicating that other whales were spouting in the same direction.

The crew were rushing with eager haste to the boats, each man to the one to which he belonged. The captain went away in one ; the whale-master and two of the officers in the others,—for five only were lowered.

Walter and Alice were on deck, as eager as any

one.　Walter was about to slip into one of the boats, when the first mate saw him.

"No, no, my lad; the danger is too great for you. The captain has not ordered you not to go; but I am right sure he would not allow it."

Walter felt much disappointed, as he was very anxious to see the sport.　He would not have called it sport for the poor whales, had he witnessed the mighty monsters writhing in agony as harpoons and spears were plunged into their bodies.

Away dashed the boats as fast as the hardy crews could lay their backs to the oars, the captain's boat leading, while the ship was heading up towards them. All hands on deck watched their progress, till they looked mere specks on the ocean, although the backs of the whales and their heads could be seen above the surface as they spouted up jets of breath and spray.

Walter was surprised to see the third mate and surgeon with pistols in their belts and cutlasses by their sides, while Nub and Tidy and several other trustworthy men gathered aft, also with cutlasses, pistols, and muskets in their hands.

"Why are you all armed?" asked Walter.　"I thought there was no fear of the mutineers playing any tricks."

"We obey the captain's orders," answered Mr. Lawrie.

"I thought that as Hulk is dead, and the boatswain is away, none of the rest would venture to mutiny."

"The boatswain is cunning as well as daring, and while the captain and most of the other officers are away, he might come back and induce those he has won over to take possession of the ship," answered the surgeon. "Your father is right to take precautions, though there may be but little chance of anything of the sort happening."

"We must not tell Alice, or she may be alarmed," observed Walter. "If she observes that you are armed, I will tell her that our father directed it should be so."

The captain's boat had in the meantime reached one of the whales, just at the moment that the monster, rising above water, had begun to spout. Two of the boats remained with him, while two others went in search of another whale. The captain's boat dashing up rapidly towards the creature, he stepped to the bows, harpoon in hand. Hurling it with all his force, he fixed it deeply into the body of the whale; while one of the other boats coming up, a second harpoon was struck into its body.

"Back off, all!" was the cry, and the crews pulled away with might and main. The lines were run out to get to a distance from the now infuriated creature, which, seeing its foes, gave signs of making at them with open mouth; but they, pulling round towards the tail, avoided it; and the whale, no longer seeing them, lifting its flukes, dived far down into the depths of the ocean. The first lines being nearly run out, others were added on, which also rapidly ran out—a few fathoms only remaining. A third boat, which had been keeping pace with them, was now called up, that her lines might be added to those already out. Just then, however, the lines slackened, and the crews quickly hauled them in. It was a sign that the whale was once more coming to the surface. The mighty creature soon appeared, sending out from its spout-holes jets of blood and foam, and dyeing the water around with a ruddy hue. Again the boats approached, hauling themselves along by the lines made fast to its body, to inflict further wounds with the spears ready in the officers' hands, when the whale again made towards them. It soon stopped, and began to lash the water furiously with its flukes, writhing and rolling in agony. Once more it ceased struggling, apparently exhausted; and the boats dashing up, more spears were struck into its body. The pain caused by the fresh wounds made it leap above the surface, and roll and lash the water with its flukes with greater violence than before, till the whole sea around was a mass of foam tinged with blood. The whale was in its "flurry." These mighty exertions could not last long, and at length it lay an inert mass on the surface. Another whale was captured much in the same manner; when the boats, taking the creatures in tow, pulled towards the ship, the crews singing in chorus a song of triumph.

All on board had been eagerly looking out for their arrival. At length both were towed up, one being firmly secured by lashings to one side of the ship, and one to the other side, preparatory to the work of cutting in and trying out; that is, taking off the blubber or fat which surrounds the body, and boiling it in huge caldrons on deck.

Walter eagerly examined the monsters which had been brought alongside. They were sperm whales, which produce the oil so much valued for making candles. The head, as it was lifted out of the water, looked very much like the bottom end of a gigantic black bottle. This, the mate told him, was 'called the snout, or nose, and formed one-third of the whole length of the animal. At its junction with the body was a huge protuberance, which the mate called the " bunch " of the neck; immediately behind this was the thickest part of the body, which, from this point, gradually tapered off to the tail, or " small." At this point was another protuberance, of a pyramidal form, called the " lump," with several other small elevations, denominated the " ridge." The end of the small was not thicker than the body of a man; it then expanded into the flukes, or, familiarly speaking, the tail,—the two flukes forming a triangular fin somewhat like the tail of a fish, but differing from it inasmuch as it was placed horizontally. The two flukes were about twelve feet or rather more in breadth, and six or seven in length. The whole animal was about eighty-four feet long, and the extreme breadth of the body between twelve and fourteen feet; thus the whole of the circumference did not exceed thirty-six feet. The mate said he had seldom seen whales larger. Though the upper part of the head was very broad, it decreased greatly below, so that it resembled somewhat the cut-water of a ship; thus, as the animal when moving along the surface raises its head out of the water, it is enabled to go at a great speed, the sharp lower part of the jaw performing the service of the stem of a ship. The mouth extended the whole length of the head, the lower jaw being very narrow and pointed,—no thicker in proportion than the lid of a box, supposing the box to be inverted. It had but a single blow-hole, about twelve inches in length, resembling a long S in shape. In the upper part of the head, the mate told him, there is a large triangular-shaped cavity called the "case," which contains oil of great lightness, thus giving buoyancy to the enormous head. This oil is the spermaceti; and from the whale alongside, the mate said that probably no less than a ton, or upwards of ten large barrels of spermaceti, would be taken out. The throat, he asserted, was large enough to swallow a man, though the tongue was very small. The mouth was lined throughout with a pearly white membrane, which, when the whale lies below the surface with its lower jaw dropped down, attracts the unwary fish and other sea-creatures on which it feeds. When a number swim into the trap, it closes its jaw, and swallows the whole at a gulp.

"You see, Walter," observed the mate, "the sperm whale differs very much in this respect from the Greenland whale, which has a remarkably small gullet, and a quantity of whalebone in its gills, through which it strains its food, so that nothing can get into its mouth which it cannot swallow. Now, the sperm whale has no whalebone in its jaws, and could manage to take in a fish of fifty pounds, or, for that matter, one of a hundred pounds, provided it had no sharp prickles on its back.

"Now, look at the eyes, how small they are, compared to the size of the animal. They have got eyelids, though; and they are placed in the most convenient spot, at the widest part of the head, so that it can see around it in every direction. Just behind the eyes are the openings of the ears; but they are very small,—not big enough to put in the tip of your little finger. Just astern of the mouth are the swimming paws; not that the whale makes much use of them, for it works itself on by its flukes, but they serve to balance the body, and assist the female in supporting her young."

While Walter had been looking at the whales, the crew had been busy in preparing for the operation of " cutting in," or taking off the blubber.   Huge caldrons, or " try-pots," had been got up on deck, with pans below them for holding the fire.

The first operation was to cut off' the head ; which being done, it was hauled astern and carefully secured with the snout downwards.   Tackles being secured to the main-top, were brought to the windlass, when one of the crew being lowered on to the body of the whale with a huge hook in his hand, he fixed it into a hole cut for the purpose in the " blanket," or outer covering, near the head.   Others being lowered to assist him, they commenced cutting with sharp spades a strip between two and three feet broad, in a spiral direction round the body.   This strip, as it was hoisted up by the tackles, caused the body to perform a rotatory motion, till the whole of the strip or " blanket-piece" was cut off' to the flukes ; which " blanket-piece," by-the-by, the mate told Walter, was so called because it kept the whale warm.   As soon as this was done, the shapeless mass, deprived of its fat, was allowed to float away, to become the prey of numberless sea-fowl and various fish.   A hole being now cut into the case of the head, a bucket was fixed to a long pole and thrust down, and the valuable spermaceti bailed out till the case was emptied, when the head was let go, and, deprived of its buoyant property, quickly sank from view.

The next operation was to boil the spermaceti, and to stow it away in casks. The blanket-piece being cut up into small portions, they were thrown into the try-pots; the crisp pieces which remained after the oil was extracted, called " scraps," serving for fuel. This last operation is called " trying out."

Four days elapsed before both the carcasses were got rid of, and the oil stowed away in casks in the hold. Fortunately the weather remained calm, or the operation would have taken much longer. This was considered a very good beginning, and the captain hoped he should hear no more grumbling.

We must rapidly pass over the events of several weeks. Two ports in the northern part of Peru were visited, in order to dispose of to the inhabitants some of the goods brought out, and to obtain fresh provisions. It was a work of some risk, as the *Champion* would have to defend herself against any Spanish men-of-war which might fall in with her. After this, she touched at the volcanic-formed Galapagos Islands, situated on the line, at some distance from the continent. Here a number of huge tortoises were captured,—a welcome addition to the provisions on board. The ship remained some time in port, that the rigging might be set up, and that she might undergo several necessary repairs. From this place she sailed northward, touching at the Sandwich Islands,—then in almost as barbarous a condition as when discovered by Captain Cook.   The inhabitants, however, had learned to respect their white visitors, and willingly brought them an abundance of fresh provisions.   Captain Tredeagle was too wise not to take precautions against surprise.   Some of the worst of the crew, however, grumbled greatly at not being allowed to visit the shore, and showed signs of mutinous intentions; their ringleader, as before, being the boatswain.   By constant watchfulness and firmness the captain managed to prevent an actual outbreak; and having taken on board an ample supply of fresh provisions, and filled up with wood and water, he sailed for the south-west, —intending to try the fishing-grounds off the Kingsmill and Ellis's groups, and thence to proceed to New Guinea and the adjacent islands.

After the *Champion* had been some weeks at sea, a sail was seen to the westward : whether a friend or a foe, could not be discovered; but she was apparently of no great size.   The crew loudly insisted that chase should be given, and that she should be overhauled, many even of the better disposed joining in the cry.

"I warn you, my men, that if a foe, though small she may be strongly armed, and you may have to fight hard for victory—not probably to be gained till several lives have been lost."

"We want prize-money, and are ready to fight for it," shouted the crew.

"I am willing to please you, though it is my belief

that we shall be better off in the end if we keep to
our proper calling. Even if we come off victorious,
our crew will be weakened; and while we are repairing the damage we receive we might be filling our
casks with oil."

" One rich prize will be worth all the whales we can
catch," shouted the crew.

The captain yielded, and all sail was made in chase
of the vessel in sight. The stranger soon discovered
that she was pursued, and set all the canvas she could
carry to escape.

The *Champion* sailed well, and carried a strong
breeze with her, while the vessel ahead had but a light
wind. The former soon came up with the chase, which
hoisted French colours. She was a brig, and from her
appearance many thought that she was a man-of-war.
If so, though much smaller, she might prove a formidable antagonist, or turn out a Tartar. It was too
late, however, to escape, and their best chance of gaining the victory was to put a bold face on the matter. Shot and ammunition were got up from below,
the guns were run out, and the crew went to their
quarters ready for battle. Many surmises were hazarded
as to the character of the vessel. It soon became evident that she was not a man-of-war; but she might
be a privateer, and if so, would prove a tough customer.
That such was the case was soon evident. She now
got the breeze ; but instead of setting all sail to escape,

she hauled her wind, and stood away on a bowline, manœuvring to obtain the weather-gage. This Captain Tredeagle was too good a sailor to let her obtain ; and seeing that she could not do so, she stood boldly towards her antagonist.

Captain Tredeagle told Walter and Nub to carry Alice down below, to remain in the lower hold, the safest part of the ship. She was very unwilling to go, and begged that she might stay on deck to share the danger to which he might be exposed.

"It is impossible," he answered. "I should have my thoughts fixed on you instead of on the enemy ; and should you be wounded, I should never forgive myself."

"Come, Miss Alice. Enemy soon begin to fire, and time you out of harm's way," said Nub, taking her hand to lead her below.

"May I return, father?" asked Walter. "I cannot bear the idea of hiding away while there is fighting going forward."

Captain Tredeagle hesitated. "I must not place my son out of the way of dangers to which the rest of the crew are exposed. They will look down upon him if I did."

"You may return," he answered.

"Thank you, father, thank you," said Walter, springing after his sister and Nub.

He soon came back. "Alice is now all right," he said. "Nub has been telling her that we probably shall not have much fighting, as the battle will soon be over, and we shall no doubt take the enemy."

The brig was soon within range of the whaler's guns, and showed her readiness for the fight by firing the first shot, which came crashing through the bulwarks, and striking one man to the deck.

"Give it to them, my lads!" cried Captain Tredeagle; and the whaler's broadside was fired at her opponent with an effect scarcely expected—one of the shot going right through the brig's fore-top-mast, sending it with all its sail and rigging overboard. The English crew cheered lustily. Captain Tredeagle ordered the helm to be put down, intending to shoot ahead of the brig and rake her; but before he could do so, she fired her broadside, which came sweeping across the deck, killing two men and wounding three others. It was her last effort, however; for the whaler, passing ahead of her, poured in her broadside in return, rending her main-mast, and killing several of her crew. Finding that all resistance was useless, the French colours were hauled down.

Walter's first impulse was to rush below to Alice. "Good news! good news!" he exclaimed; "we have taken a prize! Hurrah! hurrah! You may come up into the cabin; but you had better not go on deck, for there are sights there you would not wish to see."

Walter was right, for the three men lately killed lay stark and stiff on the deck, which was sprinkled in many places with blood ; while three others severely wounded were under the doctor's hands. Besides this, a portion of the bulwarks was knocked away ; and, what was of still more consequence, two of her boats were almost irretrievably damaged.

A boat was lowered, and the first mate pulled away to board the prize. The damage she had received was severe ; besides which, a number of her crew had been killed and wounded. The captain and two of his officers had also lost their lives. The prize was of less value than was expected, as she had only a small assortment of articles on board, for the purpose of trading with the natives. Captain Tredeagle's own crew would of necessity be weakened to carry her into port ; the nearest to which he could send her being Sydney in New South Wales. Some time must also be spent in rigging jury-masts and refitting her for the voyage : so that, whatever others might have thought, he very much regretted having fallen in with the brig, the battle proving, as in most instances when nations or people fall out, a loss to both parties. He gave the command to the third mate and six hands, all that could be spared ; and they would have, besides navigating the brig, to look after the prisoners, most of whom remained on board.

Fortunately the weather remained calm, though even then it took three days to prepare the brig for the voyage. A third of her crew were received on board the *Champion*, they having volunteered to join her. Both vessels then made sail, the *Champion* accompanying the prize. They had not got far, however, when the look-out at the mast-head gave the welcome cry of "There they spout! there they spout!"

"Where away?" asked the captain.

"On the weather bow," was the answer.

The captain made the signal for the brig to proceed on her voyage, and ordered the *Champion's* sails to be braced sharp up, to stand towards the whales which were seen to windward. There was a fresh breeze, which seemed likely to increase. After making a couple of tacks the ship was hove-to, and the captain ordered two boats to be lowered,—he going in one, and the second mate in the other. Away they pulled after the whales, which, however, caught sight of them, and went off in all directions. The captain made chase after one, which, taking several turns, at length came towards him. Ordering his men to lie on their oars, he stepped forward, waiting till the whale, a huge bull, came near enough, when with unerring aim he struck his harpoon deep into its side. The whale, smarting with pain, turned round, almost upsetting the boat, and away it went dead to windward at a tremendous speed right against the sea, which flew from the bows, covering her with showers of foam.

The second mate, who had gone away after another whale, observing the course the first was taking as it came by, dashed up and fixed his harpoon into the other side of the monster. Away went both the boats, towed with undiminished speed, till in a short time neither could be seen from the *Champion's* deck. Scarcely had they disappeared when several more whales were seen spouting at no considerable distance to windward. The opportunity of catching them was not to be lost, and Mr. Shobbrok ordered the two remaining boats to be lowered,—he going in one and the fourth mate in the other, leaving the ship in charge of the surgeon.

Walter had long been anxious to see a whale actually caught; and not allowing the mate time to refuse him, he jumped into his boat.

"Do let me go," he exclaimed. "The whales are not far off, and we shall soon be back with a prize." The men in their eagerness had shoved off and were giving way. Walter sprang aft to the side of the mate, who was steering. "You won't be angry with me, Mr. Shobbrok," he said; "I promise not to come again, if you object."

"I trust that no accident will happen, my boy," answered the mate. "It was for your own good alone that I wished you to remain on board, otherwise I should have been glad of your company, and given you the opportunity of seeing a whale caught."

A whole school of whales was in sight, several of them spouting together. The mates steered for them.

making sure of getting hold of a couple at least. Some were spouting, others sounding, and others just coming up again to breathe. Mr. Shobbrok steered for one which had just made its appearance above water; while the fourth mate's boat made way towards another huge monster which had already been blowing for some seconds.

The first mate's boat approached the whale he had selected. Stepping to the bows, he plunged his harpoon into the creature's side; and then taking one of the lances he thrust it deep into its body, singing out as he did so, " Back off, all !"

At that instant Walter heard a cry from the direction of the other boat. He looked round, when what was his horror to see that the boat had been struck by the whale and lifted into the air! The next instant down it came, dashed into fragments, while those in it were sent flying in all directions. The first mate, in his desire to go to the rescue of his shipmates, was on the point of heaving his own line overboard with a drougue fastened to it, when the whale he had struck, lifting up its huge flukes, sounded, nearly dragging him overboard as he let out the line. The men were backing out of its way, when suddenly it slewed round its tail. The men, well knowing their danger, made every effort to escape, and believing that they had got to a safe distance, and that the whale had gone down, pulled back to the assistance of their drowning shipmates.   Just then a tremendous blow was felt, and the boat, struck amidships, was thrown into the air as the other had been, and smashed to fragments.   The two men in the centre of the boat must have been killed instantaneously.   Walter felt stunned for a moment, but, recovering his senses, found himself struggling in the water, and close to the broken stern of the boat, to which he clung fast. Only one person remained floating above the surface. Walter called to him; and Mr. Shobbrok's voice answered, " Hold on, my lad; I'll be with you anon."

Walter saw that he was towing some of the fragments of the boat.   The whale had disappeared, possibly having carried down some of the men in his mighty jaws.   The first mate, after considerable exertion, reached Walter.

"Thank Heaven, you have escaped!" he said, helping him up on to the wreck of the boat.   Fortunately the second line remained. attached to it.

"We must put together a raft, Walter, and try to get back to the ship," said the mate.   By means of the line he set to work, and lashed together the different pieces of the boat which he managed to pick up, till he had formed a raft sufficient to support Walter. The fragments of the other boat still remained floating at no great distance.   Pushing the raft before him, he shoved it on till he reached the spot, when, collecting them, with the assistance of four oars he had

DESTRUCTION OF THE WHALE-BOAT.

picked up he formed a still larger raft, on which he, as well as Walter, could sit securely. He had also got two other oars with which to urge on the raft. Thus a considerable time was occupied, and it was now evening; before long it would be quite dark, and the difficulty of finding the ship much increased; they had less chance, also, of being picked up by either of the two other boats on their return to the ship.

Walter had not uttered a word of complaint, and had done his utmost to assist the mate. He could not help feeling how wrong he had been in getting into the boat, knowing, as he did, that his father would certainly have objected; and should he not find them, how grieved he would be on getting on board the ship to discover that they had not returned. The accident had occurred at too great a distance for those remaining on board to see what had happened, though they might, perhaps, conjecture that the boats had been destroyed.

The sun soon set, and darkness rapidly coming on, shrouded the far-distant ship from sight. The mate and Walter had done their utmost to impel the raft towards her; but gathering clouds obscured the sky, and they had no longer the means of directing their course.

"It will be impossible to reach her during the night," said the mate at length. "We are as likely to be pulling away from her as towards her; and I have a notion that the wind has shifted more than once. The best thing we can do is to lie on our oars and to wait patiently till the morning. Take care, however, my boy, that you do not drop asleep and fall off. Here, make a couple of beckets, and slip your arms through them; they will awake you if you move in your sleep."

"I have no wish to go to sleep," said Walter; "I feel too anxious to do that."

"You must not trust too much to that," said the mate. "Nature may be too powerful for you; and you will be all the better for the rest."

Still Walter insisted on endeavouring to keep awake. He was sitting up trying to pass the time with talking, when suddenly he exclaimed, "Look! look, Mr. Shobbrok! Where can that light come from?"

The mate gazed for some time, and then said solemnly, "Walter, I am afraid the ship is on fire."

CHAPTER IV.

AFTER the boats had left the ship, Alice remained on deck, attended by Nub, watching their progress. Now and then Mr. Lawrie came and spoke to her, but she was so eager that she could scarcely reply to what he said. Away dashed the two boats dancing over the waves, and were soon almost lost to sight, though Alice saw that they had reached the spot where the whales had been seen spouting. They had been gone some time when she saw Tidy come from below and speak in a hurried, anxious tone to Mr. Lawrie. He then hastened away, as if not wishing to be seen by his shipmates. Soon after the surgeon came to her, and begged that she would go into the cabin.

"Let me help you, Missie Alice," said Nub. "Better aff dere dan on deck."

Alice saw that something was wrong, but could

not make out exactly what it was.   She went, however, as Mr. Lawrie requested her; and taking up a
book endeavoured to read, but not with much success.
She saw Mr. Lawrie come in and put a brace of pistols
in his belt.   Nub and Tidy, with three or four of the
other men, did the same.   This, of course, made her
very anxious.   Several times she asked Nub if the
boats were in sight, but always got the same answer:
" No signs of boats yet, Missie Alice."   Poor girl,
she felt very forlorn with both her father and Walter
away.   Nub came in and placed the tea-things on
the table, and she made tea.   At last Mr. Lawrie came
in, apparently in a great hurry, and somewhat agitated.
Of course she asked him if the boats were in sight.

" I hope they soon will be," he answered.

" Is there anything the matter ?" she asked.

" I hope it will not be of much consequence," he
replied evasively; and without saying more, quickly
went again on deck.

It was now getting quite dark.   Nub lighted the
cabin-lamp.

" You had better take a book and read, Miss Alice,
and dat pass your time till de captain return."   Alice
found it almost impossible to keep her eyes on the
page.   Presently she heard some loud shouts and cries,
and the stamping of feet, and pistol-shots.

That there was fighting going forward on deck she
felt sure, but she dared not go up to ascertain.   The

noise increased—there was more firing—then Nub rushed into the cabin.

"Oh, what has happened?" she asked.

"I come to take care of you, Miss Alice," he answered. "De prisoners and de bad men who mutiny before try to take de ship from de surgeon and us, and dey are now fighting; and Mr. Lawrie told me to come to take care of you."

"Oh, thank you, Nub. How I wish my father was on board, to help poor Mr. Lawrie. What will he do?"

"He fight like brave Scotchman," answered Nub; "and he soon make de mutineers ask pardon. Don't be afraid, Miss Alice; de captain soon come, and all go right."

Nub, however, was more sanguine than the state of the case warranted. Mr. Lawrie, aided by the true men, had managed to drive the mutineers forward; but they were too numerous to allow him to hope for victory, unless the loyal part of the crew away in the boats should speedily return. For a short time all was again quiet; but the mutineers were merely gathering to make another rush aft. Several who had before been faithful joined them; and now again began to utter the most savage cries, this time shouting out, "Overboard with all who oppose us! Down with the officers! Death to our enemies!" They were already on the point of dashing aft to execute their threats, when thick smoke was seen ascending from the fore-hatchway, a bright flame shooting up directly afterwards in the midst of it.

"Fire ! fire ! fire !" shouted both parties of the crew.

"My lads, we must try and put it out, if we don't want to be burned alive," exclaimed the surgeon, addressing those about him. Then turning to the mutineers, he shouted out, "You men who are about to attack us,—if you have any sense left in you, I entreat you for your own sakes to assist in extinguishing the fire."

"Ay, ay, sir," cried the boatswain ; and then addressing his own party, he exclaimed, "There's sense in what the doctor says. Let's put the fire out first, and settle our differences afterwards."

All hands turned to and tried to save the ship ; but the fire had already made so much progress below that there appeared little probability of their succeeding. The buckets were collected and filled ; the hatches torn off ; and the boatswain, heading a party of the boldest, went below, while the others passed the buckets to them. Mr. Lawrie and the other officers exerted themselves to the utmost, he setting a good example by his courage and activity. Dense volumes of smoke, however, continued to ascend both from the fore and main hatchway ; while flames which had at first only flickered up occasionally now burst forth through the fore-hatchway, circling round the foremast and catching the rigging and sails.

Nub, in the meantime, who would have willingly worked with the rest, considered it his duty to remain with Alice, every now and then putting his head out of the companion-hatch to see how matters were proceeding. At last he came back, his countenance exhibiting anxiety rather than terror. "De ship will be burned; no doubt about dat, Missie Alice," he said; "and de sooner we get away de better. You help me, and we make raft on which we float till de captain comes back to take us. Don't be afraid, Missie Alice; no harm will come to you, for God will take care of us better dan we can take care of ourselves. Still, we do what we can."

"I will do whatever you advise, Nub," answered Alice, endeavouring to overcome her alarm. She did what every truly wise person under such circumstances would do—she commended herself and her companion to the care of God. She then took Nub's hand, who led her up the companion-ladder to the poop. Having obtained an axe, he immediately began to cut loose the hen-coops, spars, and gratings, and the lighter part of the wood-work of that part of the ship. Securing them to ropes, he forthwith lowered them over the side. Fortunately at this time the wind had fallen completely, so that the ship was making no way through the water. Placing Alice in one of the ports, from which she could leap if necessary into his arms, he descended, and began lashing

together the spars and gratings and pieces of wood-
work which he had thrown overboard. He could
only do this in a very rough manner, as he knew that
from the rapid progress the fire was making there was
no time to be lost. He would have called the surgeon
and Tidy to his assistance, but he was afraid if he did
so that the rest of the crew would take possession of
the raft he had commenced. His great object was to
save Alice, leaving the others to do the best they
could for themselves. He had put materials together
sufficient to bear his and her weight. While he was
working, it occurred to him that it would be necessary
to get some provisions; and securing the raft, he
sprang on deck by means of some ropes he had hung
overboard for the purpose, and rushing into the cabin,
he got hold of a small box of biscuit, a bottle of
wine, and an earthen jar full of water. With these
prizes he again descended to the raft. On his way
he observed that the surgeon and the rest of the
people were still labouring in vain endeavours to put
out the fire, and he could not help shouting to Mr.
Lawrie, " You had better build a raft, sir ; no use
trying to put out the fire."

Whether or not Mr. Lawrie heard him he could not
tell. As he was getting over the quarter, he caught
sight of a boat's sail, which he threw on the raft.
Having deposited his provisions in a hen-coop in
which a couple of fowls still remained, he sprang up

A COLOURED HERO

again to assist Alice down, as he had a feeling that she would be safer on the raft than on board the ship. He had secured a boat-hook for the purpose of catching hold of the articles he threw overboard, and was stretching out his arm to reach a piece of timber which had floated away, while Alice was holding on to a rope close to him, when a thundering sound echoed in their ears.

"O Nub, what is that?" cried Alice in a terrified tone, gazing at the fearful scene before her.

"Ship blow up, I s'pose," answered Nub, working away energetically. "Hold on, Missie Alice; no harm come to you,—we shove off directly."

An explosion had, indeed, taken place in the fore part of the ship, scattering destruction around, blowing up the deck, and sending all on that part into the water, killing some and fearfully mangling others. The fire now burst forth with increased fury, enveloping in flames the whole of the fore part of the ship. Nub, fearing that another explosion of still more terrific character would occur should the fire reach the chief magazine, which it would do, he thought, before long, shoved off with his young charge, so precious in his sight, to put as great a distance as possible between her and the danger he apprehended. He had already fastened together several pieces of wood, which he had not time to secure as perfectly as he desired; and on his way he picked up many more such fragments, as well as some casks which had been on deck, and were sent overboard by the explosion. Without loss of time he began lashing them together, soon forming a raft which he considered would be able to withstand a tolerable amount of knocking about should the sea get up.

Nub was not destitute of humanity, but though he heard the cries of his shipmates as they struggled in the water, he continued labouring away at the raft without attempting to go to the rescue.

"Oh, poor men! cannot we help them?" exclaimed Alice.

"Dey take care of demselves, Missie Alice," answered Nub. "My business is to sabe you."

"Oh, don't think of me," exclaimed Alice. "I cannot bear the thoughts of their perishing if it is possible to save them."

"It not possible, den," answered Nub; "unless I run de risk ob losing you." And he worked away as before.

The flames had now burst forth from all sides of the ship, affording him sufficient light for the purpose. Having preserved a stout spar to serve as a mast, he fixed it firmly at one. end of the raft, staying it up with the remainder of the rope, with the exception of a piece which he kept for halyards. The sail was already attached to a light yard, so that he had only to secure it to his halyards and hoist it up. This he did, bringing the sheet aft, where he placed himself, with an oar to serve as a rudder.

His great object was to get to a sufficient distance from the ship, to avoid the danger of another explosion. By this time the cries from the drowning men had ceased; and had he thought it safe to venture back to the ship, it would probably have been too late to save them. What had become of the rest of his ship-mates he could not tell. He fancied, indeed, that he heard the sound of voices; but if so, they must have been on the other side of the ship, and were thus shut out from view.

A light breeze having now got up, the raft made tolerable way, and soon got to some distance from the ship; but still fearing that the fragments might reach them and injure Alice, Nub stood on. Now and then he cast a look at the ship. It appeared to him that the flames were not making such rapid progress as at first. "After de fire burn out, we go back, Missie Alice; but still I tink we safer here dan on board de ship," he observed. "S'pose we near and de ship go down, den de oder men get on de raft and sink her."

Nub, indeed, knew that there were two dangers to be apprehended. Should the ship blow up, he and Alice might be injured by the fragments, which would probably be sent to a great distance from her; while, should she go down, the raft might be drawn into the vortex and sink with her. He could not tell at what distance they would be free from either of these two dangers; and this made him stand on much further than was in reality necessary.

. On and on he went. It seemed foolish to him to stop short of a spot of positive safety. The fierce flames were blazing up from every part of the ship, making her appear much nearer than she really was. The wind was increasing, driving the raft rapidly before it; and as the sea got up and rolled under the raft, Nub saw that the only means of preserving it from being swamped was to continue on his course.

On and on he sailed. The sea rose higher and higher, and the clouds gathered thickly in the sky. His great fear was that the seas would break aboard and sweep Alice off. To prevent so fearful a catastrophe, he begged her to let him fasten her to a hencoop, which he lashed tightly down in the centre of the raft. "Don't be afraid, Missie Alice; don't be afraid," he kept continually saying.

"I am not afraid for myself," answered Alice; "but I am thinking how miserable poor papa and Walter will be when they get back to the ship and find that I am gone. They will not know that you are taking care of me, and that we are safe on a raft. And then, if Mr. Lawrie and Dan Tidy should escape, they will not be able to say where we are gone, as they did not see us get away.   For their sakes, I wish that we could go back."

"Dat we can't do, Missie Alice ; for, if I try eber so hard, I not pull against such a gale as dis," answered Nub.

Alice was silent ; she saw that Nub's reason was a true one.   Though she had assured him that she was not frightened, she felt very anxious and alarmed about her own fate and his.

The thunder rolled, the lightning flashed, and the seas tumbled the raft so fearfully about, that had it not been put strongly together it would speedily have been broken into fragments, and she and her companion left without any support on which to preserve their lives.   The burning ship appeared further and further off, and even should the storm cease it would be almost impossible to get back to her.   At length there came a loud roar which sounded above the noise of the thunder.   The flames seemed to rise higher than before in the sky ; and even at that distance the masts, spars, and rigging could be discerned, broken into fragments, and hanging, as it were, above the fire.   Then after a few minutes all became dark !

"Dere goes de ship to de bottom," exclaimed Nub ; "I hope no one on board her.   De people had time to get away on a raft if dey got deir senses about dem."

"Indeed, I hope that Mr. Lawrie, and honest Dan Tidy and the others, managed to escape," cried Alice.

"But oh, Nub, do you think papa and Walter can have been on board ? "

" No, I tink not, Missie Alice," answered Nub. " Dey too wise to stay when de ship was burning like dat. Dey knew well enough dat she would go up in de air when de fire reach de magazine, which has just happened. Dey eider not get back, or put off again in time."

" But they will think that we were blown up, should they not have visited the ship first," said Alice; " and that will break their hearts."

" I hope not, Missie Alice. Dey know dat I had got to take care of you, and dat I got head on my shoulders, and would not do so foolish a ting as to stay on board and be blown up if I could get away. Don't be unhappy, derefore, about dat."

" I will try not," said Alice, " though it is very, very terrible."

" No doubt about dat, Missie Alice," answered Nub ; " but tings might be worse, and if de raft hold together in dis sea it will swim through any we are likely to have. Already de wind down, and it grow calmer. Suppose now we had been close to de ship when she blow up, we much worse off dan we are now. Suppose de people had made me work to put out de fire, den I had not built a raft, and we blown up,—dat much worse dan we are now ; or suppose de sea had washed over de raft and carried us away, den also we much worse off dan we are now; or suppose I had not got de biscuits and de water, den we starve, and much worse off dan we are now: so you see, Missie Alice, we bery fortunate, and hab no right to complain."

"Oh no, I am not complaining," exclaimed Alice; "I feel that we have been very mercifully preserved, and I trust that we shall be saved, though I cannot say how that is to be."

"No more can I, Missie Alice, 'cept the captain find us, or one of de oder boats; and den we have a long way to go before we reach land, I s'pose; but dere are many islands in dese seas, and perhaps we get to one of dem where we find cocoa-nuts, yams, bananas, and plenty of oder tings to eat; and den perhaps de captain build ship, and we get back some day to Old England."

By such like remarks honest Nub tried to amuse the mind of the young girl, and draw her thoughts from the fearful dangers which he saw clearly enough surrounded them. He knew perfectly well how difficult it would be for the boats to find them in that wide sea, low down as they were on the surface of the ocean. Though they might float many days, their provisions must come to an end, while their supply of water was fearfully limited, and would soon be exhausted. He resolved to touch but the smallest drop himself, that he might have more for her.

Nub was unwilling to increase his distance from the

place where the ship had gone down, as the further he
went away the less chance there was of the boats
coming up with them.   Still there was too much sea,
he considered, to make it safe to lower the sail; for
though the raft floated lightly over the waves, should
its progress be stopped he feared that they would break
on board.   The wind, which had subsided for some
time, again increased, and the danger he had apprehended became greater.   He had stepped the mast in
a hurried, and therefore imperfect manner, while he
had not stayed it up as he could have wished.   As it
was very necessary to remain at the helm, he could
do nothing to strengthen it.   All he could say was,
"Hold on, good mast! hold on!" as he saw it straining and bending before the breeze.   In what direction
he was going he could not tell.   Land had been seen the
day before, and he might be running towards it; but
then, again, the attempt to get on shore might be more
dangerous than to remain on the raft.   He also knew
well that the inhabitants of the islands in that part of
the world were generally savage cannibals, who would
murder Alice and him without the slightest compunc-
tion; or if their lives were spared, that they would
probably be reduced to the most abject slavery.   Though
he could not keep these thoughts from entering his own
mind, he did his best to cheer up the little girl by
assuming a confidence which he himself did not feel.

The sky still looked wild and threatening, the wind

blew stronger than ever. Suddenly there came a sharp report and a cracking sound, and in an instant the mast was broken sharp off, the shrouds torn away, and, with the sail, carried overboard. Nub sprang forward to secure it, but it was too late ; the raft, with the impetus it had received, drove on, and the sail was irretrievably lost. Happily at the same instant the wind suddenly dropped, and though the seas dashed the raft alarmingly about, none washed over it.

Alice, hearing the noise, and seeing Nub's agitation, became frightened. " Oh, what has happened ? " she exclaimed, for the first time giving way to tears. Nub did his utmost to quiet her alarm by assuring her that they were in no greater danger than before, and begged her to hold fast to the hen-coop, lest any of the seas which were tumbling about around them should break on the raft and sweep her overboard. Nub did his best with the long oar he had fixed as a rudder in the after part of the raft to keep it before the wind, so that it still drove on, though at much less speed than when the sail was set. Happily, soon after the last violent blast, the gale began sensibly to abate and the sea to go down, and when at length the long wished-for morning came it was almost calm. As soon as it was light enough Nub looked anxiously around in the hopes of seeing some of the boats approaching from the direction of the ship ; but no object was visible on the wild waste of waters, the raft appearing to float in the midst of a vast circle bounded by the concave sky, without a break on either side.

Alice felt very tired and sleepy, for she had not closed her eyes all the night; and Nub himself began to get excessively hungry. This reminded him of the provisions he had stowed away in the hen-coop, and he bethought him that Alice would also want some breakfast. He could now venture to leave the helm; and going to the hen-coop, he got out some biscuits and the wine and water.

"Here, Missie Alice," he said; "will you take some breakfast? It will do you good and raise your spirits. When people hungry dey always melancholy."

"But I am not melancholy, Nub, though I cannot say that I am merry; and I am not especially hungry, but if you think I ought to eat I will do so."

"Yes, yes; you will get ill if you don't eat," said Nub, offering the biscuits, and pouring out a little wine and water into a cup, which he had slipped into his pocket as he left the cabin.

Alice thanked him, and was going to eat. "Stop!" she murmured. "I have not said my prayers this morning, and I was going to begin breakfast without saying grace."

"Oh, Missie Alice, you are an angel," exclaimed Nub.

"I forgot all about saying my prayers, and I am sure an angel would not have done that," she answered.

"Oh, how ungrateful I was; but it is not too late." Before she would touch anything, she knelt down and offered up her short morning prayer, adding a petition that she and Nub, and all others she loved or was interested in, might be preserved from the dangers which surrounded them. Rising from her knees, she then reverently said grace, and ate some of the biscuit with a better appetite than she had supposed she possessed. Nub took a very small portion, and merely wetted his lips with the wine and water to quench the thirst he was already beginning to feel. He gave Alice, indeed, but a small allowance, wishing to make it last as long as possible, as he knew that they might have to remain on the raft for a long time. Again and again he looked round to see if any one was coming to their rescue; but no object being in sight, he sank down, intending to watch over Alice, who, overcome with weariness, at length fell asleep. Though he himself wished to keep awake, before long his eyelids closed, the slow up and down movement of the raft having the effect of making both the occupants sleep soundly.

The solitary raft lay on the waste of waters. Hour after hour passed by, and still the little girl and faithful black slept on, watched over by One who ever cares for the helpless and distressed who trust in Him. Hungry sharks might have jumped up and seized them in their maws; huge whales might have struck the raft with their snouts, and upset it as they rose above the water; or birds of prey might have pounced down and struck them with their sharp beaks;—but from all such dangers they were preserved, while a veil of clouds covered the sky and sheltered them from the burning rays of the hot sun of that latitude.

At length Nub started up. He had been dreaming that Alice had fallen overboard, and that he had plunged in after her to save her from a hungry shark. For a few moments, so confused were his senses, he could not tell what had happened; then finding himself on the raft, and Alice sleeping close to him, he recollected all about it. His first impulse was to stand up and look round, in the hope of seeing the boats; but, as before, not an object was in sight.

"Well, well, I s'pose de boats come in good time," he said to himself, sitting down again with a sigh. "We must wait patiently. If any land was in sight I would row to it, for though de raft might move very slowly, we should get dere at last; but now, though I pull on all day, I get nowhere. Better wait till God sends some one to help us. Perhaps when de breeze gets up again another whaler come dis way and take us on board." Nub looked at Alice. She was sleeping calmly; and knowing that the more she slept the better, he would not awake her. He himself felt very hungry, but he did not like to eat except she was sharing the meal. He could not, however, refrain from

nibbling a piece of biscuit, to try and stop the gnaw-
ings of hunger. Several times he stood up and gazed
anxiously around; sitting down, however, on each
occasion with a sigh, and saying to himself, as before,
"No sail, no boat. Well, well, help come in good
time."

At length Alice awoke, and seemed even more surprised than Nub had been to find herself on the raft.
He at once got out the biscuits, and begged her to eat
several, and to take a little wine and water.

"But you are not eating any yourself, Nub," she said.

"I have had some; but I take a little more to keep
you company," he answered, not telling her that he
had before merely nibbled a small piece. In the same
way he merely wetted his lips with the liquid, though
he would gladly have taken a cupful.

Another night was coming on. Just before the sun
sank beneath the horizon, Nub took a last look round.
Alice glanced up in his face.

"Can you see anything?" she asked in an anxious
tone.

"No, noting, Missie Alice. Perhaps to-morrow de
boats come," he answered. "We not despair; we got
food and water, and we tank God for dem."

"I will say my evening prayer," said Alice, kneeling down with her arms on the hen-coop. Nub reverently placed himself on his knees by her side, and repeated the words she used.

"I will now sing a hymn," she said, re-seating herself on the hen-coop. From that solitary spot on the desert ocean arose to heaven a sweet hymn of praise, Nub, who, like many negroes, could sing well, joining with his voice.

Darkness came down over the deep, shrouding the raft with its sable canopy. Alice, having slept so much during the day, could not for some time close her eyes; so Nub did his best to amuse her. She talked to him not only of the past but of the future, and of the hope of deliverance. Nub calculated that their stock of provisions would last, if he could manage to exist without eating more than he had hitherto done, at least for four or five days; this would give Alice enough to keep up her strength. But should help not come at the end of that time he must, he knew, die of hunger; and though she might live a few days longer, what could she do all alone on the raft? This thought made him very sad, but he tried to put it from him.

At last Alice fell asleep, and the sea remaining calm, he thought it best to follow her example, that he might endure his hunger and obtain the refreshment which sleep would give him.

Another day broke. It was spent almost as the previous one had been. No sail hove in sight, and the raft floated calmly as at first. He had thought the loss of the sail a great misfortune, but for the last two days it would have been of no use except to afford some shelter to Alice ; and perhaps, like other things which people at first look on as misfortunes, the loss might prove ultimately advantageous.

With Nub's assistance Alice could move about a little on the raft, to prevent her limbs from becoming benumbed. Frequently she begged him to let her stand upon the hen-coop, that she might look around to watch for any sail which might heave in sight ; each time, however, only meeting with disappointment. The arching sky and circling expanse of water were, as before, alone visible.

Towards evening Nub became more anxious. He did not like the look of the weather. Dark clouds were gathering overhead, and the sea rose and fell in ominous undulations, which he fancied betokened a storm. Still he could do nothing. He felt his own helplessness ; and this God often designs should be the case, that men may place their entire dependence on Him who alone can afford help in time of need.

Nub did not speak of his fears to Alice, who at length fell asleep while he sat watching by her side, ready to hold her fast should the sea get up as he expected it would do. He was mistaken, however, in his anticipations of evil; for though the threatening appearance of the weather did not go off, the ocean remained as calm as before.

Another day came round. Nub was constantly on his feet looking about for the expected sail, as there was a light breeze, which might have brought one towards them. Hour after hour passed by and no sail appeared.

"Will a ship neber come?" frequently ejaculated Nub. He was losing patience, and it was but natural. "The biscuits and water will soon be all gone, and den what shall we do?" he thought to himself; but he did not say that aloud, lest Alice might be alarmed.

"I am sure that the boats, or a ship, will find us to-morrow," said Alice.

"Why do you tink dat?" asked Nub.

"Because our biscuits are coming to an end," said Alice calmly; "and, Nub, I see that you eat very few of them, and you are growing weak and thin. You ought to take twice as many as I do, as you are twice as big ; and yet I am sure that you eat much fewer."

"How you know dat, Missie Alice?" asked Nub.

"Because the last time you served them out I counted the number you took ; and while you gave me four, you only ate two yourself."

"Well, you bery cunning girl," said Nub, trying to laugh. "But den remember you are growing, and want food more dan I do. I have only to eat enough to keep body and soul togeder ; and you have not been accustomed to hardships as I have since I can remember ; so you see dat it's right I should give you more dan I take myself."

Alice did not quite understand Nub's reasoning, but

she felt very hungry, and was thankful to obtain the food.

"Now, Missie Alice, I am not going to eat any more of de biscuits," said Nub. "De next food I take will be one of de fowls."

"But how can you light a fire to cook them?" asked Alice.

"I eat dem raw! Much better eat dem dan die."

Poor Alice shuddered. Nub knew that it was high time to kill one of the fowls, for though their troughs were full of food when he lowered the coop on to the raft, it had long since been exhausted. Alice turned her head aside when Nub put one of the fowls out of its misery, and eagerly drank up the blood to quench the burning thirst from which he was suffering. He did not offer her any, as he knew that while any wine and water remained she would not touch it. He felt in better spirits, and much stronger, after this meal.

He also imbibed some of the hope which inspired Alice, that they might be relieved before long. Still, when the sun went down again, and the night once more began, his spirits drooped. He could no longer keep awake as he had done on the previous night, and as soon as she had closed her eyes his head began to nod, and he fell asleep. He slept soundly, for the raft moved quietly about. Nothing occurred for several hours to disturb him. At length he was startled by a loud peal of thunder. He looked up. The sky was overcast; a vivid flash of lightning darted from the clouds, followed by another terrific peal, which awoke Alice.

"Oh! what is the matter?" she exclaimed.

"A thunder storm," he answered. "But de sea calm, and de lightning not hurt us." It required firm faith, however, to believe that such would not be the case.

At times the whole heavens were lighted with vivid flashes, while the thunder roared and crashed on every side. This continued for some time. Nub stood up and looked around him. Alice saw him gazing intently to windward; she rose and took his hand.

"What is it you see?" she asked.

"It may be only de white top of a wave," he answered.

There was a cessation of the lightning in that part of the heavens for a minute or more, but Nub kept looking steadily in the same direction. Presently another vivid flash darted across the sky, lighting up a wide portion of the ocean.

"Dere! dere now! I see it again!" exclaimed Nub. " Yes, Missie Alice, yes, dat is a sail; I am sure of it. Dere it gone again; but you will see it soon, if you look with all your eyes. Alice did look with might and main, waiting for another flash. Presently the heavens were lighted up more brilliantly than before, the glare falling fully on a white sail, which seemed at no great

A FEARFUL NIGHT

distance off. Once more all was dark; but Alice and Nub continued to gaze in the direction where they had seen the sail, in the expectation that it would re-appear. They waited in vain. They raised their voices together, and shouted, in the hope of being heard by those on board. Nub's voice, however, was weak and hollow; Alice's was almost as loud, and far shriller.

"Dey cannot hear us," said Nub at length. "Dey too far off." Still he stood and gazed, and again and again shouted out. His fear was that the boat (for such, he conjectured, was the object he had seen, and which appeared to be running before the wind) might pass in the darkness either on one side or the other, and that he and his beloved charge might be left to perish on the waste of waters. He waited for some time.

"Dey must be bit nearer now," he said at length. "We try to make dem hear." He and Alice again lifted up their voices, and shouted till they could shout no more.

"Hark!" cried Nub, "I tink I hear a voice."

CHAPTER V.

E left Walter and Mr. Shobbrok on their hastily-constructed raft at the moment they had discovered that the ship was on fire. Having now a light from the burning ship to direct their course, they got out their oars and urged on the raft with all the strength they could exert. They had succeeded in fixing the bow of the shattered boat to one end of it, and they were thus able, in the calm water, to make far better way than they would otherwise have done. They were in a terrible state of anxiety. Walter more than ever blamed himself for having left the ship. Had he remained on board, he might have been able to assist Alice; and should she perish, he could never forgive himself. There were no boats on board, they knew, and the people would scarcely have time to construct a raft without an officer of experience to direct them. They rowed and rowed with all their power, and it was evident that they were approaching the ship.

"The fire seems at present to be confined to the fore part of the ship," observed Mr. Shobbrok. "If so, we may have time to assist in forming a raft for saving ourselves and the rest. If I had been on board, I would have set every man with axes to cut away the upper works and mizzen-mast, and we should soon have materials for the purpose."

"I am thinking of poor, dear Alice," exclaimed Walter. "How dreadfully frightened she will be! Oh, what shall I do should anything happen to her?"

"We must trust to Him who will, if He thinks fit, find the means of preserving her," said the mate. "Row away, Walter; we must not think about what may happen, but exert ourselves to the utmost to do our duty, and that is to get on board as soon as possible. Row away, my boy, row away."

Walter did not need any incitement to labour; but, though he was not aware of it, while he was talking he had actually relaxed his efforts.—(Not an unusual circumstance. People, when talking, too often forget to *do*. There is no lack of talkers in the world. Doers are much rarer. We want our readers to belong to the latter class.)—Taking Mr. Shobbrok's advice, Walter did not utter another word, but rowed away as hard as he could. Their united exertions made the raft move at a considerable rate through the water.

They were still at some distance, when Mr. Shobbrok, who was guiding the raft, and in order to do so had to look towards the ship, uttered an exclamation of grief.

"O Walter, the fore-part has blown up!" he cried out, "and must have sent many of the poor fellows to the bottom.   But pull on! pull on! we may yet be in time to save your young sister."

Walter said nothing, but his heart was almost breaking with anxiety.

"The flames are not spreading as fast as I thought they would," said Mr. Shobbrok.   "We may still be in time."

On they rowed, till at length they got near enough to have seen any one remaining on the deck of the ship; but not a person appeared, although the mizzen-mast was still standing, and the flames had not yet reached the poop.

At length they got under the quarter, and making fast their raft by means of a rope which hung down, they hauled themselves on board.   Walter rushed into the cabin, but Alice was not there, and no one was to be seen.

"Don't be cast down, Walter," said Mr. Shobbrok. "It is evident that they must have built a raft and left the ship.   We must do what we can, while time is allowed us, to build one for ourselves.   We must be quick about it, for before long the fire will reach the magazine, and we must take care to be at a safe distance before then." Saying this, he rushed into the cabin, and returned with a couple of axes. One he gave to Walter, and the other he took himself, and they both began cutting away at the taffrail and quarter rail. He then sprang aloft, and telling Walter to stand from under, with a few strokes brought the gaff, the cross-jack, and mizzen-top-sail yards down on deck, while he at the same time cleared the mass of the running rigging, preserving the most perfect coolness and exhibiting the most wonderful activity. He soon collected ample materials for the purpose he had in view. The spars were light, and were soon cut into the lengths he required; and ably seconded by Walter he quickly hove them overboard, secured to ropes to prevent them from floating away from the ship as she moved through the water. Having collected their materials, they descended upon their former raft and began at once to lash the pieces of timber closely together, so as to form an oblong and compact raft.

"Take care, Walter, to secure every lashing properly," said Mr. Shobbrok; "it is better to spend a little more time about it now, than to find our raft come to pieces in the first heavy sea we encounter."

The mizzen-royal, which had been sent down at nightfall, remained on deck, and the mate had lowered it on to their first raft. The framework having been formed, he once more sprang up on deck.

"You remain, Walter; I will be back in a moment," he sang out.

Walter was very anxious while he was gone, for he had not forgotten what Mr. Shobbrok had said about the magazine. He soon heard him crying out,— "Take hold of this, and see it does not capsize." Looking up, he found that a basket was being lowered. He placed it on the most secure part of the raft. Directly afterwards Mr. Shobbrok lowered down a hammer and a large bag of nails.

"I must see what more can be got," he cried out. Directly afterwards he sprang over the side and descended rapidly on to the raft.

"Shove off, my boy, shove off! there's not an instant to be lost!" he exclaimed; and he and Walter, seizing the oars, pulled away on their former raft, towing the one they had just formed after them. As it floated lightly, they managed to make fair way, though by this time the sea had somewhat increased, the wind having suddenly got up. They had not got more than two cables length from the ship when a loud roar announced that the magazine had exploded; the foremast and main-mast, which had hitherto stood, fell over the side, while the mizzen-mast shot up into the air. They narrowly escaped from some of the smaller pieces of the burnt fragments of the ship, which came down on the raft.

"There goes the *Champion*," cried Mr. Shobbrok.

"It's a sad ending; but sadder for those will it be who come to look for her, and find only a blackened wreck floating on the water."

As he spoke, the stern of the ship lifted out of the water, while the burning bows dipping beneath the surface, she gradually descended into the depths of the ocean, and ere a minute was over, had disappeared from sight.

"We may be thankful that we got away in time," sighed the old mate. "Well, well, I thought we should have got home safely in her; but it was God's will. We must trust to Him, and not despair, whatever happens."

"I try to do so," said Walter; "but I wish I knew what had become of dear Alice and our father. If he has not yet visited the ship, it will well-nigh break his heart when he does come back, to find her gone. He will think we are all lost."

"If he has not visited the ship, he will not be certain whether she has gone down,—though, to be sure, that would be almost as bad; for he will suppose that the scoundrel of a boatswain and the French prisoners have got possession of her and made off,—knowing to a certainty that we should never have left the spot till he had returned," answered the mate.

"Then I hope that he has visited the ship," said Walter; "and now I think of it, he must have seen the fire at a great distance, and would have come back as fast as he could.   He might easily have passed us in the dark without seeing us.   Perhaps his boat and the other took the people off, and he has Alice safe with him."

" I don't think that," said the mate ; " for from what I observed when I was on board, I am sure that they must have made a raft.   The main and main-top-sail-yards, and all the spare spars on deck, and a good part of the bulwarks and the hatches and gratings, were gone ; had they been left, I should at all events have seen the burnt ends.   I took it in at a glance, though I did not tell you so at the time."

" But that does not prove that the boats did not visit the ship," observed Walter.   " They could not carry all the people.   I rather think that my father did come back, and had the raft built under his orders."

" Well, well, lad," answered the mate, " as I said before, we will hope for the best ; and as soon as it is daylight we must set to work and secure our raft better than it is at present, or it will not stand the sea we are likely to have on before long."

By this time the wind had greatly increased, and the sea was tumbling the raft about from side to side in a way which would have made it impossible for any one but a practised seaman, as was the mate, and an active boy like Walter, to keep their footing.   Dark clouds had gathered in the sky ; the lightning flashed and the thunder roared.   Still the mate and Walter did not lose courage, but exerted themselves to keep the materials with which they intended to complete their raft together.   Happily, however, though the weather was so threatening, the sea did not continue to increase, and towards dawn it once more sensibly abated.

"Now, Walter, while we have got a lull, let us set to work to finish this raft of ours," said Mr. Shobbrok.

"Ay, ay," answered Walter; "tell me what to do, and I will do it as soon as we have got light enough to see with."

"We shall have that before long : the first streaks of dawn are appearing in the sky," observed the mate.

"Then I hope we may get a sight of the boats, for they are not likely to have run far from the ship," said Walter.

As the light increased sufficiently to enable them to see objects at a distance, they stood up and took an anxious glance around; but the horizon on all sides was unusually obscured, and their view consequently limited.   Walter, whose young eyes were keener than those of the mate, fancied that he caught sight of an object which looked like a boat's sail away to leeward, but if such was the case it soon disappeared.   He made out, however, on the part of the ocean where the ship had gone down, numerous pieces of wreck, casks, and spars, and other articles, which, escaping burning, had floated ; but they were too far off to enable him to distinguish clearly what they were.

"Come, lad, let's turn to and work," said the mate.

The first thing they did was more completely to secure the spars and pieces of timber which formed the frame-work of their raft.   They then took the wreck of the boat to pieces and nailed the planks down on the centre, so as to make a thick flooring, which enabled them to walk about and keep their feet out of the water, though it here and there still spouted up through the interstices of the planks.   They also gave it greater buoyancy by sinking some of the casks they had secured under the framework, and firmly securing them.   They then fixed two oars at either side of one end of the raft, and stayed them up, so that a sail might be hoisted between them.   Some time was thus spent, for the sea tumbled them about a good deal, and it was no easy matter to work.   It was necessary, indeed, to keep all the articles lashed together till they were wanted, or they would have been washed away.

They had been too eagerly employed to think of eat-ing ; at length, however, when their task was accom-plished, Walter looked up and said, "Are you hungry, Mr. Shobbrok ? "

"I think you must be," answered the mate.   "We will see what the basket contains, for I tumbled into it whatever I could get hold of in a hurry, and I am greatly afraid that there is not as much food as we could wish for."

The mate and Walter sat down on the centre of their raft and anxiously examined the contents of their basket. There was a small piece of cooked salt beef, a few biscuits, and part of a Dutch cheese; a scanty supply for two persons with little prospect of obtaining more till they could reach land. There were, however, several bottles, but what they contained it was difficult to say without opening them: one certainly had oil in it, two were full of red wine, and two others of a white liquid, as it appeared when they were held up to the sun.

"I hope it may be water," exclaimed Walter; "for I am very thirsty already."

"I am sorry to say that it's not," answered the mate; "for they are tightly corked up. It must be gin, which is at all events better than nothing."

"I would give both of them for a bottle of water," said Walter.

"We must try to do without it, however, and endure thirst as long as we can," said the mate. "Let us be thankful for what we have got."

Walter and the mate each ate one of the biscuits and a small piece of the meat and cheese; but they did not take much meat, for fear of exciting thirst. Walter took a very little wine.

"We must husband our stores, to make them last

longer. I will tell you what we will do to prevent ourselves suffering from thirst—I have known the plan to succeed, and enable people to go many days without drinking, without being much the worse for it. We will dip our clothes twice a day in the water, and our skins will thus soak up as much moisture as we absolutely require; though I will allow it would be pleasanter if we had a little cold water to pour down our throats."

They both did as the mate advised, and found much benefit from it. It has been known, indeed, under similar circumstances, to preserve the lives of people who might otherwise have perished. The mate, however, cautioned Walter on no account to drink the salt water, however tempted by thirst, as it has a powerful effect, and in many instances has produced madness. Walter promised strictly to follow the mate's advice.

"I give it to you now," said the mate, "because there is no saying what may happen to me. You are young, and may survive, while I may knock under from the hardships we may have to endure. I would give my few remaining years of life to know that you were safe, and restored to your father."

"Oh, don't talk thus, Mr. Shobbrok," said Walter; "I hope that you may live and get back safely to Old England."

The mate had waited near to the spot where the ship had gone down, on the possibility of the boats returning, but the day was now drawing on, and they did not appear.

"There's no use in remaining here longer, I am afraid," he said at length. "We will make sail, and run before the breeze. There's land away to the eastward, though I'm afraid it's a long way off; however, if we can get there, we may obtain food and water, at all events. As far as I can judge, it's the only thing we can do under present circumstances. Perhaps we may be picked up by a ship, as whalers frequent these seas."

Walter of course agreed to the mate's proposal, and accordingly the sail was hoisted between two oars, a third oar serving as a rudder. The breeze freshened, and the raft ran swiftly over the water. Night at length approached. Walter felt very drowsy, and could with difficulty keep his eyes open, though he made strenuous efforts to do so. The mate observing him, said, "Lie down, Walter; you are less accustomed to long watches than I am. Get some sleep, my lad; and when I think you have had enough of it, and should the weather continue moderate, I will call you, and you can take a spell at the helm."

Walter thankfully did as the mate advised, and was soon in the land of dreams, and far away in old England. He once, when a little boy, had had a fever, and he thought he was lying on his bed as he then did, with his fond mother watching over him, and giving him cooling draughts, and singing a sweet song he loved to hear. He was awakened at length by the old mate calling him. His mouth felt dreadfully parched. What would he not have given for a cup of that refreshing beverage which he had dreamt of in his sleep!

"Come, Walter," said the mate, "you may take the helm; and mind you don't fall overboard. An hour's sleep will set me to rights, and then you shall have some more rest."

"I will give the old man more than an hour's sleep," thought Walter, as he got up and took the oar in his hand.

"Keep her before the wind," said Mr. Shobbrok, lying down; "and if there is any change, call me immediately."

Walter steered on as directed, keeping the raft before the wind, and watching the stars which ever and anon shone out between the passing clouds. He felt almost sure that the wind had shifted several points, and that he was now steering much more to the north than at first. It was very light, and the raft made but little progress. He suspected that the old mate had purposely allowed him to sleep on till near daylight; and he determined to return his kindness by not arousing him, but allowing him to awake of his own accord. Mr. Shobbrok, however, was so accustomed to awake at the hour he intended, that before long he got up, and smilingly said, "Well, Walter, I hope you

are the better for your rest; I can honestly say that
I am. And now, I dare say that you are ready for
breakfast."

Walter confessed that he was; but when he tried
to get the salt meat and dry biscuit down, he could
scarcely swallow it. How he longed for a cup of cold
water! A little wine which the mate served out
slightly relieved him, but he soon got thirsty again.
They both tried the effect of wetting their clothes;
but that was only a partial relief. When the sun
came out, and its rays struck down with fiery heat
on their heads, they both began to suffer painfully.
Wine enabled them to swallow their food, but it was
water they wanted. The wind fell, and the raft lay
rocking about, making no progress. They neither of
them felt much inclined to talk. While Walter took
the helm, the mate, with his hammer and nails, gave
a few finishing touches to the raft, and added fresh
lashings to the parts which he thought required to be
better secured.

The next night passed away much as the first had
done. The mate told Walter he must keep the first
watch. Walter fancied that he should be able to
let the mate have a good long spell of sleep; but he
was mistaken, for in less than a couple of hours
the old man got up and insisted on his lying down;
and when he awoke he found that daylight had returned. They were both by this time beginning to

suffer greatly from want of water. Mr. Shobbrok kept his thoughts to himself, but he knew too well what must be the result. Both wetted their clothes; their thirst continued to increase; they felt, however, that it would have been much worse had they not adopted that course. The day wore on, and poor Walter gave signs of severe suffering though he did not complain aloud. The wind had fallen to a dead calm, and the raft floated motionless on the water; then, the sail being useless, the mate lowered it. Ceasing to look out for any sail in sight, for he knew that none could approach, he pounded up some biscuit and moistened it with wine; but even then Walter could scarcely get it down his throat. The old man gazed on the lad with pitying eye and sorrowing heart, as he saw that he could not much longer endure his sufferings. He himself, strong as he was and inured to hardships, began to feel the agony of thirst; his lips were parched, his mouth dry. He wetted Walter's clothes and his own, and he washed his mouth out frequently with salt water, bidding Walter do the same; but they found their throats become almost immediately afterwards as dry as before.

The sun again went down, and the comparative coolness of night somewhat relieved them. The mate feared that Walter would not be able to endure another day. The stars shining brightly from the sky were reflected on the mirror-like surface of the deep. All around looked calm and peaceful. Walter soon fell asleep. "He will forget his sorrows, poor boy, and will be the better for it," thought the mate as he sat watching by his side; yet he could not help dreading that it might be his young friend's last sleep here below. "Well, well, he is a true Christian lad, and will be saved much pain and sorrow, and many trials. God knows what is best. He takes those he loves most; though, if the captain survives, it will go well nigh to break his heart." These thoughts occupied the mind of the worthy mate, till, overcome by weariness and exhaustion, he himself lay down, resting his head on a piece of timber which served as Walter's pillow. He soon fell asleep, and seldom, perhaps, had he slept so soundly. He was awakened at length by a bright glare in his eyes; and starting up, he found that the sun had just risen out of his ocean bed. The whole sky, however, was quickly obscured; for dark clouds hanging low down were gliding across the heavens. The mate watched them eagerly, for he saw that in several directions they were sending down copious showers on to the still calm surface of the ocean. Now on one side, now on another, he saw the rain falling, but none came near where the raft lay. He would not arouse Walter—who was still sleeping—knowing how the sight would tantalize him; but he knelt by his side, and prayed that the rain might reach them. Then he stood up and gazed around, hoping against hope that a sail might be in sight; but not an object was to be seen. On every side to the edge of the horizon the sea presented the same glass-like surface. The clouds were coming from the north-east, and a breeze would probably spring up from that direction. He stood watching the clouds, and while he watched he bethought him of a plan for catching the rain should it come at last. Two or three of the boat's planks were still not nailed down; he took one of them, and with his knife split it into thin strips; these he fastened together so as to form a large hoop; then casting off the sail from the yard, he placed it over the hoop, and allowed it to sink down in the centre, thus making a large basin. He next considered how the precious water, if caught, could be preserved,—when he recollected that he had secured a small empty water-cask under the stern of the raft. He at once cast loose the lashing which held it, and hauled it on board; and it apparently made but little difference on the buoyancy of the raft. After some difficulty he got out the bung, and held it with the hole downwards, to be sure that no salt water had got within; and lastly, he placed it in readiness to be filled.

He had just accomplished his task, when, looking to windward, he exclaimed, " Thank Heaven, it's coming !" He now touched his companion on the arm. " Rouse up, my lad," he said; " we are not forsaken."

Walter slowly raised his head.

" There, there !" added the mate; " look at yonder

blessed shower ! It will reach us before many minutes are over. I can almost see the drops as they splash into the salt sea."

Poor Walter crawled to the other end of the raft, to hold up the hoop as the mate bade him. The shower approached, its course marked by a line of hissing bubbles. The sound of the drops, as they struck the surface of the ocean and bounded up again, could be heard. It reached them sooner than they expected. They raised the sail which had been prepared to catch it. Down came the precious rain, quickly filling the sail; while they eagerly opened their mouths, that not a drop more than they could help should be lost. But as the water rose in the sail, they could no longer help dipping down their heads and taking a long refreshing draught. It produced an almost instantaneous effect on Walter, whose strength seemed suddenly to return. "Oh, how merciful God has been to us!" were the first words he uttered. "I now feel sure that we shall be saved; but last night I had begun to fear that we were doomed to perish."

"I thought the same," said the mate; "but it was wrong of us. Under all circumstances, however hopeless, we should trust in God."

The cask had been placed directly under the centre of the sail, in which the mate making a small hole with the point of his knife, the water ran through into it. So rapidly descended the rain, that it was quickly filled. Had they possessed another cask, they would gladly have filled it; but they could not venture to withdraw any of the larger casks from beneath their raft; and they trusted that the supply they had now obtained would last them till land was made, or they were relieved by a passing ship. "At all events," said Walter, "we may hope to get another shower to replenish our cask of water when this is exhausted."

"You must not count too much on that, my lad," answered the mate.

"What think you, then, of throwing away some of the wine or spirits, and filling up the bottles with water?" asked Walter.

"I should be sorry to throw it all away; for, though the water is the most precious liquid of the two, the wine may yet be of great service to us, as it is the only medicine we have got. I am willing to empty one bottle of wine and one of spirits; but we will keep the rest in case we need it."

On this the mate drew two of the bottles out of the basket. He looked at them, evidently doubting whether he was acting wisely in throwing the contents away. At the bottom of the basket he discovered a large cup which he had before overlooked. He half filled it with wine; then casting an affectionate look at the bottle, he exclaimed, "It would be a pity."

A WELCOME SHOWER.

And putting it to his mouth, sailor-like, he took a few hearty gulps. "Now, Walter," he said, "before we throw the wine away, just take some biscuit and this bit of beef. It will give you the strength you want so much; and then, to my mind, some wine and water will help to make it go further than it would otherwise do."

Walter very willingly did as the mate advised, and ate the biscuit and beef with more appetite than he had felt since they had been on the raft. The mate then handed him a cup of wine, which he had diluted with water. Walter thankfully swallowed the liquid.

"Now, it has done you good, has it not?" said the mate.

Walter nodded.

"I knew it would; and instead of throwing the wine away, we will fill the bottle up with water. We shall then have a mixture all ready. Now, as for the rum, that's bad by itself, I know; but, mixed with water, it will help to digest our dry biscuit and cheese, and any other food we may obtain,—which, if we do get any, we shall have to eat raw."

The mate was a temperate man, and had never been drunk in his life. But what are called temperance principles were not known in those days. He took his share of biscuit and beef; then pouring some rum into the cup, mixed it with water from the sail, afterwards filling up the rum bottle with water.

He evidently felt satisfied that they had not yielded to their first impulse and thrown the wine and spirits away.

"Now, to my mind, Walter, both the wine and spirits are given to us as blessings; and what we have got to do is not to abuse them. If we had a disorderly crew, I would stave in every spirit-cask on board sooner than let them get drunk. But our case is very different; and as neither you nor I are likely to take more than would be good for us, and having a wine-cask full of the more precious liquid, I am sure we should be wrong in throwing away what may, under present circumstances, help to preserve our lives."

All this time Walter and the mate had been kneeling with the sail, still half full of water, between them. The rain had ceased. They looked affectionately at the precious fluid. It might be long before they could get any more. Once again they each dipped down their heads and took another long draught. The mate suddenly exclaimed,—"We will still make use of it. We will first bathe our heads and faces, and then wash our clothes, to get some of the salt out of them. It will make us feel more comfortable, and help to keep the scurvy at bay. At present I feel like a Yarmouth bloater."

Walter was greatly refreshed by his ablutions. He then thoroughly washed his shirt, and wringing it out, hung it up to dry. The old mate afterwards performed the same operation. At length they allowed the water to escape from the sail. Scarcely had they done so when, a light breeze springing up, they hoisted it and stood on to the westward. The raft made but slow progress; and though the voyagers no longer suffered from thirst, they could not help feeling anxious as they looked after each meal at the scanty supply of food which remained. The meat was almost exhausted, and scarcely half-a-dozen biscuits were left, while their piece of cheese had been reduced to very small dimensions.

"We have a bottle of oil," said the mate, as he saw Walter gazing anxiously into the basket. "That will help to keep life in us; though train oil was never much to my fancy."

"Nor to mine," said Walter. "But our biscuits would prove more nutritious if we were to soak them in it; though I confess that I would rather eat them as they are."

"We will try your plan," said the mate; and accordingly, the next time he served out provisions, he broke up some biscuit into the cup, and poured a little oil upon it. Walter made a wry face as he took his share; but he ate it notwithstanding, owning that, although the taste was not pleasant, it seemed to go much further than dry biscuit itself. The mate being of opinion that there was no use in dying by inches, gave Walter rather more of the meat and cheese than perhaps was prudent—he taking a much less quantity himself.

Another day passed away, and the only food remaining were the biscuits, with the oil, which, nauseous as it tasted, was not to be despised. The calm continued. The old mate felt conscious that he himself was growing weaker and weaker, and he feared that poor Walter would begin to suffer even more severely before long. There was just wind enough to waft on the raft; but many days must pass before they could possibly reach land. Wine and water would help to sustain them, and they might even gnaw the leather of their shoes.

"Well, well," thought the mate, "I won't alarm the lad; and Heaven may send us aid when we least expect it."

CHAPTER VI.

THE raft glided on over the smooth surface of the ocean. The old mate was standing up steering, while Walter, already feeling the pangs of hunger, was lying stretched at his length in the shade cast by the sail; for the intense heat of the sun, which was striking down from an almost cloudless sky, was almost insupportable. Mr. Shobbrok constantly looked around on every side.

"Any vessel in sight?" asked Walter, sitting up. A shake of the head was the answer he received; and lying down again, he closed his eyes. Once more he sat up, and seeing the mate casting an eager glance around, he asked him what he saw.

"Dolphins or bonitoes playing about. If we had a harpoon, we might chance to get hold of one."

"Could we manage to manufacture something that would answer the purpose?" asked Walter.

"Nothing that would be of use, I am afraid," said

the mate. "But see, Walter, see! there comes what I have been praying for."

Walter looked in the direction the mate was pointing out, and saw a large covey of flying-fish darting towards them. First a couple, then three, then four more, fell directly on to the raft. Walter and the mate quickly secured them. As most of them appeared to be directing their course some way ahead, the mate allowed the raft to glide on, by that means being able to knock down four more, which would otherwise have flown over it—the remainder quickly disappearing beneath the surface. The two voyagers collected the fish which lay on the raft.

"I wish we could keep them alive," said Walter.

"That's more than we can do. We must be thankful that we have got these ; and He who sent them to us may send us more when we require them. And now, my lad, the sooner we get some of them down our throats the better, for you want food, and so, I confess, do I."

"What! eat them raw?" exclaimed Walter.

"Ay, lad ; and for my part I could almost eat them alive. But I will try how I can make them more fit for you to swallow. Hand me that bit of board and the axe. Now, just get out some biscuit and the oil."

Walter gave the articles to the mate, who, kneeling down, cut off the heads and tails of the fish, and sepa-

SAVED FROM STARVATION.

rated the flesh from the bones. He then mashed it up with some biscuit, moistening it with some oil till he had made a thick paste.

"Now, try this. But first let us thank God for sending us the food; and may He feed our souls as well as He feeds our bodies." Saying this, he put a large lump into his own mouth, and quickly swallowed it, adding another portion in like haste, for he was in truth famishing. Walter found the mixture far more tolerable than he had expected, for he had got accustomed to the taste of the oil. The meal was soon finished, and was washed down with some wine and water. Both the mate and Walter found themselves much stronger after the meal, and did not fail again to return thanks to God for sending it to them. They then collected the rest of the fish, which they cut open, and, at the mate's suggestion, hung up in the sun to dry; reserving two to eat fresh at their next meal. The heat of the sun and the nature of their food made them very thirsty, and Walter especially was much inclined to drink freely from the water-barrel.

"Remember, my lad," said the mate, "that won't last for ever, and we must take care to economise it. Just take a little now and then when you feel overcome with thirst. To my mind, under our circumstances it would be as wrong to keep drinking away at our water-barrel as it is for a man to spend his fortune without thinking of the future.   That's our chief wealth just now."

Walter, after this, followed the mate's example, and only took a mouthful at a time, when he felt his throat unusually dry.

Onward they sailed, not always in a straight course ; for they were obliged to keep before the wind, which occasionally shifted a few points of the compass. They were several times tantalized by seeing other coveys of flying-fish rising out of the water, and darting fifty feet, and sometimes even one hundred feet, over the surface ; but none came near them.   They saw also dolphins and bonitoes swimming near them, and occasionally caught sight of a large shark, with its black fin just above the water.   Now and then a bonito came so near to the raft, that had they possessed a harpoon they could easily have caught it. The mate, indeed, could not resist the temptation of giving one of them a blow on the head with his oar, hoping to stun it ; but the creature, notwithstanding the heavy thump it had received, darted off, and was lost to sight.   "If I had been wise, I should have had a running bowline ready, and we would have caught the fellow," said the mate.   "I will have one for the next, and if we are quick about it we may get him on board."   The rope was prepared, and Walter kept eagerly on the watch ; but the wished-for opportunity, as is often the case when once a chance has been lost, did not return. Two or three big fish came swimming by them, however, but too far off to be caught—apparently to have a look at the strangers passing across their domain.

The end of another day was approaching, and the weather, hitherto calm and fine, gave indications of a change.

"Provided we get a good stiff breeze from the eastward, I shall be thankful," said the mate.

"We shall the sooner reach shore or fall in with a ship; and although our raft will stand a good deal of sea, I would rather be in a good whale-boat under such circumstances," said Walter.

"So would I, lad; but we must be contented with what we have got. That's my opinion, and it's about the best a man can have. Now, Walter, I want you to take the helm," said the mate. "I expect to have a pretty long watch at night, and a few winks of sleep will enable me to stand it. Call me if it comes on to blow harder than at present—as I expect it will—or if you see anything which you cannot quite make out."

Walter quickly went to the helm, for the food he had taken had greatly restored his strength, and enabled him to stand up firmly. The mate lay down, and before Walter could count thirty the old sailor was fast asleep.

Walter steered on. Although clouds were already

gathering in the sky, the wind continued moderate, and he hoped that the mate would be able to take a longer spell of sleep than he had expected to do.

The sun went down with a fiery red appearance, and scarcely had it sank beneath the horizon when the gloom of night came sweeping over the deep. The wind shortly afterwards began to increase; but still, as the raft did not tumble about much, Walter considered that he was right in not calling the mate. Presently, however, a vivid flash of lightning darted from the clouds, followed almost immediately by a crashing peal. Mr. Shobbrok started up. "Why, Walter," he said, "you should have called me when the weather changed."

"The storm has only this instant burst on us," answered Walter. "I wished you to have as much rest as possible. I do not feel myself inclined to go to sleep."

"I suppose not, my lad," said the mate; "but I will take the helm, at all events, and you can stand by the halliards. We must take a reef in our sail, if it comes on to blow much harder."

The wind, however, did not greatly increase, and they stood on. The lightning continued to flash and the thunder to roar, but the sea remained calm. Frequently the whole heavens were lighted up altogether; then only in one direction, and now in another. Walter, who had never seen such vivid lightning or heard the thunder roar so loudly, very naturally felt somewhat alarmed.

"Is the lightning likely to strike us?" he asked at length.

"I think not, my lad. We have but little iron about our raft; and though iron is said to attract it, we are so low down on the surface that I believe it will pass harmlessly over our heads. A large ship, with her taunt masts, would be in much greater danger than this small raft. We must trust to Him who rules the winds and seas, and the lightning also. It won't do to be sometimes trusting Him and sometimes not. It's as easy for Him to save us out of a great danger as out of what we call a small one. Not that I think we are in any especial danger now; nor shall we be as long as the sea remains calm."

Walter's anxiety was greatly relieved by the mate's assurances. He sat down on the raft. They had been steadily running on for some time, when a vivid flash lighted up the sky and all the ocean to the westward.

"I saw something floating on the water, right ahead," said Walter. "What it was I cannot exactly say, though it seemed to me to be like a piece of wreck, and I thought for the moment that I saw people on it."

"Keep a bright look-out then, my lad," answered the mate. "We shall probably have another flash presently, and then you will see clearly. Stand by to lower the sail, that I may have a look at it too."

Walter cast off the halliards, and tried with all his might to pierce the gloom.

"There! there!" he exclaimed, letting go the halliards as another flash darted from the sky. "It's a raft with two people on it. We are close upon them."

A hail came from the raft uttered by two voices.

"O Mr. Shobbrok, that was Nub's voice, and Alice's too! I am sure of it," exclaimed Walter, scarcely able to speak from excitement. He then, lifting up his own voice, shouted in return—"Is that you, Alice? Is that you, Nub?"

"Yes, yes," answered Nub; "praise Heaven, we all right! Is dat you, Massa Walter?"

"Yes," answered Walter.

"O Walter! O Walter! is it you?" cried Alice.

"I am Walter, and Mr. Shobbrok is with me," he shouted.

"Here, Walter, take the helm," cried the mate, "but work away on the starboard side; I will get a rope ready to heave to Nub."

Walter did as directed, and their raft was soon brought up alongside the other, when Nub, having secured the rope hove to him, in his eagerness forgot the difference of their rank, and sprang forward with delight to embrace the old mate. Walter sprang on to the other raft, and quickly had his dear little sister in his arms. They no longer thought of the thunder roaring or the lightning flashing around them as they

MEETING OF THE TWO RAFTS.

eagerly recounted to each other their adventures. It seemed for the moment, indeed, that all danger to them was over. They soon, however, inquired of each other news of their father, and the fear that he might be lost, or might be hopelessly searching for them, soon made them feel the reality of their position. Nub in the meantime had told the mate all that had happened on board, and his belief that a large raft had been formed, and that the rest of the people had got away from the ship. He told him also that he had seen nothing of it. It was possible, however, that the captain's boat might have fallen in with it; and if so, they would certainly have proceeded together towards the land.

"Our poor, poor father! how unhappy he will be at not finding us," ejaculated Walter and Alice together.

"He will not give up all hopes of your being restored to him; so don't fret too much about it, my dear Miss Alice," said the mate, anxious to comfort her. "He will know very well that Nub would not have deserted you; and he will have heard from the people on board that Walter went off with me; and very likely he will guess something like the truth. And not knowing our boat was destroyed, he will fancy that I picked you up, and that we have made our way in a well-found whale-boat towards the shore."

"I hope he may think so," answered Alice. "I

will try not to be too anxious about him ; and perhaps we shall meet each other before long."

"That's it, Miss Alice," said the mate. "Hope for the best. 'Hope still in God,' as He Himself in the Bible tells us to do, and don't be cast down."

The night had been much further spent than those on the raft supposed. The thunder gradually rolled away to the southward, and soon afterwards the sun arose in the clear sky, shedding a brilliant glare across the water. Directly the light appeared the mate exclaimed, "Now, Walter,—now, Nub, as we have doubled our numbers, we must turn to and increase the size of our raft."

"As you think best, Mr. Shobbrok," answered Walter.

"Anything you tell me do, I do," said Nub.

"Well, we will pull your raft to pieces, and put the bow and stern on to ours, and raise our bulwarks."

"Ay, ay, mate," answered Nub ; and they immediately set to work. It was an operation requiring a good deal of skill, as it was necessary to lash the fresh timbers very securely, or they would prove a source of much danger; for should the sea get up, and should they break loose, they would be thrown upon the raft, and thus endanger the safety of those on it. A portion of Nub's raft was composed of spars, one of which was found long enough to serve as a mast, instead of the two oars which had hitherto done duty as such; and they would now be of much use in impelling on the raft. The mast was securely fixed between the two cross spars, fastened at either end to the raised sides, and it was then well stayed up, so that the whole sail bent to a yard could now be hoisted up. The casks were then lashed securely to the two sides of the raft as well as to the bow and stern; and when all was finished, the mate declared that he believed their craft would weather out a heavy gale as well as many a ship at sea. He might have said much better than many, which, over-laden and leaky, go helplessly down into the depths of the ocean without any land in sight or help near, the hapless crew perishing miserably.

It was nearly mid-day when all was completed. Nub had not uttered a complaint. At last he could not help exclaiming, "Oh, Mr. Shobbrok, can you give me just one mouthful of water? I give de last to Missie Alice, and she not know I go all de time without any."

"Of course, my lad, of course," answered the mate, filling a cup from the cask. "We must be careful of it; but I know what you are feeling, and there would be no use in giving you just one mouthful."

Nub drank the water, and, heaving a sigh as he smacked his lips, he exclaimed, "Dat is delicious!"

"Now I think of it, we have not breakfasted. Miss Alice and Walter must be pretty hungry, and thirsty too," said the mate.

"I am not very thirsty, but I should like to have a few of the biscuits Nub and I brought," answered Alice.

Nub looked downcast. There were only two remaining. He had not let Alice discover this, that she might not know how close run they were for food. For many hours he, honest fellow, had eaten nothing. The mate, suspecting this, gave Alice the biscuits with a cup of wine and water, and then beat up some more fish, oil, and pounded biscuit, which he shared with Walter and Nub. The latter thought the food especially good, and would have been perfectly ready to eat twice as much of it had it been given to him. Some more wine and water restored the strength of all the party, but poor Nub wanted something besides food. For many a long hour he had not closed his eyes. He told the mate so, and asking his leave, threw himself down on the deck. Almost before his head reached the piece of wood Walter had placed for a pillow, he was fast asleep. Alice was very nearly as sleepy as poor Nub; and the mate saying he would steer, Walter sat down on the deck, and taking her in his arms, she also in less than a minute closed her eyes, feeling far happier than she had done since she had left the burning ship. Having perfect confidence in the mate, it seemed to her that they had now only to sail on till they reached the shore. Happily, she little thought of the dangers before them, or knew that the scanty stock of provisions they possessed would not last long, and that before many days were over famine must overtake them.

The wind remained light but variable, and now coming from the southward, they could only steer a north-westerly course. The mate feared that it might shift to the west; if so, they would have to lower the sail and trust to their oars. Their progress in that case would be very slow, as neither Walter nor Nub had much strength for rowing. As before, he himself intended to steer during the night; so, on the approach of evening, telling Walter to take the helm, he lay down, making his arm serve as a pillow for Alice. Before closing his eyes, he gave the usual charge to Walter to call him should there be any alteration in the wind; which, of course, Walter faithfully promised to do. Walter stood bravely to his post till he found his head nodding, and the stars at which he was gazing dancing before his eyes; and reluctantly he was on the point of calling Mr. Shobbrok, when the mate, lifting up his head, told him to take charge of Alice, while he resumed his place at the helm.

All night long the old sailor stood steering the raft, allowing his young charges and Nub to sleep on.

"The black deserves his rest," he said to himself; "and it's much better that those two dear young ones should forget their sorrow and troubles; they will have enough of them, I am afraid, before long."

Again the sun rose—another day, which promised to be like the last. The remainder of the flying-fish was eaten in the same manner as before. Alice could not manage to get down the unsavoury compound, and contented herself with some hard biscuits soaked in wine and water. Though they were saved from the suffering which thirst would have caused them, hunger stared them in the face. In vain they watched the shoals of flying-fish in the distance; none came near them. They had no hooks or lines, nor any means of replenishing their stock of provisions. The mate did not allow the rest of the party to discover how anxious he felt; indeed, he blamed himself for feeling anxious, and continually kept saying, "God cares for us. He will take care of us, I am sure. He won't let these young ones perish." Still the thought arose, "How is that to be? It's more than I can tell, unless He sends a ship to pick us up." No sail, however, appeared in sight. Hour after hour passed away. The mate looked round and round the horizon, in the hope that one would appear; but again the sun went down, and the raft floated slowly on amid the darkness of night.

Except a little biscuit reserved for Alice and Walter, no substantial food remained for the next day, though the oil, wine, and spirits might assist to keep them alive for some time longer. The mate and Nub steered on watch and watch during the night, as they agreed to let the young people sleep as long as they could.

The mate felt perfect confidence while Nub, who was an excellent sailor, was at the helm, and he was thus able to take more rest than heretofore. The latter part of the night was darker than usual, for a thick mist rested on the calm ocean. Morning was approaching, when Walter awoke, and springing to his feet, offered to take the helm, that his companions might have more rest.

"No, thank you, lad; Nub and I have had sleep enough, and we wish that you and Miss Alice should have as much rest as possible," answered Mr. Shobbrok.

Alice, on hearing her name, started up, and inquired if anything had happened. But before the mate could reply, Nub shouted out, "Land! land!—land right ahead!"

All the party, naturally highly excited, looked out, endeavouring to pierce the gloom; but either the mist had risen for a moment, enabling Nub to see the land, or his eyes, still heavy with sleep, had deceived him. A light breeze was still driving on the raft. They got out the oars, and endeavoured to impel it faster. They had not gone far when Nub again cried out, "There! there! There it is!"

"Is it an island, or is it the back of an enormous whale?" exclaimed Walter. "I see a flag flying on the highest part, and people moving about."

"Are you sure that those are people?" asked the mate. "I see a flagstaff and flag clearly enough; but if those are human beings, the flag must be a very large one, such as no whale-boat carries."

"Can papa be there?" exclaimed Alice, who was seated on a piece of timber in the centre of the raft.

"Little doubt about dat," said Nub, turning round to her. "Cheer up, Missie Alice; cheer up. We soon get dere. But whether it is land, as Massa Walter says, or one bery big whale, is more dan I can tell. It look to my eye like a whale; but I cannot see its head or its tail,—and whales got both, unless dey are cut off." Nub, in fact, was greatly puzzled at the appearance of the seeming island. He did not take into consideration the deceptive effect produced by the light mist which pervaded the air, making objects seen through it magnified and distorted, as it floated imperceptibly by.

"I cannot quite make it out even now," observed the mate. "There's a flag, there is no doubt about that; and there are creatures of some sort moving about— but to my eyes they look more like birds than men. The curious mist which hangs over the water plays strange tricks; and I have over and over again been deceived, and so have many others; but I see the flag as clearly as if it was not more than a cable's length from us."

"It seems to me that the people are stooping down or carrying huge bundles on their backs," observed Walter. "Perhaps they are digging or building huts.

IS IT AN ISLAND?

I suspect, from their numbers, that the whole crew, whom we supposed embarked on the big raft, are there. We are near enough for them to hear our voices, though, as they are so busy, they have not as yet made us out." On this Walter shouted and waved his hands.

"I thought so. There go your men, who were so busy digging and building!" exclaimed the mate. As he spoke, a number of birds rose in the air and flew shrieking away, soon being lost to sight in the clouds of mist which hung over the ocean to the west; and revealing, scarcely a quarter of a mile off, an enormous whale, or marine monster of some sort, floating on the surface, with a small flagstaff and flag sticking in its back.

CHAPTER VII.

S the voyagers were anxious to reach the
creature which lay before them, they got
out the oars, the mate and Nub pulling,
while Walter steered.

"I see some harpoons and spears sticking in the creature's back," exclaimed Walter.

"They will be of use, if we cannot get anything
else from it, as we shall be able to kill any dolphins or
bonitoes which swim near us," said the mate.

"I tink me get some slices of meat out of de back
of de creature," said Nub.   "We no want food now."

"We shall find it rather high-flavoured and somewhat tough," observed the mate; "but it will keep
body and soul together; and we must not be par-
ticular."

Walter, though very hungry, felt no inclination to
eat whale's blubber, especially if the creature had been
dead for some time,—though he had heard that the

Eskimos consider it dainty food, and eat it in vast quantities.   Poor Alice, who had been unable to swallow the mixture of flying-fish and oil, shuddered at the thought.

"I see a quantity of gear hanging about the creature's head," said Walter; "and that makes me suppose that it must have been fast to a ship.   If so, it cannot be a fish my father has struck; and some other whaler besides ours must be in the neighbourhood."

"I am of your mind," said the mate.   "We shall know for certain, when we get alongside, by the harpoons.   However, the idea gives me hope that we shall obtain assistance before long."

The voyagers were gradually approaching the monster, which was certainly not a sperm whale, though it was of enormous size, floating far higher out of the water than does that creature.   They therefore came to the conclusion that it was of a rare and hitherto unknown species.*   A quantity of gear with some large floats hung about its head, while the harpoons sticking in it had their lines attached.   The only way to account for this was, that the people who had attacked it had fancied that it was dead, and that it had suddenly revived and broken loose from them.

The whale was soon reached, when the raft was

* The author confesses that he has had some difficulty in understanding the descriptions in the old journal from which the tale is taken. From its evident truthfulness and general accuracy, he would not feel justified in altering them. But the illustration beats him, and sets at defiance all the accounts in his books of natural history. He must therefore leave his readers to judge for themselves.

made fast to a couple of the harpoon lines which hung from its body.   It was no easy matter to climb to the top of its back; but the mate, bidding Alice remain on the raft, hauled himself up by the lines which hung from it, Walter and Nub following his example.   On reaching the top of the whale's back, the mate examined the flag.

"This is an American piece of bunting," he exclaimed.   "It shows without doubt that it was killed by the boats of one of their whalers.   There are a good many of them in these seas at present, and they are not the fellows to abandon a fish they have once caught."

"Dat is what I was tinking," observed Nub.   "I don't tink any Englishman eber kill such a 'straordinary-looking fish as dis."

"I have seen a good many, but never one like it," said the mate.

"I only hope it good to eat; and de sooner me cut some blubber and cook it, de better.   Mr. Shobbrok, you got tinder-box and flint and steel?"

"Yes," answered the mate, "I always carry them; though, as we cannot light a fire on the raft, I have hitherto made no use of them.   But how do you propose lighting one on the top of the whale, Nub?"

"We get up some pieces of wood from de raft, and den, with de blubber, we soon have one blazing fire," answered the black.   Descending to the raft, he took

one of the pieces of plank and began to chop it up.
"We soon have some dinner for you, Missie Alice," he
said while so employed. "You stay quiet on de raft,
and not fancy you going to starve any more." Having
performed his task, he secured the wood in a bundle,
and hoisting it on his back, he climbed up again.

During Nub's absence the mate and Walter looked
anxiously around them, in the possibility of any boats
being in sight. None were to be seen; but they
observed several objects floating about, apparently
pieces of wreck, spars and casks,—and among them a
sea-chest, which seemed of large size, as it rose considerably above the surface.

"We must try and get hold of that," said the mate.
"It may contain articles of value to us, though I am
afraid we are not likely to find any food within it."

"I would rather have a cask of biscuits or flour, or
beef or pork," observed Walter.

"I doubt whether we shall find such," said the mate,
"for I observe that the casks float high out of the
water. But has it struck you, Walter, what must
have happened?"

"I was thinking that these things must have come
out of our ship and floated away here," answered
Walter.

"They cannot have come so far by this time," said
the mate. "I think that I can unravel the mystery.
This whale was attacked by the boats of a ship, some

of which were probably destroyed by the monster.   It
was then towed alongside, when she was either capsized in a storm, or, receiving damage from some other
cause, she went down, and the articles we now see
floated up out of her.   Possibly she was struck by
some large whale, and her bottom or sides stove in ;
such a thing has occurred before now.   I remember
some years ago a big whale off the coast of New
Zealand which went by the name of New Zealand
Tom.   He was a monster, and capable of sending any
ship to the bottom.   I was in one of the boats of the
Adonis whaler when, in company with a dozen others,
we went one morning to chase that very whale.   Most
of us got near enough to drive our harpoons into its
body ; but it made us pay dearly for our sport, for
before breakfast it had knocked nine of our boats to
pieces, and we were obliged to return to our respective
ships.   Some weeks passed before we again got sight
of the creature ; when, in company with several other
boats, we again attacked it, and this time came off
victorious.   You will scarcely believe it, but we found
eight harpoons in its body belonging to as many different ships, which had chased it at various times.   Big
as it was, there are others as big, and even fiercer.   I remember meeting a man who had belonged to the American whaler *Essex*.   All the boats but one were on one
occasion away with the larger portion of the crew, leaving only the doctor and a few others on board, when they

caught sight of an enormous sperm whale coming towards them, as if not seeing the ship; suddenly lifting its flukes up in the air, it sounded, throwing the water over the deck, when they felt a tremendous blow, as if the ship under full sail had struck a rock. The blow broke off some of the keel, which was seen floating up to the surface. The whale quickly rose again, and was observed at a short distance from the ship; when, what was the horror of those on board to see it come swimming directly at them with the greatest fury! It struck the bows a tremendous blow, staving them in. A cry arose that the ship was sinking; and so she was. The water was rushing into her like a mill-sluice; and the people had scarcely time to get into the remaining boat when she capsized, the casks in her hold for a time keeping her up. The people in the other boats, seeing their ship going down, pulled back and managed to get a small quantity of provisions; but before they had obtained as much as they required down she went, leaving the boats to find their way to land as best they could. They steered for the coast of Peru— the event happened on the other side of the Pacific— but only one boat, with three men in her at their last gasp, was picked up; they happily recovered, and were able to narrate what had happened. The rest of the poor fellows must have perished, as none of the other boats were ever afterwards heard of. Now, it's my opinion that something of the sort I have described has happened to the ship which had got hold of this whale; though what has become of her crew is more than I can tell."

"I trust that our fate may not be that of the unfortunate crew of the *Essex*," said Walter.

"I trust not, lad," answered the mate; "I shall be sorry I told you the story, if it affects your spirits. We shall do very well if we can get provisions,—and four people are more easily fed than forty,—so don't think about it. Here comes Nub with a bundle of wood, and we will see if we can light a fire and cook some blubber; but I wish we had some more delicate food for your dear young sister."

Nub, who had brought the axe, having chopped off several pieces of skin from the fattest part of the whale's back, made a pile of the wood and placed the dry skin on the top of it. The mate then produced his flint and steel, and striking a light, set fire with a match to the bottom of the pile.

"While de fire blazes up, I cut some nice pieces of blubber," said Nub; and setting to work, he soon produced several lumps, which he stuck at the end of some other sticks brought for the purpose. The oil which oozed up out of the whale's back made the flames rapidly blaze up. Each of the party then held the blubber—which sputtered and hissed more vehemently than the fattest of bacon in a cook's frying-pan—to the fire. The odour was certainly not pleasant, but

A STRANGE COOKING-PLACE.

Nub sniffed it up, exclaiming, as he bit off a piece,
"Oh, dis bery fine ; it soon make us quite strong and
fat, and we go a week without eating anyting else."

Walter did not feel quite satisfied on that point ;
however, he managed to get down a few mouthfuls.
Having roasted a piece as nicely as he could, he hurried
down with it to Alice.

"If you think I ought to eat it, I will," she said ;
"but it does not smell nice."

"I am afraid we are not likely to get anything else
at present, and it's our duty to try and keep up our
strength. It will, I hope, have that effect, though it
may taste disagreeable at first."

Alice, who was really ravenously hungry, overcame
her repugnance to the unattractive food, and ate it up ;
taking at the same time, to help it down, a small piece
of biscuit which had been reserved for her. Walter
then climbed up again and joined the party on the
whale's back.

The skin and blubber affording ample fuel, they
were able to keep up their fire and cook a considerable
quantity of blubber ; for to eat it raw in its present
condition they felt would be impossible, but toasted in
thin slices it would, they hoped, keep for some time.
They tried several portions, and agreed that the most
eatable were those on either side of the hump. As the
chest and casks did not appear to be drifting away
from the whale, they agreed that it was not necessary

to put off expressly to get hold of them. Having cooked as much blubber as was likely to keep till it was consumed, they carried it down to the raft, where it was stowed away in the hen-coop, which was considered cooler than any other place. The mate proposed that while they were alongside the whale they should take the opportunity of more firmly securing the fresh part of the raft, as they had now a favourable opportunity for doing so. This took them some time, but they were well satisfied when the work was done.

"And now, my lad, we must not go away without the harpoons and spears, for I have hopes, by their means, of getting a good supply of food. We may catch bonitoes and other big fish with the harpoons; and with the spears we may strike any smaller ones which come within reach."

"I have been thinking, Mr. Shobbrok, that if we could manage a lamp, we might, on a calm evening, attract the fish to the side of the raft, as is often done, I have read, by savages, who then spear them; and the blubber will afford us oil for the purpose."

"Bery bright idea, Massa Walter," exclaimed Nub. "De hole where we made de fire is full of oil, and me fill up two of de empty bottles with it; den, as we have no saucer for de lamp, suppose you take one of your shoes,—it will hold de oil for de purpose."

"I will gladly give up both my shoes," said Walter.

"So will I mine," exclaimed Alice ; "if they are of any use."

"We need not deprive you of yours, Miss Alice," said the mate ; "I must insist rather on mine being taken. And for a wick, we have only to pick a rope to pieces and twist it up lightly."

Nub, taking the two empty bottles, climbed up again on the whale's back. He found even more oil than he had expected, and filling the bottles, lowered them on the raft. He was about to descend, when he was seen looking eagerly out on the other side of the whale.

"What is it?" asked the mate.

"A sail! a sail!" he shouted, clapping his hands, and dancing frantically about at a great risk of slipping off into the water. The mate and Walter quickly climbed up, anxious to ascertain the truth of Nub's assertion.

"Dere! dere!" he exclaimed. "To the south. Dere she comes! Missie Alice and Massa Walter soon be safe!"

"That's not a ship," observed the mate. "If you look steadily, you will see that it's a long way on this side of the horizon, and but little raised above the water. It would not appear so distinct as it does if it was the top-gallant-sail of a ship, hull down. That's the sail of a boat or a raft ; and before long it will be near at hand."

Alice eagerly inquired what they were looking at. Walter having told her what the mate said, could with difficulty persuade her to remain on the raft, so anxious was she to climb up to see the object in sight.

The party on the whale's back stood watching the sail; but instead, however, of it coming directly towards them, as they had expected it would do, it was seen, when about a mile off, to be steering a course on which it would pass them scarcely nearer than it then was. Walter seized the flag out of the whale's back and waved it over his head, shouting at the top of his voice, as did the mate and Nub, to attract attention; but apparently they were not seen, and certainly could not have been heard.

"It is more than I can make out, what they are about," observed Walter. "They must have caught sight of the whale, and whether that's a boat or a raft, it's surprising that they should not have come nearer to have a look at us. They seem to have a pretty stiff breeze out there, and it would not have taken them much out of their way."

"I am sure that it is a raft," said the mate, "as, with the breeze they have got, and that large sail, a boat would move much faster through the water than they are doing. Depend on it, those are the *Champion's* people, and they have got some reason for not wishing to communicate with us. I am pretty sure they fancy that this whale was killed by the captain, and that, not finding the ship, he returned to it. I may be wrong, but I think I am not much out in my calculations."

"But suppose you are wrong, and my father is on board the raft, could not we shove off and overtake it?"

"As it is almost dead to windward, we should not have the slightest chance of doing so; and see! they are still holding their course. If they had wished to communicate with us, they would have lowered their sail; and they must see the smoke of the fire, even should they not make out the flag,—though they could scarcely have failed to do that."

"I tink I could swim much faster dan our raft could pull against de wind," said Nub; "supposing de captain on board, den I tell him dat Massa Walter and Missie Alice on de whale, and he sure to come."

"You had better not make the attempt, Nub," said the mate. "You will have a long swim before you can reach the raft; and if you fail to do so, you will be exhausted before you can possibly get back."

"Neber fear, Mr. Shobbrok," he answered. "If I get tired I can rest on one of dose casks, or perhaps I find some spar or piece of timber which keep me up;" and before the mate or Walter could stop him, Nub had slipped off into the sea on the opposite side to that to which the raft was secured, so that Alice did did not see him. Nub struck out boldly, and made rapid way. The mate and Walter stood watching him.

"That black is indeed a first-rate swimmer," observed the mate. "Heaven protect the brave fellow."

Nub, however, had not got more than two or three cable's lengths from the whale when he was seen to turn, while he furiously beat the water with his hands and feet, at the same time shouting out loudly.

"Oh, what are those black-looking things moving about on either side of him?" exclaimed Walter.

"Those are sharks' fins," answered the mate. "He must have caught sight of them; and he knows well that, should he get tired, they will attack him."

"O poor Nub! poor Nub! Can he escape them?" exclaimed Walter, wringing his hands and looking the picture of despair. "O Mr. Shobbrok, can we do nothing to save him?"

"We can only shout and try to frighten the sharks, as Nub is doing," answered the mate.

"Oh, I will do that," cried Walter; and he began to shriek and jump frantically about in a way which made the mate begin to feel anxious on his account: still Mr. Shobbrok himself shouted at the top of his voice, and then bethought him of cutting pieces of blubber and throwing them as far away as possible, in order to attract the savage creatures and to draw their attention off from the black. The plan seemed to succeed, and several of them were seen to dash forward and spring out of the water to catch the blubber before it reached the surface. Nub, meanwhile, was making rapid way towards the side of the whale.

"Now, Walter," said the mate, "do as I have been doing, while I get a harpoon-line ready to haul the black out of the water; but take care, my dear boy, that you don't slip off."

Walter did as the mate told him, still continuing to shriek out as loudly as before. Bending the end of one of the lines to the centre of a spear, Mr. Shobbrok let it drop into the water, where it floated; while he stood by to haul up Nub as soon as he caught hold of it. Walter continued in the meantime cutting off pieces of blubber and throwing them towards the head of the whale, and as long as he did so the sharks remained on the watch for the delicious morsels. At length Nub reached the spear, and grasping hold of it, endeavoured to haul himself up; but he was evidently greatly exhausted by his rapid swim, and the dread he had experienced of being seized by one of the monsters swarming around. The mate, who had begun to haul him in, called Walter to his assistance. They had got the black half out of the water, when they saw several of the dark fins gliding towards him. How poor Walter shouted and shrieked!—while he and the mate hauled away with all their might, every instant dreading to see the savage creatures tear at Nub's legs. With all their strength they hauled away, when, just as Nub's feet were clear of the water, two enormous sharks rose with open mouths above the surface to seize him. Happily they were disappointed, for the creatures in their eagerness rushing against each other, missed their aim, their heads nearly touching the soles of his feet—which, as may be supposed, he quickly drew up; while the mate and Walter, hauling away, got him fairly up to the top of the whale's back. As soon as he was safe, Walter threw his arm around him, exclaiming, " Have the creatures bitten you, Nub? Have you really escaped them? oh, why did you go— oh, why did you go ?"

" Yes, Massa Walter, I quite safe, neber fear," answered Nub, panting for breath. " Dey no hurt me, though dey would have liked to eat me up as they did the blubber which you and de mate threw to dem.; no doubt about dat."

" I am thankful that you have got back safe, Nub," said the mate. " It was a bold attempt, but it would have been a vain one; for I am as sure as I stand here that the captain is not on board the raft out there."

" Oh, where can my father have gone, then?" exclaimed Walter, who was still in a state of unusual excitment, into which, weakened as he was by famine, the alarm he had just experienced had thrown him.

" Your father is in his boat, be assured of that, Walter," answered the mate calmly; " and now, the sooner you go on the raft and join your sister the better." Still Walter did not go, but again seizing

NUD'S NARROW ESCAPE.

the flag, kept waving it ; but the raft glided on, moved by the strong wind, which now reached the part of the ocean on which the whale floated. The mate himself could not help standing to watch it, but it rapidly got farther and farther off. At last, taking Walter's arm, he said, "Come, we must waste no more time here ; Nub and I will help you down to the raft."

Walter made no resistance, but allowed himself to be lowered down, the mate and Nub following him. Alice threw her arms around his neck when she saw him, exclaiming,—"What has all that noise been about? I have been so frightened. Why did you not come and tell me?"

The mate briefly explained what had happened ; while Walter, with apparent calmness, added a few remarks ; and, soothed by his sister's voice, he soon appeared to recover, and Mr. Shobbrok had no apprehensions about him. The mate told him to lie down and rest, which he at once did. The raft being on the lee side of the whale, he and Nub then hoisted the sail.

"Oh, Massa Shobbrok, we have forgotten de harpoons!" exclaimed Nub.

"So we have," answered the mate. "In my anxiety about Walter I forgot them."

"Den I go up and get dem," said Nub ; and he again climbed up the side of the whale. He had lowered down a couple of harpoons and three spears, when the mate, who had in the meantime cast off the lines

which had secured the raft to the whale, in his anxiety
to lose no time, sprang up to pull out another spear
which had been fixed nearer the tail; Alice, who was
standing near him, taking hold of the line still attached
to it.   At that moment, from some unknown cause,
the monster body began to move, and before either
the mate or Nub could descend, over it rolled; while
Alice, in her terror still holding on to the line, was
lifted from her feet and dragged into the water.   The
sail, no longer under the lee of the huge carcass, filled,
and away glided the raft, leaving the poor little girl,
with the mate and Nub at some distance from her,
struggling in the water.

CHAPTER VIII.

THE huge monster rolling over, slowly sank head foremost into the depths of the ocean ; possibly from the oil in the case by some means or other having escaped, thereby depriving it of its buoyancy—an occurrence which occasionally takes place when, after a hard chase, a whale has been captured, and the victors are about to tow it in triumph to their ship ; losing in consequence several hundred pounds worth of oil.

The mate and Nub found themselves dragged a considerable way under water ; but quickly coming up again, as they were striking out they caught sight of the raft driving before the wind, and poor Alice struggling in the water at some distance from them. Horror-struck at the sight, they swam towards her, their hearts beating with anxiety lest they should not be in time to reach the spot ere she sank beneath the surface, or was seized by one of the ravenous sharks from which Nub had just before so narrowly escaped. Happily the savage creatures had darted down after the whale, eager to seize the strips of blubber which had been cut off its back. So busily were they engaged, that they did not take notice of the human beings thus left to their tender mercies. The mate had been on a part of the whale nearest Alice, and was thus the first to approach her. Seeing the impossibility of reaching the raft, he shouted to Nub and told him to swim after it; he himself intending to assist Alice, who was stretching out her arms and piteously calling to him for help.

Walter, who had gone off into a state of dreamy unconsciousness as he lay stretched on the raft, on hearing Alice shriek out at the moment she was dragged into the water, started up, his senses completely bewildered, and instead of lowering the sail, stood waving his hands, and incoherently shrieking out to her to come to him. The mate shouted to him to lower the sail; but he did not understand the order, and continued leaping frantically about the raft, waving his hands and shrieking as before. The consequence was that the raft got further and further away, at a rate which gave but little hope that Nub would overtake it. The mate's brave heart almost died within him at the thought that not his life only, but that of the little girl and Nub, would be sacrificed. Nub was exerting himself to the utmost. Never had he swam so

A DIRE MISHAP.

fast. But he soon saw that all his efforts would not enable him to overtake the raft. Again and again he shouted to Walter to lower the sail: Walter only shrieked louder in return, calling him to come to his help—and Nub expected every moment to see him leap into the water, when, in all probability, he would be drowned. Still the brave black persevered.

"Lower de sail, Massa Walter, lower de sail!" he shouted; "you all right if you do dat. De mate save Missie Alice, so no fear about her. Lower de sail! Oh, de poor boy gone mad!"

In vain Nub shouted; Walter only waved his hands more frantically, till, overcome by terror, he sank down exhausted on the raft, and Nub saw that it would be impossible to overtake it while it continued running at its present speed. The only hope was that the wind might drop, or shift, and bring it back to them. This, however, was barely probable; the breeze was blowing fresh, and the light raft, having now no longer their weight on it, skimmed swiftly over the surface. Still Nub persevered in endeavouring to obey the mate's orders; he was ready to swim on till he sank exhausted. Happily he was as much at home in the water as on shore, and by turning on his back or treading water, or swimming in a variety of other ways, could keep up for several hours together.

He turned his head round and saw that the mate had reached Alice, and was supporting her in his arms.

"De mate swim well, I know, so he keep up de little girl while I go after de raft," he said to himself, and he again made way ; but though he swam rapidly, the raft skimmed along at a still faster rate, and had he not even yet trusted to the possibility of either a change of wind or a calm, he would have given up the attempt as hopeless. He thought, too, that Walter might perhaps regain his senses, and do what alone could preserve his own life and that of his friends. Left by himself on the raft, he must inevitably perish as well as they. Inspired by this hope, the gallant black pursued his course undaunted by the recollection of the shoal of ravenous sharks which he knew were in the neighbourhood, or by the want of any object, as far as he could see before him, on which to rest. Fearful as was his condition, it was to become still more terrible. He had just glanced round and shouted to the mate and Alice to keep up their courage, when, as he again turned his face towards the raft, he saw, not twenty fathoms from him, a hideous head, such as the morbid imagination sometimes pictures during a dreadful dream. The front was of immense width, with large, savage eyes glaring out at either side ; while below appeared a large mouth, full of formidable teeth ; the body, as Nub knew, being in proportion to the size of the head. It was indeed an enormous specimen of the hideous zygæna, or hammer-headed shark, so frequently observed about the coast of the South

Sea islands, and scarcely less voracious and formidable than the terrible white shark, the sailor's hated foe. Its body was comparatively slender, but its head was dilated on each side to a prodigious extent,—the form being that of a double-headed hammer, from which it takes the name of " the hammer-headed shark."

Nub gazed at the creature, but his courage did not fail him. It had apparently only just come to the surface to gaze about it, and had not yet discovered the human beings floating near. The black had often seen the shark bravely attacked by the natives of Otaheite and other islands, who encounter it fearlessly as they swim off through the raging surf, and never fail to return victorious to the shore. There was no time, however, for consideration, for with a few turns of its tail the monster might be up to him. He had, fortunately, a large, sharp sheath-knife sticking in his girdle ; he drew it, and keeping his eye on the shark, he struck out so as to gain a position rather behind the creature's head, which was turned from him. At the same moment that Nub caught sight of the zygæna the mate also saw it ; he fully expected that it would dash at the black and seize him in its dreadful jaws. The shark, however, was either of a sluggish nature, or perhaps gorged with food, for its head remained above water without moving from the spot where it had at first appeared. The mate endeavoured to prevent Alice from seeing the hammer-head, but her eyes unfortunately fell on it. "Oh, Mr. Shobbrok, what is that dreadful creature?" she cried out. "Will it kill poor Nub? Oh, what can we do! what can we do!" She did not appear to think so much of her own and the mate's danger as of that of the black. The mate, for a moment, was almost unnerved, for he felt his utter inability to defend himself or the little girl should the monster attack them; still, like a brave man, he summoned up all his courage, and considered how he could possibly tackle it and defend Alice. He looked around to see if there was any spar or other floating object near at hand on which he could place her while he fought the shark. Could he find a spar, he would push it in the shark's mouth as it swam towards him; he had likewise his clasp-knife hung round his neck, but the blade, he feared, was too blunt to be of much service; he opened it, however, and held it in his teeth ready to use. As he glanced round he saw the chest which he had observed when on the back of the whale, but it was too far off to be of any avail in the present emergency. In the meantime he had kept a vigilant watch on the hideous hammer-head, to be ready for an encounter should it dart towards him. He had also been watching the proceedings of Nub. He soon saw that the black was manœuvring to gain an advantage over the shark, which did not appear to observe him. Poor Alice, overcome with terror, had almost fainted in his arms; he urged her to keep up her courage. "Don't be afraid, Miss Alice; don't be afraid, my child," he said soothingly. "There is a big chest not far off, which will serve as a raft for you, and it will support Nub and me while we swim alongside it. See—see! Nub is going to tackle the shark; and he well knows, depend on it, what he is about. I have heard that the natives in these parts do not fear the creature, terrible as it looks, and I don't see why we should. Come, we will swim towards the chest, and Nub will join us when he has finished off Jack Shark, —which he fully intends doing, depend on that."

The mate, as he spoke, began to swim in the direction of the chest; but he soon found that, having Alice to support, he could make but slow progress; he therefore recommenced treading the water, turning his face towards the shark, that he might be the better able to encounter it should it make a dash at him. He now saw that Nub, having got close to the creature, his long knife in his hand, was swimming up alongside it. He expected, in another moment, that he would plunge his weapon into the shark's body; but instead of that, what was his surprise to see him suddenly leap on its back and dig the fingers of one hand into its left eye. If the hammer-head had been torpid before, it now made ample amends by its sudden activity; off it darted along the surface, Nub holding up its head to prevent it from diving, while with his right hand he struck his knife with all his might sometimes before

him and sometimes behind him, inflicting deep wounds
in its back and sides.   It seemed surprising that the
zygæna could endure them, but its wonderful vitality
is well known—the terrific gashes which Nub inflicted
in no way impeding its rapid progress.   At first it
seemed to be coming towards the mate and Alice ; and
though it would not have been able to bite them, it
might have inflicted a blow which would have stunned
them both.   Nub, however, managed by hauling at its
head to turn it, and it swept by, forming large circles
round and round the spot where they floated.   Its
speed, however, from its loss of blood, began somewhat
to diminish, and Nub could evidently guide it with
greater ease than at first. Seeing this, the mate shouted
to him, " Steer the brute, if you can, to yonder chest,
and bring it up to us as soon as possible."

"Ay, ay, massa," answered Nub ; "I finish de
brute off soon.   It not got much more go in him.
Cheer up, Missie Alice ; I no tink dis a steady horse
for you, or I ask you to have a ride on it." *

This remark did more than anything else to restore
Alice's courage, for she knew that the black felt perfectly certain of gaining the victory.   Nub, who had
already deprived the monster of sight, continued to dig
his knife into its head, guiding it towards the chest,

* The author must express the surprise he felt when he met with the account of
Nub's wonderful ride on the zygæna. However, it was too good to be omitted,
though he must leave his readers to judge of its probability. He would advise any
of them who may visit the new British possession of the Fiji Islands, should they
fall in with one of the monsters, not to attempt a similar exploit.

FIGHTING FOR LIFE

which he thus rapidly reached. He then, turning half round while he held up its head, stuck his knife as far back as he could reach behind him, persevering in his efforts till all movement in its tail had ceased.

"Dere, you go and feed your ugly cousins!" he exclaimed, giving it a last dig,—when, leaping from its back, he threw himself on the top of the chest; while the shark, its life almost extinct, rolled over on its back with its head downwards.

Taking off a lanyard attached to the chest, Nub secured it to the handle at one end, and after resting for a few seconds, again threw himself into the water and struck out for the mate and Alice.

"There, my dear child, I told you so; the brave black has killed the shark, and he will soon have the chest up to us. It will serve as a boat for you," said Mr. Shobbrok.

"But where is Walter? What has become of the raft?" exclaimed Alice, who had hitherto been unaware of her brother's unhappy condition, and had not noticed that the raft had glided far away from them.

"We must try and overtake Walter as soon as we get you safe on the chest," answered the mate. "It will be a long swim; but we must hope to get something to support ourselves, for I fear that the chest will not hold us all."

"Oh, what can have made Walter sail away again?" asked Alice; and then another thought seemed to strike her, as the mate did not immediately answer. "Oh, tell me, Mr. Shobbrok," she exclaimed,—"was the raft drawn down by the whale, and has my dear brother been drowned?"

"The raft is all right, and I hope Walter is on it," he answered, after a minute's hesitation. "We may come up with it before long. Don't think any more about it just now. See Nub; he's bringing the chest to us,—and a fine large sea-chest it is too, and by-and-by we will open it, and ascertain what it contains. I suspect that it's a carpenter's chest; though, as it floats high out of the water, it cannot contain many tools, but it may possibly have some which will be useful to us when we get on shore."

"When will that be, do you think?" asked Alice.

"There's no saying exactly, but we will hope for the best," answered the mate evasively. "See, here comes Nub. He will soon be up with us, and we will then begin our voyage."

The mate had no little difficulty in speaking; for, strong as he was, the exertion of treading the water so long was very considerable. He was very thankful when at length Nub got up to them.

"Here is de chest," exclaimed the black. "Now de sooner Missie Alice on de top of it de better." Fortunately there were several turns of rope round the chest, by means of which Nub held to one side, and the mate balancing it, enabled Alice to climb up

NOVEL USE OF A CHEST

on the other. He then told her to lie down along it, exactly in the centre, so that it might be as well balanced as possible. "All right, Missie Alice?" asked Nub, looking up at her while he grasped the rope fastened to the chest; the mate, who required a few minutes' rest, supporting himself on the other.

"Yes, I feel very secure," said Alice; "and I only wish that you and Mr. Shobbrok could get up and sit on it also."

"We should roll it over if we did, and tumble you into the water," said the mate. "It will afford us ample support if we merely hold on by each side. Are you all right, Nub?"

"Yes, yes, Massa Shobbrok; all right," answered Nub.

"Then off we go," cried the mate; "and I hope that before long we may come up with the raft, or that the captain's boat, or some stranger, may pick us up." Saying this, the mate took hold of one of the beckets which Nub had secured for the purpose, and struck out boldly to the westward.

Only strong swimmers and very determined men could have kept up as they did. It is true that the chest afforded them some support, but they had thus only one hand to swim with; still they made considerable progress, shoving on with their feet and striking out with the hands left at liberty. The wind was fair and the water smooth, or they would have been unable to make any progress. On and on they swam. When the arm they were using for propelling themselves grew weary, they shifted sides; by which they were able to continue their exertions much longer than they would otherwise have done. Alice remained perfectly still, though she now and then spoke to the mate or Nub. The former found it very difficult to answer her questions, as again and again she asked when they should overtake Walter, or how far off the land was likely to be. "Oh, how I wish that we were near enough to see it!" she added.

"It may cheer you to know that when I was on the top of the whale I fancied that I caught sight of some high land away to the westward," answered the mate. "It was very faint, and as I felt uncertain, I did not like to run the risk of disappointing you; but I have been thinking over the matter, and am persuaded that it was land. If it was, we shall have a better chance than I had hoped for of reaching it before long."

"You thought dat land, Massa Shobbrok; so did I. Hurrah! Swim away, boys! swim away! We soon get over de sea!" shouted Nub, endeavouring to raise his own spirits, as well as to encourage Alice. Thus they went on, but the mate could not help secretly feeling that the probability of their escaping was small indeed.

CHAPTER IX.

O two men could have conducted themselves more heroically than did the mate and Nub to save the young girl left under their charge. Neither of them allowed her to discover how weary and exhausted they felt by their prolonged and almost superhuman exertions. Now and then they stopped, and holding on with both hands to the chest, allowed their bodies to float on the water, thus obtaining some relief. The water was so warm that they did not feel any benumbing effects from being so long in it. After resting for a time, they would again strike out, Nub always commencing with a laugh and a negro song, though he seldom got further than—

"Swim away, boys, swim away;
We get to land 'fore end of day."

Then he would cry out, "I tink I smell de flowers and de fruit already." Mr. Shobbrok spoke but little, except occasionally a word or two to cheer up Alice. She did not experience the anxieties of her older companions, for it did not, happily, enter her head that they might after all fail to reach the shore. She could not help thinking about Walter, however, and wondering how it was that the raft had run away with him. She kept her eyes ahead, looking out for the land; but though her vision was remarkably keen, she could not discover it. She thought, however, that she could distinguish, far away, the white sail of the raft; and so undoubtedly she could, but she forgot that all the time it was going further and further from them.

The mate had at first had another cause for anxiety. It was that they might be espied and followed by some of the sharks which they had seen in the neighbourhood; but as they got further away from the spot, he began to hope that they had escaped them, and that the creatures were too much occupied with the carcasses of the whale and the zygæna to follow them.

They had thus been going on for two hours or more, when Alice exclaimed, "I see something floating ahead !"

"What is it like ?" asked the mate anxiously.

"It seems to me like another chest, or a cask perhaps. If you will lift your head a little out of the water, you will see it clearly."

The mate drew himself up till his head was as high as the chest.

"It's an empty cask," he exclaimed; "and will serve to rest one of us, though it will not assist us while towing the chest."

They swam towards it, and found that it was a large empty cask—probably one which had floated out of the American whaler which had gone down.

"Now, Mr. Shobbrok, you get on de cask; you want rest more dan I do," said Nub. "But take care dat you not roll round and round. It no easy matter to sit on an empty cask in de water."

The mate tried to do as Nub advised, but he found that the cask would roll round, and that the only way he could rest on it was by throwing himself length-wise along it—though he had considerable difficulty in keeping it steady. He was thus, however, able to regain his strength.

When he found himself somewhat recovered, he re-signed his place to Nub, who managed by working his feet on either side to sit across it, holding on to the chest. Scarcely had he taken his seat when he ex-claimed,—"Oh, I can smell de flowers and de fruit! Here come de land-breeze; but den it will drive us back faster dan we came along."

Nub was right. In another minute a strong breeze, smelling of the earth, blew in their faces; and the water, which had hitherto been calm, was soon rippled over with small waves, which rapidly increased in height, hissing and bubbling around them. This was excessively trying to the mate, who could with difficulty keep his head above the foam which drove in his face. His heart began to fail him, for while the breeze continued the little hope he ever had of reaching the land must be abandoned. All he could do was to hold on to the chest, which Nub balanced on the opposite side, without attempting to make any progress. He was, for the first time, beginning to lose hope of saving the little girl, when he was aroused by hearing Nub exclaim,—

"Hurrah! here come de raft! De wind catch her sail, and drive her back. We soon see Massa Walter, and I hope he soon see us."

"I see him! I see him!" cried Alice, lifting up her head.

The mate raised himself also; and then, sure enough, he caught sight of the raft skimming along at a rapid rate over the seas.

Whether Walter saw them or not, they could not tell; but they supposed that he had recovered his senses, and was steering the raft,—and that, finding the breeze in his favour, he was endeavouring to reach the spot where he had left them. He might remember the chest and casks and other objects floating about, and believe that they had been able by such means to support themselves. There could be

THE RAFT IN SIGHT

little doubt, by the steady way in which the raft approached, that Walter was at the helm, though, as he was steering a course rather on one side, it was probable that he had not yet discovered them. As the raft drew nearer, Nub exclaimed,—

"I will swim away and cut him off, or else maybe he will pass us."

"Let us first try what hailing will do," said the mate; "we will all shout together."

"Ay, ay!" answered Nub. "I give de time."

All three, raising their voices, shouted as loud as they could, Alice's shrill note reaching almost as far as the others.

"Once more," cried Nub; "and sure dis time he hear." Again they all cried out, even louder than before.

"Dere! dere, Missie Alice, he see us!" exclaimed Nub, looking down at the little girl as he spoke. At that moment the sheets were let go, and Walter was seen eagerly looking out to discover whence the voices came. The raft now came gliding up towards them, Walter having gone back to the helm to steer it.

Nub was the first to spring on board, and then having made fast the chest, he lifted Alice safely on to the raft, where she was received in Walter's arms. The almost exhausted mate was then dragged on board by Nub. The first thing Mr. Shobbrok did was to haul down the sail, that the raft might not be driven further away from the land ; he then turned towards Walter, not to find fault with him for running away, —for he was well aware that the poor lad could not help it,—but to ascertain the state of his mind.

Walter had placed Alice on her usual seat, and now sat by her side. He looked up at Mr. Shobbrok. "I cannot tell you how it all happened," he said in a low voice. "I only remember seeing Alice in the water, and shrieking out for some one to help her, when I fell down fainting on the raft. I was unconscious of what happened further, till I found myself alone on the raft, which had at that instant been taken aback by a strong breeze from the westward. I felt full of dismay and grief, but as calm and self-possessed as I ever had been. I considered what was to be done. My first thought was to go in search of you. I lowered the sail, got the raft round, and again setting the sail, steered away to the eastward, fully prepared to perish should I not find you ; and oh, I cannot express how thankful I am to find you again ! "

"I am sure he is," said Alice, jumping up and kissing Walter.

"I am certain of it too, my lad," said the mate. "We don't blame you ; and can only be thankful that, through God's mercy, your senses were so wonderfully restored."

"Yes, Massa Walter, we bless Heaven dat de shark

not eat us, and dat we find you ; and now all go well."

Both the mate and Nub felt too much fatigued just then to speak more ; so having secured the chest and cask, they threw themselves down to rest, as they could not attempt to row against the breeze then blowing, with their strength exhausted as it was.

Alice was scarcely less weary than they were, not so much from exertion as from alarm and anxiety. Her clothes soon dried in the hot sun, and then she too lay down. Walter, who was now apparently quite recovered, sat by her side, watching her till she dropped off to sleep. The wind did not much affect the raft, but it was all the time slowly drifting further and further from the shore. The little girl's slumbers were disturbed by the terrible scenes she had gone through, and now and then she cried out, " Oh, save him ! oh, save him ! Where is Walter? where is Walter ?"

Walter, on hearing his name pronounced, took her hand. " Here I am, all safe," he said in a soothing tone. " I am very, very sorry that I caused you so much alarm ; but it's all right now. We shall soon reach the land, I hope ; and then we will build a boat, and go in search of our father and the rest."

Alice, who was still scarcely awake, did not understand what he said. Suddenly she started up. " O Walter, where are we ?" she exclaimed, looking wildly about her. " I thought you had gone away again, and were never coming back. You will never leave me, will you?"

"I should be miserable without you," he answered. "No, I never will leave you, if I can help it, till we find our father—though Mr. Shobbrok and Nub take the best care of you they possibly can : had it not been for them, we should both have been lost."

"Don't think that it's we who take care of you, my children," said the mate, who had been awakened by their voices. "There is One above who alone has the power to do so. We are only the instruments in His hands."

"But we do what we can, though," said Nub, sitting up ; "and now I tink the wind begin to fall, and we get out de oars."

"We had better take some food first," said the mate. "The young people must be hungry, and I am pretty sharp set myself."

"What you like to have, Mr. Shobbrok ? Roast beef, boiled mutton, pork pies, or plum pudding?" asked Nub, trying to make Walter and Alice laugh, for he observed how sad they both looked. "Well, if we can't have dem, we have whale blubber; it bery good for dem dat like it. Take a lilly bit, Missie Alice."

Poor Alice's lip curled. She recollected how nauseous she had found it in the morning. Nub got out some of the blubber, which the rest of the party swallowed without making faces. Fortunately there was still a small portion of biscuit, and this enabled Alice at length to get down enough of the food to sustain her strength. They had still the wine and water; but, alas! there now remained only sufficient biscuit to afford her another meal. " After that has gone, what can we give the little girl to eat?" thought the mate. " Well, well, she has been sustained hitherto, and we must not anticipate evil."

Nub having stowed away the rest of the blubber, the oars were got out, and while Walter steered, he and the mate began to urge on the raft towards the shore. Their progress, however, was very slow, as when they stood up their bodies acted the part of sails, and they were driven back almost as fast as they advanced. Several birds were flying overhead, a sign that land could not be far off; while, as they looked around, they saw here and there fish of all sizes rising out of the water.

" We may get hold of one of these fellows if they come near us," said the mate. " Our time may be better spent in preparing the harpoons. Lay in your oar, Nub, and we will set to work."

They all eagerly sat down, and in a short time two harpoons were fitted with lines, while spears were also got ready for use. Scarcely were their preparations completed when the land-breeze died away ; and a sea-breeze shortly afterwards setting in, the sail was once

more hoisted, and the raft steered for the land.   All
the party kept a bright look-out ahead on either side,
in the hope of seeing a fish and getting near enough
to catch it.   The mate and Nub stood with their harpoons in their hands ready for instant use ; the importance of catching some creature made them vigilant ; the strong flavour of the blubber assured them
that it would not keep much longer.   They had got a
short distance, when Alice exclaimed, " See, see ! what
is that curious fish ?"   She pointed to a spot a short
distance on one side, her sharp eyes detecting what
had escaped the observation of the mate.   As she
spoke, there rose from the surface a creature with a
long white polished piece of bone or ivory at the end
of its snout, which might be well likened to a sword,
and having two fish of considerable size spitted on it ;
at the same moment two large frigate-birds were seen
in the sky, flying rapidly down to deprive the fish of
its prey.

" That's a sword-fish," exclaimed the mate ; " and
we must try to get it before those frigate-birds succeed
in stealing the smaller fish from it.   Lower the sail,
Nub ; get out your oar and pull away.   Starboard
the helm, Walter.   That fellow will not dive as easily
as he may expect to do with those fish on his nose."

Nub pulled away with all his might, thus bringing
the raft close up to the spot where the sword-fish,
which had run its pointed weapon, perhaps uninten-

UNEXPECTED SUPPLIES.

tionally, through the fish, was struggling to get them off. The mate stood with his harpoon ready; it flew from his hand, and was buried deeply in the creature's body. In vain it tried to escape. The fish impeded its progress; and Nub coming to the mate's assistance, the line, which had run out some way, was hauled in; after which Nub, seizing the animal's snout, in spite of its struggles held it fast, and drew off the two fish, which he threw on the raft.

"Dere, we got dem safe, at all events. Dey make a good dinner for you, Missie Alice," he exclaimed. "Now, Massa Walter, you take de spear and stick it into de sword-fish's belly." Walter thrust in the weapon, and in another instant the creature's struggles ceased, and it was hauled up on the raft.

"Thank Heaven," said the mate. "We have now got food enough, if it will last so long fresh, for two or three days; and could we but smoke it, we should each of us enjoy two hearty meals a day for a week to come. However, it may, at all events, keep for some time if dried in the sun. Hoist the sail, Nub; Walter, do you steer, while the black and I cut up the fish."

The frigate-birds, disappointed of their prey, had flown off, but were hovering overhead ready to seize the entrails as they were thrown overboard.

The fish hauled up on the raft was about ten feet long, of a bluish-black above, and silvery white below, the skin being somewhat rough.

"I have seen them much bigger than this one," observed the mate; "but it's as well that we did not catch a much bigger fellow, for we should have had some difficulty in handling it. I have known these fellows attack a whale, and run their beaks right into its side, while the thrasher sticks to its back; and between them they manage to kill the monster, though I believe the sharks benefit most by the hunt. I have seen them caught in the Mediterranean by harpoons, especially off the coast of Sicily. The people in those parts are little better than idolaters, and when they go out fishing they sing some old heathen song which they fancy attracts the sword-fish. They won't utter a word of their own language, for fear that the creatures should understand them; but certain it is that the fish follow their boats, when they stand ready with their harpoons to strike them. The flesh is good eating, and very nourishing when cooked; as we shall find it, I hope, though we have to eat it raw. There's another sort of fish which I have fallen in with in these seas, and a curious creature it is. It is called 'the sail-fish,' for it has got a big fin on the top of its back which it can open or shut like a Chinese fan; and when it rises to the top of the water, the wind catches this sail-like fin and sends it along at a great rate; and at its chin it has got two long lines, which I suppose serve it to anchor by, to the rocks in a tideway, when lying in wait for its prey."

"What a curious sort of creature it must be," said Alice; "how I should like to see one!"

"Perhaps we may, when we get closer in-shore," answered the mate; "and we will try to harpoon it, if you don't object to our eating it afterwards."

"Oh, no, no; that I would not," answered Alice. "I only wish some flying-fish would come on to the raft; I would willingly eat them raw. I remember what a foolish remark I made about the matter when we were on board the *Champion*. I little thought how very thankful I should be to catch some of the beautiful creatures for the purpose of eating them."

"I no tink Missie Alice need eat de fish raw," said Nub. "I manage to cook it."

"How so?" asked the mate. "We have no hearth nor fuel."

"I find both," said Nub, in a confident tone. "Look here, Massa Shobbrok. We get some bits of board. I put dem down on de middle of de raft, and we damp dem well; den I take de skin of dis fish and put it on de top of dem, doubled many times; den I take some of de dry pieces of blubber, and I pile dem up; den I get some chips from de sword-fish, and fix dem close to de heap; and now I set fire to de heap, and de fish toast; and I give it to Missie Alice and Massa Walter to eat."

"Oh, thank you, Nub; but Walter and I shall not

like to eat cooked fish while Mr. Shobbrok and you are eating it raw," said Alice.

"We see, Missie Alice, if we got enough for all," answered Nub.

"Your plan seems a good one, Nub," said the mate. "We will try it, at all events."

Nub set to work and prepared the hearth, and by putting on only a few pieces of blubber at a time, he was able to keep up a sufficient heat to cook some small pieces of fish, which Alice and Walter gratefully ate. There were a few pieces over, which he insisted that the mate should take, he himself humbly saying that raw fish was "good enough for black fellow." The mate and Walter stood by ready to throw water on the raft should the fire burn into the wood; but though it nearly consumed the skin, it only charred the boards beneath it.

There was still some blubber remaining, with which Nub proposed to cook another meal for Alice on the following day. Part of the sword-fish was now cut up into thin strips, which were hung up along the yard to dry in the sun, as they would thus, it was hoped, keep longer. They had now such food as they could require; though, eaten without any condiments, it was not palatable, nor altogether wholesome. It would, however, keep them from starving, and they were thankful. They knew that many voyagers, under similar circumstances, had been much worse off than they were.

They had been so much engaged that they had almost forgotten the chest which had been the means of saving Alice. Walter, looking at it, asked the mate if he would like to have it opened.

"Though I do not expect to find much within it, still there may be something that will prove useful to us," answered the mate.

Not being very heavy, though of considerable size, it was easily hauled up on the raft. It was a more difficult matter to get it open, for they were afraid of breaking their axe should they attempt to prize the lid off. Walter proposed to use one of the spear-heads, which might be driven under the lock with a hammer. The attempt was immediately made, and succeeded better than they anticipated. It was, as the mate had suspected, a carpenter's chest. In the upper part was a drawer containing boat-nails, brad-awls, gimlets, and other small tools. The centre part, which had contained the larger tools, was empty; but below, under a sort of false bottom, were found a fine and a coarse saw, some parcels of large heavy nails, two cold irons, and several pieces of iron of various shapes, which altogether had served to ballast the chest while in the water.

"I don't know that in our present circumstances we can make much use of these things," observed the mate; "but if we get on shore on an uninhabited island, they will serve us either for putting up a house, or for building a boat, and we may be thankful that we obtained them; and should the sea get up, the chest will also serve to add buoyancy to the raft."

By this time it was almost dark, and the wind had again begun to drop. As night drew on it was a complete calm. The mate and Nub rowed on for some time; but they found that they were overtaxing their strength, and were obliged to desist, hoping to get a breeze from the eastward the next day.

They had now less fear of want of food than of want of water. Their stock of the latter necessary of life had already begun to run short. The mate, therefore, proposed that they should reduce their daily allowance, though they gave Alice as much as she would consent to take.

The party on the raft had been so accustomed to the sort of life they were leading, that it no longer appeared strange to them. Now and then Walter woke up, and saw the stars shining brightly overhead, and reflected on the wild ocean around him; then he went to sleep again almost with the same sense of security which he had felt on board ship. He began to fancy that the raft would stand any amount of sea, and he fully expected to reach the shore at last. Alice slept on more calmly than on the previous night, the comparatively wholesome meal she had taken making her feel more comfortable than before.

Now the mate took his watch, now Nub his; and as Alice opened her eyes, she saw either one or the other on the look-out, so she soon again closed them, feeling as secure as did Walter. Towards morning both were awakened by finding the raft tossing about far more violently than it had hitherto done. The mate was steering, and Nub was attending to the sheets with the sail hoisted only half-way up.

"What's the matter?" asked Walter.

"We have got a stiffish breeze, and it will carry us the sooner to the shore, if it does not come on to blow harder," answered the mate. "But do you and Miss Alice sit quiet; the weather does not look threatening, and if the wind brings us some rain we may be thankful for it."

"But the wind may throw the surf on the shore, and we may find it dangerous to pass through it," observed Walter.

"Time enough to think about that when we get there," said the mate. "Either there was no land in sight yesterday, and we were mistaken when we fancied we formerly saw it, or a mist hanging about it hid it from our view."

"Perhaps we see it when daylight come back," observed Nub; "and dat just begin to break astern."

The dawn gradually increased. Nub kept eagerly looking out ahead. "I see someting!" he exclaimed suddenly. "It either a rock or a boat."

"That's not a rock," said the mate, "or it would be hidden as the sea washes over it."

"Den dat a boat," cried Nub. "Can it be de cap'en's?"

"Our father's boat?" cried Walter and Alice in chorus.

"It may be," said the mate; "but I think not. We shall soon know."

Eagerly they all watched the boat.

"You must not raise your hopes too high," said the mate at length. "If that boat had people on board she would be pulling towards us, but by the way she floats on the water I am pretty certain that she's empty. Yes, I am confident of it," he added. "In another minute we shall be up to her, and till then there is little use hazarding conjectures on the the subject."

The raft approached the boat. "Furl the sail!" cried the mate. Walter and Nub did so, and the raft glided up alongside the boat, which was half-full of water, and much shattered. Nub seized hold of the bows, while Walter jumped in, and with his cap began to bail out the water.

"What boat is it?" asked Alice.

"One of the *Champion's*—no doubt about that," answered the mate; "but don't be alarmed, Miss Alice, at there being no one on board. It's strong evidence, in my opinion, that the people have been

A PRECIOUS PRIZE.

taken out of her, and that the boat, being water-logged, has been abandoned. Bail away, Walter. We shall soon free her from water, and then as soon as the sea goes down we shall haul her up on the raft, and see what we can do with her. That carpenter's chest was not sent us for nothing, for the tools are just the sort we want for the work ; and, look here ! the planks we nailed on to the bottom of the raft are exactly suited for repairing her. I scarcely dared to pray for a boat like this ; but now she has been sent us, we may have good hope of reaching the shore, which I own I began to doubt we ever should."

" Ay, Massa Shobbrok, you can never pray for too much," said Nub. " I always pray for what I want ; and if it no come, I know it not good for me."

" Do you think this is papa's boat ? " asked Alice.

" No, Miss Alice. I know this is Morgan the second mate's boat, which accompanied the captain's ; and we may hope that the same vessel which received both crews on board may pick us up."

Walter having reduced the water in the boat, sail was hoisted, and she was dropped astern, Nub jumping in to assist in bailing out the remainder. At present she was too sorely battered and leaky to be of any use. Their fear was that the weather might get worse, and that she might after all have to be abandoned. However, as the day advanced, happily the wind fell and the sea went down. As soon, therefore, as they had breakfasted they hauled the boat up on the raft; and though she occupied the larger portion of it, there was still room for Alice to sit near the mast. All hands then set to work to repair her,—Walter and Nub acting under the direction of the mate, who performed the more difficult parts of the task. The boat-nails found in the chest were invaluable, but, of course, without the planks which had been preserved, nothing could have been done.

" Now, lads," said the mate, " before we begin we must see what amount of material we have got, and fit it to the parts for which it is best suited. A little time spent in this way will be time saved in the end, and enable us to accomplish what we might not otherwise have the power to do."

They worked away, scarcely allowing themselves a minute to rest or to take food. The boat had apparently been damaged by the flukes of a whale, several planks on one side having been broken in. These were first repaired, and her bottom made sound; and then other injuries she had received at the bow and stern were put to rights, either by fixing in new planks or by nailing others over the damaged places. There was still wood enough remaining to run a weatherboard all round her, thus to enable her the better to go through any bad weather she might encounter during the long voyage she would possibly have to make. Lockers were then fitted to the bow and stern, in which provisions might be stowed, and so prevent the risk of these being wetted should the sea break into the boat.

Darkness found them still engaged in the task. Their intention was, next morning to make a step for the mast and to build a little cabin aft for Alice.

As there was not room to lie down on the raft, the boat was propped on it; and they all got into her, having also stowed away on board the cask of water, the remaining biscuits, the bottles of wine, two harpoons and spears, and a portion of the fish. Walter and Alice occupied the stern sheets; the mate lay down amidships; while Nub, who was to keep the first watch, sat in the bows. Nub, finding himself in a boat, felt much more secure than he had done on the raft. He had kept the morning watch, and had been working hard all day. It is not surprising, therefore, that when he ought to have been sitting with his eyes wide open he allowed them to close, and fell asleep. The mate himself, though generally very wakeful, experienced a feeling of security he had not for long enjoyed, and slept more soundly than usual. It was almost a dead calm when they lay down, and the sea was perfectly smooth; no vessel could run over them, for none could approach without wind; indeed, unless to be prepared for a change in the weather, it seemed almost needless to keep watch.

Some hours, probably, had passed, when suddenly

the voyagers were awakened by a loud roaring sound, and by feeling the boat lifted on a sea and sent surging forward.   They all started up, the mate and Nub looking around them, while Walter held Alice in his arms, thinking something terrible was about to happen.

"Out with the oars!" cried the mate.   "Walter, ship the tiller."   He was instantly obeyed, fortunately for them; for should such another sea as that which had washed the boat off the raft catch her broadside, it might roll her over and over.   By great exertions the mate got her round, head to the sea, and there he and Nub were able to keep her.   But what had become of the raft?   In the darkness it could nowhere be seen.   Perhaps it was afloat near them, or it might, deprived of their weight, have been turned over and knocked to pieces by the seas.   Happily, most of the articles on which they depended for existence were in the boat; but their mast and sail had gone, with the chest, and the greater portion of their tools.   In vain the mate and Nub looked around on every side in the hope of seeing it.   Could they find it, even though it should be sorely battered, they might hang on to leeward of it by a hawser, and thus, in comparative security, ride out the gale; as it was, they must keep their oars moving all night to prevent the seas from breaking into the boat.   They were, fortunately, rested; and the flesh of the nutritious sword-fish had restored their strength.

"Pull away, boys; pull away!" sung out Nub. "It's a long lane dat has no turning. We better off dan on de raft, which de sea would have washed over ebery moment. Here we pretty dry—only have to keep de oars moving. Pull away, boys; pull away!"

"That's the right spirit, Nub," said the mate. "I only wish that I could sing as you do."

"I sing to cheer up Missie Alice," said Nub in a low voice. "I don't tink I could sing oderwise."

Walter had learned to steer well, and kept the boat's head carefully to the seas, so that she rose over each of them as they came hissing by. The wind was blowing on the land; and though the boat's head was turned the other way, she was in reality drifting towards it. Without a sail they could not attempt to put her stern to the seas, and they must therefore remain in their present position until the weather should again moderate: when that might be it was impossible to say. However, the mate and Nub, being happily inured to hard work, could keep on rowing for many hours together.

Thus the night passed away; and when daylight returned, the rolling seas hissing and bubbling around them were alone to be seen. They naturally looked out for the raft. The boat had just risen on the crest of a rolling wave, when Nub exclaimed, "I see de raft on de larboard hand,"—and he pointed with his chin to indicate the direction; "but it look bery much knocked about."

" But I see it on the starboard bow," exclaimed Walter. " It seems to me as if it had kept perfectly together, though the mast has gone."

" How can that be ? " exclaimed the mate, looking round in the direction towards which Nub was pointing. " Yes, you are right, Nub; that's our raft, sure enough. And now, Walter, I will try to get a look at what you say is a raft." The mate managed, while pulling, to slue himself sufficiently round to look in the direction in which Walter pointed. " Sure enough, Walter, that's also a raft," he exclaimed,—" a much larger one than ours ; but whether or not any people are on it I cannot make out.'

CHAPTER X.

WE must now go back in the order of events, and return to the *Champion*. After the boats had gone away on the expedition which was to end so disastrously, Mr. Lawrie, the surgeon, was walking the deck, meditating on the responsibility he had undertaken, when Dan Tidy came up to him and whispered,— "Hist, sir! things are not going on altogether straight below, I'm after thinking; and if we don't keep a bright look-out, we shall have the boatswain and the Frenchmen running away with the ship, and leaving the captain and the rest of the people in the boats to get back to her if they can. The only chance is that they come to loggerheads together; for they have been quarrelling away for the last hour, though what about, for the life of me I cannot make out."

"Then, Tidy, call the true men aft, and I will arm

them, and be ready for whatever may happen," said the surgeon quietly.

Tidy did as directed; and the man at the helm being one who could be trusted, a cutlass and a brace of pistols were given to him. Scarcely had these arrangements been made when a number of men came rushing up the fore-hatchway, some shouting in English and others in French,—showing the surgeon that, although they might before have been quarrelling, they were now united for one common object. He guessed that their intention was to get possession of the helm, as he saw some of them squaring away the fore-yards.

" If a man advances abaft the main-mast, or touches a brace, we fire ! " he cried out.

" Knock him over ! " cried out a voice, which he recognized as that of the boatswain. " Do as I told you."

" You, my brave fellows, who are resolved to stand faithful to the captain, be ready with your firearms," cried the surgeon. The boatswain and the others with him on this uttered loud shouts of derision, and several shots were fired at the surgeon and his supporters. He was compelled now to give the order to fire in return. Two of his men had been wounded; and three or four of the mutineers fell from the steady fire poured in on them. The rest, led on by the boatswain, now made a fierce onslaught on the surgeon—

he and Tidy being knocked over; but his party, standing firm, drove back their assailants, and he was able to recover his feet. A second attack was about to be made, when loud cries of " Fire! fire!" arose from below, and smoke and flames were seen issuing up the fore-hatchway. The danger threatening had the effect of calming the fury of the mutineers, while Mr. Lawrie's earnest appeals induced them to exert themselves in putting out the flames. Indeed, had not the explosion which has been described taken place, they might possibly have succeeded. For a few moments they stood aghast; but the boatswain, who had already shown his courage, rallied the survivors around him, and urged them to assist him in building a raft. " It's our only chance of saving our lives," he shouted; " and the sooner we set about it the better." Most of the men, obeying him, began cutting loose such spars as could be most easily got at, and launching them overboard. They then, with axes, cut away the bulwarks and other materials for forming a raft; while Mr. Lawrie and his party still made desperate efforts to extinguish the fire. The boatswain showed himself a thorough seaman, by the skilful way in which he put the raft together; and he had finished it before the flames had gained the mastery—thanks to the labours of the surgeon and his party, who, though they could not extinguish, had kept down the fire. Mr. Lawrie, who had not forgotten Alice, was hurrying aft with the intention of trying to save her, when some of the mutineers caught him. "Come along, sir!—come along!" they shouted; "we want a doctor among us, and cannot leave you behind;" and, in spite of his struggles, he was dragged to the side and lowered down on the raft. Dan had made a dash into the cabin, but only in time to see Nub and Alice floating away on a raft from the wreck. Notwithstanding the bruises he had received, he rushed forward in the hope of saving his life, and, unseen by the mutineers, he lowered himself down among them.

Mr. Lawrie's first inquiry on being placed on the raft, and just as they were shoving off, was whether they had brought any provisions. "If we leave the ship without any, we shall only be seeking a more lingering death than we should have found on board," he exclaimed.

The cry arose from those near him, who saw the sense of his remark,—"What provisions have we got?" Search was made, when it was found that they were actually leaving the ship without a particle of food or a drop of water!

"This will not do," cried the boatswain. "Who will volunteer to go back and get what we want? I'll lead the way!" Saying this, he sprang up the side, followed by several of the more daring of the crew. They made their way to the after-hold. A cask of beef was got up; but the men, breaking into

the spirit-room, insisted on having some rum. One
of them, wiser than his companions, managed to lower
down a couple of breakers of water, while the rest
were occupied in getting up three casks of rum;
precious time, which should have been employed in
searching for more provisions, being thus wasted in
procuring what would too likely prove their destruction. The spirit-casks had just been lowered down,
when the flames, bursting out with greater fury, made
them dread another explosion.

"Shove off!—shove off!" was the general cry;
and the men who had been labouring on the deck for
the good of the others had barely time to spring on to
the raft, when the ropes which held it to the ship were
cut, and they shoved away from the side.

By this time a strong breeze had sprung up; the
sail was hoisted, and the raft, passing under the stern,
glided rapidly away from the ship. Though it was
large enough to support the people on it, they found
it necessary that each man should keep a certain place
in order to balance it properly. The boatswain took
the command, and insisted that all the rest should
obey him. His own people seemed willing to do so; ·
but the Frenchmen, who equalled them in numbers,
from the first showed an evident inclination to dispute
his authority, under the leadership of their own boatswain, a man not dissimilar to him in character. Capstick had sense enough to know that he must assert

his authority, and keep the Frenchmen in check, or they would very probably take the raft from him.

"I see what these fellows are after, Mr. Lawrie," he said to the surgeon, who was seated near him. "You will stick by me, I know; for it will come to a fight before long, when, if we don't gain the upper hand, we shall all be hove overboard."

"Then I would advise you to get rid of the rum-casks at once," said the surgeon. "I see that your people are already eyeing one of them as if they were about to broach it; and if they get drunk, which they certainly will, we shall be in the Frenchmen's power."

"I believe that you are right, sir; but I would not like to lose so much good rum," answered the boat-swain, who was himself much too fond of liquor. "I will see what I can do, though."

"Avast there, lads," he shouted to the men. "If we wish to save our lives, all hands must be put on a limited allowance of provisions and spirits. I cannot say how far off we are from the land; but it may be many a long day before we get there."

"We will think about that to-morrow," answered one of the men. "We are thirsty now, after the hard work we have been doing, and we want a glass of grog or two to give us a little strength."

The boatswain expostulated; but he himself longed to have a glass of rum, and his opposition grew weaker. The cask was broached, and a cupful—a large allowance—was served out to each Englishman, including the doctor and Tidy. Mr. Lawrie, however, managed to throw some of his away, and to fill it up with water from a breaker which he had secured, and on which he was sitting—treating Tidy's in the same way. The Frenchmen, on seeing what was going forward, clamoured loudly for rum; for French sailors, and especially under the circumstances in which these were placed, generally show as strong an inclination for spirits as do Englishmen.

"Well, you shall have it if you obey orders," answered the boatswain; the grog he had taken making him more inclined to be good-humoured than before, as well as to forget his suspicions. The seamen were also willing enough to share their treasure with their companions in misfortune. The quantity they had taken at first produced no apparent ill effects, though it tended to raise their spirits and make them forget the dangerous position in which they were placed. Some became loquacious, others sang songs; and both parties shook hands, and vowed that they regarded each other as brothers and friends.

The next day, however, a change had come over their spirits. The French boatswain declared that, as he had assisted to build the raft, he had as much right to the command as Capstick, as well as to half the rum and provisions. To this the latter would not agree; but the Frenchmen, after remaining quiet for some little time, suddenly sprang up, made a dash at one of the casks of rum, and capturing it, carried it in among them.

"Let them have their way," said Mr. Lawrie. "Keep your own people sober, and if the Frenchmen get drunk, you will the more easily master them."

This advice, however, was not followed; some even of the better men making such frequent visits to the cask that several of them were utterly stupified. The Frenchmen meantime having broached their cask, many of them were soon in the same condition. The raft, however, was tumbling about too much to allow them to move,—this more than anything else preventing the two parties from coming to blows on the subjects of dispute which frequently arose. Those who had retained their senses had become hungry, and now demanded food. The doctor and Tidy had managed to knock off the head of the beef-cask, and they served out a portion to each man. It was, however, salt and hard, and tended to increase their thirst.

Thus the day wore on, and Mr. Lawrie could not help looking with serious apprehensions to the future. As yet the two parties had not come to actual blows, but it was evident that they would do so on a very slight provocation. The only person over whom he could assert any beneficial influence was Tidy, who, notwithstanding an Irishman's proverbial affection for a "dhrop of the crater," willingly followed his advice, and took only a small quantity of spirits with his share of water. Tidy had fortunately filled his pockets with biscuit when he went into the cabin to look for Alice. This he shared with the doctor, thus preventing the beef from producing the thirst which it did in the others, who ate it by itself. The Frenchmen had complained that smaller rations were served out to them than the Englishmen took for themselves, and, watching their opportunity, they suddenly rushed towards the beef-cask. Capstick and his party defended it, and soon drove them back again. Though no knives were drawn on the occasion, blows were inflicted, and two of the combatants struggling together fell overboard,—when, locked in a deadly embrace, they sank before their companions could rescue them. Their fate for a time had the effect of sobering the rest; and the doctor, in the hope of keeping them at peace, advised that the two boatswains should together serve out the beef, and see that their countrymen had equal shares.

We cannot follow the history of the unhappy men from day to day. Their provisions had now come nearly to an end. One cask of rum and a portion only of a breaker of water remained; and had not the doctor and Tidy exerted themselves, this also would have been exhausted. Several men were lying on the raft, and the doctor knew that they were dying, but he could do nothing for them. He warned the rest; but they only laughed at him, declaring that the men had only a little too much grog aboard, and would soon come round.

They had made some progress to the westward, sometimes becalmed, and sometimes considerably tossed about, when, soon after daybreak one morning, they caught sight of a dead whale floating on the surface. The boatswain steered towards it, intending, as he said, to get some blubber, which would help out their beef. But perceiving a fire on its back as he got nearer, he at once declared his conviction that the captain and his boat's crew, and perhaps those of the other boats, must be there; so he vowed that nothing should induce him to place himself in his power, telling his own people that if the captain were to take the command of the raft, he would stop their grog, and eat up the remainder of the provisions. He called on them, therefore, to stand by him while he kept the raft on a course which would carry her some distance from the whale. The Frenchmen, in the meantime, seeing the flag on the whale, and the fire burning, and believing that boats must be alongside, frantically stretched out their hands, and shouted at the top of their voices, not recollecting that they were too far off to be heard. They shrieked and shouted, and danced about, every now and then turning with violent gestures towards the boatswain, telling him to steer for the whale. He, however, took no heed of their entreaties, but, feeling dependence on the men about him, continued his

THE "CHAMPION'S" CREW ON THEIR RAFT

course till the raft had got considerably to leeward of the whale, when it was impossible to get up to it—all the oars which had been on board, with the exception of the one by which he steered, having been lost during the frequent struggles which had taken place. The Frenchmen, finding their shouts disregarded, then returned to their seats, talking together, and casting threatening looks at the whaler's crew. The boatswain and his companions laughed at their threats.

Hunger and thirst were by this time assailing them, when one of the men proposed to broach the remaining cask of spirits. In vain the doctor endeavoured to dissuade them from touching it; the boatswain offered but a slight resistance. They dragged it from the spot in the after part of the raft, where it had been stowed, and were soon engaged in drinking its contents.

"A short life and a merry one," cried the party, as they passed the cup rapidly round. The liquor soon began to take effect on their already exhausted frames. They shouted and sang songs, but their voices sounded hollow and cracked; and several rolled over, laughing idiotically at their own condition. The Frenchmen, who had been watching these proceedings, and waiting their opportunity, now rushed aft, and knocking over those who opposed them, seized the cask, and carried it off in triumph. The French boatswain endeavoured to persuade them to take only a small quantity ; but they laughed at his warnings, and were soon in the same condition as the Englishmen. Some sang and shrieked ; and others, getting up, attempted to dance, till one unhappy man in his gyrations tumbled overboard. Some of his companions attempting to catch hold of him, nearly fell in likewise. Their efforts were of no avail, and he sank almost within arm's length. The accident partly sobered some of them. Capstick, calling on the Englishmen, who were still sober enough to move, then endeavoured to regain possession of the cask, when in the struggle the bung-hole was turned downwards, and the greater portion of the contents ran out. A general fight ensued, both parties accusing each other of being the cause of the loss. Knives were drawn, and wounds inflicted. The Englishmen, however, secured the prize, and had to continue the fight to preserve it. The two boatswains stood aloof encouraging their respective parties ; while the doctor and Tidy, who attempted to act the part of pacificators, were knocked over, the Irishman narrowly escaping being thrown into the sea. The fight continued for some time, till the combatants, many of them badly wounded, sank down utterly exhausted. The doctor, notwithstanding the hurts he had received, wished to do his duty, and went among them to examine their hurts. His sorrow was great when he found that no less than five were dead,—chiefly, he believed, from the effects of the spirits they had drunk ;

while several more were in a state which showed him that, even should help speedily come, they were too far gone to recover. Before the sun rose next morning, not a dozen people remained alive on the raft.

The doctor and Tidy had agreed to keep watch and watch, to protect each other, and they were thus able to preserve a little of the water and a small piece of beef which remained in the cask. It might be supposed that the fearful results of the drink would have been a warning to the survivors; but their desire for liquor was as strong as ever; and as soon as they awoke, they insisted on again attacking the rum-cask. A common misfortune seemed at length to have united the two parties; but their leaders stood aloof from each other. The men, however, began sharing the rum out equally among themselves. This went on for some time, till, the liquor running short, they commenced quarrelling as before. The doctor urged Tidy to take no part in any dispute. "Our countrymen are as much to blame as the Frenchmen," he observed. "If we assist our boatswain, we shall be guilty of their death." Tidy's Irish spirit, however, would hardly allow him to follow the doctor's advice.

It had now fallen perfectly calm. Mr. Lawrie, over-come by the heat, had fallen fast asleep, and Tidy, who had undertaken to keep watch, was dozing by his side. Most of the party were by this time reduced to such a state of weakness that very few appeared likely to survive much longer. Evening was rapidly approaching, when suddenly the doctor was awakened by hearing the Irishman exclaim, "Faith, sir, they are at it again; and if they are not stopped, one or both of them will get the worst of it." The doctor started up, when he saw the two boatswains standing facing each other at the further end of the raft. Each had a drawn knife in his hand. The Frenchman was at the outer end of the raft, while two of his countrymen, the only men among them able to exert themselves, were standing near him. "Hold! What murderous work are you about?" shouted the doctor. But his voice came too late; the combatants closed as he spoke, stabbing each other with their weapons. The next moment the Frenchman, driven back by the English boatswain, was hurled bleeding into the water. His two countrymen, who had hitherto remained looking on, sprang to his assistance. One of them, losing his balance, fell overboard; while the boatswain, seizing the other by the throat, stabbed him to the heart. Then turning round with fury in his eyes, he shrieked out, "I will treat every man in the same way who interferes with me!" No one, however, appeared inclined to do so. The sun, already dipping, disappeared beneath the horizon as the scene of blood was concluded; and the boatswain, who seemed suddenly to have been excited into savage fury, sank down exhausted on the raft.

WAR TO THE KNIFE.

Some more hours passed away, when Mr. Lawrie, Tidy, and the boatswain alone remained alive of all those who had lately peopled the raft. The surgeon did his utmost to restore the wretched boatswain, binding up his wounds, and pouring a little of the remaining spirits and water down his throat. It seemed surprising, considering the injuries he had received, that he had not succumbed as the others had done. He evidently possessed no ordinary amount of vitality. A few scraps of beef remained in the cask, of which the surgeon gave him a portion. He ate it eagerly. His continual cry, however, was for water.

As the night advanced, the sea got up, tumbling the raft fearfully about. Mr. Lawrie and Tidy dragged the boatswain to the centre of the raft, and it was only by great exertions they held themselves and him on. The dark, foam-crested seas came rolling up, threatening every instant to break aboard and sweep them away. The boatswain had sufficient consciousness to be well aware of his danger; and fearful must have been the sensations of that bold bad man, his hands red with the blood of his fellow-creatures, as he contemplated a speedy death and the judgment to come. He groaned and shrieked out, yet not daring to ask for mercy. The surgeon would thankfully have shut out those fearful cries from hi ears. Like a true man, he resolved to struggle to the last to preserve his own life and the lives of his companions.

Thus hour after hour went slowly by, till the gray light of morning appeared above the horizon, broken by the rising and falling seas.   Mr. Lawrie found his own strength going, and Dan was in a still worse condition.   They had no food, and not a drop of water remaining, and no land in sight.   Stout-hearted as they both were, they could not help feeling that ere long they must yield, and share the fate of those who were already buried beneath the waves.   The doctor knew, however, that it was his duty to struggle to the last, and he did his utmost to encourage poor Dan.

"Shure, Mr. Lawrie, it's myself has no wish to become food for the fishes, if it can be helped at all at all, and as long as I can I'll hold fast for dear life to the planks," he said in answer to Mr. Lawrie's exhortations.   "Maybe a ship will come and pick us up. Just look out there, sir!   What do you see?   If my eyes don't decave me, there is a boat; and she's pulling towards us."

Mr. Lawrie looked, as Dan told him; and there, sure enough, he saw a boat approaching the raft, but very slowly.   Now she was hidden by intervening seas, and now again she came into sight on the crest of a wave.

"Shure, can it be the captain's boat, or one of the other boats which have been looking for us since the ship went down?" exclaimed Dan.

On hearing the word "captain," the boatswain lifted

up his head and tried to get a glimpse of the approaching boat. "It may be one of our boats; but if it is the captain's, just heave me overboard at once, for he will hear all that's happened."

"Rest assured that if the captain is in yonder boat he will pity your condition, and not call your deeds to account," said the surgeon, anxious to soothe the mind of the dying man.

The boat got nearer and nearer, when the surgeon recognized Walter steering, with Alice by his side, and the mate and Nub pulling. They were soon near enough to hail him.

"Thankful to fall in with you," shouted Mr. Shobbrok, who just then made out the surgeon and Tidy, though he could not distinguish the boatswain. "Who's that with you?"

The surgeon told him.

"Where are the rest?" was the next question.

"Gone! all gone!" was the answer.

"Heave us a rope, and we will hold on under your lee till the water is calm enough to take you on board," cried the mate.

Tidy unrove the halliards, and made several attempts to heave the end on board the boat. At length she came in nearer, when he succeeded; and the rope being made fast, the boat floated back to a safe distance. Questions were now put and answered between them, but they could offer little consolation to each other. The surgeon had to acknowledge that they were without food and water. "If you can manage to send us a little, we shall be thankful," he shouted out.

"We have scarcely enough for another day for ourselves," was the alarming answer; "though we will share what we have when we get you on board."

It was nearly noon before Mr. Shobbrok thought it safe to haul up to the raft, when the surgeon and Tidy, exerting all their strength, and with the mate and Nub's assistance, lifted the boatswain into the boat.

CHAPTER XI.

THE mate and Nub, with their young companions, cordially welcomed the surgeon and Tidy. "We should have been more thankful to see you, had we food and water to offer," said the mate; "but we must pray that a shower may be sent down on us, and that we may fall in before long with a sword-fish or a bonito."

The weather had somewhat moderated, and casting off from the raft, they put the boat's head towards the shore. Walter, as before, took the helm, while the mate and Nub pulled away as hard as their strength would allow, neither the doctor nor Dan being able to exert themselves. As the sun got high in the sky, and distant objects could be seen, the mate stood up and looked out anxiously for the land. "I see it," he exclaimed; "but it's still a long way off. We must not despair, however, my friends." Saying this, he again sat down

"Pull away, lads; pull away!" faintly sang out poor Nub, though his strength was almost gone; for, in order that Walter and Alice might have enough, he had eaten but little food for many hours. The wind once more came ahead, and unless they continued to exert themselves, they might be blown back again a considerable distance. Nub had not spoken for some time, still pulling on; but suddenly his oar fell from his grasp, and he sank down in the bottom of the boat, while the oar, on which so much depended, fell into the water. Dan Tidy, who was sitting next to him, in vain attempted to catch it. It passed by too far off for Walter to reach. The mate in vain endeavoured with his single oar so to manage the boat as to come up with it, and in the violent efforts he made his oar almost broke in two. The helpless voyagers now floated on the wild waters deprived of the means of urging on their boat.

"What are we to do, Mr. Shobbrok?" asked Walter, as the mate stepped aft and sat down by the side of the young people.

"All we can do is to pray to God for help, for vain is the help of man," answered the mate.

"Oh yes, yes! that we will!" exclaimed Alice; and she and her brother lifted up their hands and eyes to heaven, and uttered a prayer, which was surely heard, as true prayers always are.

Poor Nub lay in the bows, too much exhausted to

move; Dan Tidy sat with his head cast down, hope almost gone, his brave Irish heart for the first time yielding to despair; while the surgeon, nearly overcome with weakness, watched the boatswain, who lay at the bottom of the boat with his head resting on one of the thwarts, holding on by the side, his groans expressing the terror and agony of his mind. Gradually the wretched man's hands relaxed their hold, and his eyes became fixed.

"He has gone to his terrible account!" said Mr. Lawrie at length. Not another word was spoken for some time.

"We must bury the man," said the mate; "the sooner it's done the better." The doctor summoned Dan to assist him, and they and the mate taking the body up, were about to let it over the side, when the latter exclaimed, "Stay! his jacket and shirt will be of use in making a sail. It's our only chance of reaching the shore." The garments were taken off the body, which was then committed to the deep; and although without any weight attached, it immediately sank beneath the surface. Not a word was spoken. The surgeon did not think for a moment of going through the mockery of a service; but they all lifted up their hearts in prayer that they might be preserved.

The boat continued drifting before the land-wind further and further from the shore, till all hope of reaching it was lost. Alice, who was seated with her brother gazing across the ocean, perhaps in the expectation of catching sight of an approaching sail, suddenly exclaimed, "Look—look! Walter! what can that be?"

"A piece of wreck," he answered; "or it's one of the rafts."

The boat was drifting directly towards it. The rest of the party turned their eyes in the direction Walter and Alice were looking.

"It's our raft," exclaimed Mr. Shobbrok, getting out the broken oar. "Walter, take the helm and steer as I tell you." They quickly neared the raft. "Heaven be praised!" exclaimed the mate, as they got close to it; "the sail and mast are still there, and also the two oars."

The boat was made fast to the raft, and the mate, with the assistance of Walter and Tidy, lifted the mast, yard, and sail into the boat, with the two oars. The chest, being securely lashed, still remained. The mate quickly opened it, and took out the tools likely to prove most useful, with an ample supply of nails. Scarcely had they been transferred to the boat, when Alice, who had been the harbinger of good tidings, exclaimed, "See! see that large fish!" Walter seized one of the harpoons, and handed it to the mate. The fish was swimming round close to the raft; the harpoon flew from the grasp of the mate, and he calling to Tidy to help him, they together in another minute brought to the surface a large bonito, which was quickly hauled on to the raft. Poor Nub, who had hitherto scarcely

MAN'S EXTREMITY

been able to open his languid eyes, dragging himself up, exclaimed, "We cook it on de raft for Missie Alice."

The suggestion was acted upon, and the lighter portions of the raft, which were sufficiently dried to serve as fuel, were cut up. The fire being kindled, large slices of the meat were arranged round it. Before they were thoroughly cooked, however, most of the starving party began to devour them, though Alice waited till the piece intended for her was done. They were still engaged in cooking the fish, when dark clouds arose in the east. How anxiously they watched them! One passed over their heads, then another.

"Here comes the rain," cried the mate. "Heaven be praised!"

The sail was stretched out as before. Down came the blessed rain. The fire was put out,—which was, however, of minor consequence; and the almost exhausted voyagers were able to quench their thirst, the cask being filled before the rain ceased. The cooked and uncooked portions of the fish were taken on board; and the mate set to work to fit a step for the mast. This was soon done; and a fresh breeze blowing towards the shore, the sail was hoisted, and the boat went gliding over the ocean. How grateful were the hearts of all on board! Food and water had been amply provided, when the blessing was least expected.

Before night set in, land was clearly seen ahead. The mate was of opinion that it was an island of no great extent, or a promontory of New Guinea. Both Nub and Tidy were greatly restored by a night's rest, and the late ample supply of food they had enjoyed. Mr. Shobbrok kept at the helm nearly the whole time, and only when the wind fell would he allow Walter to take his place, with the doctor, to keep watch while he slept. The land-wind, which blew during the morning, tried their patience; but the sea-breeze at length setting in, they rapidly approached the shore, which appeared thickly wooded down to the very edge of the water, with high ground rising at a short distance from it. A belt of coral, such as is now called a "fringing reef," against which the sea beat with considerable violence, throwing up a heavy surf, extended along the shore, making an attempt to land highly dangerous, if not impossible. The mate accordingly hauling the boat to the wind, stood to the southward, in the hope of finding some bay or inlet into which they might run. All eyes were eagerly turned towards the shore. As they coasted along, no huts or habitations of any kind were seen, nor was there any appearance of the island being inhabited. The water in the cask was by this time nearly exhausted, and the uncooked fish began to exhibit the effects of the hot sun. The day was drawing on, and the mate felt especially anxious not to have to spend another night at sea. Just as he was beginning to fear that they might have to do so, his practised eyes discovered an opening in the reef; and telling the doctor and Nub to keep a bright look-out for rocks ahead, he steered for it.

As the boat approached, the shore opened out, and the thankful voyagers soon found themselves entering a deep inlet, fringed with graceful trees down to the very edge of the water. A spot appearing, not far from the entrance, where the rocks, running out, afforded a natural landing-place, sail was lowered, and the boat being rowed carefully in, they soon reached the beach. Walter was the first to spring on shore, followed by Nub, who stretched out his arms to receive Alice from the mate. Her young heart beat with gratitude as she stood, holding her brother's hand, safe on firm land. The rest followed; and having hauled up the boat, they all knelt down and offered up their thanks to Heaven for their preservation from the numberless dangers they had gone through.

"And let us still trust, my friends, to Him who has taken care of us," added the mate. "We should always pray for protection against unseen as well as seen dangers; and it would be folly not to expect to meet with more."

The sail of the boat and the other articles in her were now landed, the mate wishing to form a tent which would protect Alice during the night. As but little water remained in the cask, and the fish was scarcely eatable, it was important to find a fresh stream or spring, and some fruit, if live creatures could not be caught, to satisfy their hunger. The doctor and Tidy set out to explore the neighbourhood for that purpose, while Walter remained to take care of Alice, and to assist the mate in putting up the tent and preparing a fire. Nub begged to be allowed to go in search of wood, observing that he had a notion on the subject, though what it was he did not say.

The mate and Walter had been very busy; the latter in collecting a quantity of dried grass and leaves to form a bed for Alice. He was thus engaged, when, looking up, he saw Nub coming out of the water, carrying on his shoulders what looked like a round basin or saucer of enormous dimensions, with long streamers down which the water trickled hanging from it.

"What can it be?" exclaimed Alice.

"It is, I suspect, a large shell-fish; a mollusc, learned people call it; and if so, the creature will afford all hands an ample meal," observed the mate.

Walter and Alice ran down to meet Nub.

"Yes, Missie Alice, bery good fish inside here," he answered. "Nuf for good supper for eberybody; only we cook it first."

The large clam—such was the species to which the shell-fish belonged—was placed on the ground.

"Where de oders?" asked Nub. "I want Tidy to help make fireplace. Dan Tidy, where are you?" shouted Nub.

Just then Dan made his appearance, with the in-

A GIGANTIC MOLLUSC.

formation that they had found a stream of fresh water running down from the hills not far off, and that the doctor had sent him back to get the cask, he himself remaining on the watch for any birds or quadrupeds which might come down to drink. The remaining contents were therefore shared among the thirsty party, and the Irishman went away with the empty cask on his shoulder; while the mate and Walter assisted Nub in building a fireplace—the materials being furnished by some masses of coral rock which lay on the beach. Fuel was then collected and arranged between the two piles of stone, and the mollusc being placed so that its edges rested on the top of them, the mate set fire to the wood.

Scarcely was the fire lighted when Dan returned with the cask. "Arrah, now, Nub, you are mighty clever; but there's one thing I think I can beat you in, and that is in blowing up a fire. Shure, they used to call me 'little bellows' at home, and set me to make the turf blaze up when the praties were put on to boil." Saying this, Dan threw himself on the ground, and began blowing away with a vehemence which soon made the sparks fly, speedily followed by a flickering flame. The sticks caught and crackled, and the smoke rose in dense volumes.

While he was so employed, the doctor arrived with a large water-fowl which he had cleverly caught, as he lay hid in the long grass, while the bird was passing by, unconscious of danger. "I will undertake the cooking of the mollusc," he said. "If the creature is cut up into small pieces, it will be much more rapidly and perfectly done. We must first open the shell, however. Walter, fetch me the cold chisel and hammer which you brought on shore."

After the mollusc had been for some time exposed to the fire, he with a few strokes opened it, allowing each half to rest on the piles of stone. Honest Nub was in no way offended at being superseded in his office of cook, and went off to collect a further supply of fuel, with which he quickly returned; while Walter employed himself in plucking the wild fowl captured by the doctor. Dan finding it no longer necessary to perform the part of bellows, got up and surveyed the mollusc with infinite satisfaction.

"Arrah, now, if there were but some praties to cook with it, we should be having as fine an Irish stew as we could wish to set eyes on. It's done to a turn now, doctor; and if you will plase to lend a hand, we will carry it to a clear place, away from the smoke, where Miss Alice can sit down and enjoy herself." Suiting the action to the word, Dan took hold of the edge of the shell, but sprang back again with a howl, wringing his burnt fingers as he exclaimed, "Arrah, now, I forgot entirely how hot it was!" The doctor could scarcely help laughing at Dan's mistake, into which he himself had, however, narrowly escaped falling. At

COOKING THE OYSTER.

his suggestion, the fire being raked away, two sticks were placed under the shell, and it was carried to a level spot, where all the party gathered round it, and thankfully ate their first meal on shore. The food was well-tasted and nutritious, though they would gladly have had some vegetable diet to take after it. All had eaten as much as they required, and still a considerable portion remained. The doctor suggested that it should be covered up with the upper shell, and kept for the next day's breakfast. As it was now getting dark, the mate advised Alice to retire to her tent, which he had erected close to the spot where they were sitting, while the rest of the party made such preparations as they deemed necessary for passing the night.

"Though we are not at sea, my friends," said the mate, "we must set a watch, to guard against the attack of wild animals or savages; for though we saw no habitations as we coasted along the shore, people may possibly inhabit the interior. If each of us take two hours apiece, we shall easily get through the dark hours of the night."

"Shure, Mr. Shobbrok, how are we to fight the wild bastes or savages, if they come, without arms?" asked Dan.

"With regard to the savages, I do not, I confess, expect a visit from them; but if any do come, we must try to win their friendship," answered the mate. "As for the wild beasts, we will at once cut some long poles, and sharpen the ends in the fire, to serve as lances. If, however, we keep up a good blaze all night, none are likely to come near us; but should any appear, the person on watch must instantly rouse up the rest."

"No fear of dat, Mr. Shobbrok," observed Nub. "If lion or tiger come, me make a precious hollobolo."

"We need not be afraid of either lions or tigers," answered the mate, "as, to the best of my belief, they are not to be found in this part of the world; but what other savage animals there are, I am not prepared to say."

Alice quickly retired to the tent her friends had arranged for her. The mate assigned their watch to each of the party,—telling Walter, however, that he must consider his over, and get a good night's rest. No one thought it necessary to provide shelter, all of them being by this time inured to sleeping in the open air. A lump of wood or a few bundles covered with grass served for pillows. The doctor took the first watch, Tidy the second, and Nub the third, while the mate chose the last, that he might arouse the rest of the party in time. There being an abundance of fuel, a large fire was kept up, which would serve to prevent any wild beasts from approaching the camp; for they, unlike fishes and insects, which are attracted by a bright light, generally show a dislike to approach a fire.

Alice and Walter were the first on foot—even before

the mate intended to call them. Alice had conceived a wish to visit the fresh stream the doctor had described, to enjoy a draught of cool water and the luxury of a bath, should a spot be found which no sharks could reach, and where no other savage creature was likely to be lying hid. Walter willingly agreed to accompany her, and to stand guard while she was performing her ablutions. The mate did not object; and when Mr. Lawrie heard of their intention, he said that he considered the place perfectly safe, and that he would shortly follow. Nub and Tim, in the meantime, collected more wood to keep up the fire, as it was important not to let it out, their stock of matches being limited. They then went down to the beach to search for more shell-fish, while Mr. Shobbrok remained at the camp to watch the fire. He and the doctor put their heads together to invent various traps, with which they hoped to catch some of the numerous birds flitting about the woods, or any of the smaller quadrupeds inhabiting the neighbourhood.

Walter provided himself with a long stick, which he hoped would be a sufficient weapon of defence against any creatures they were likely to encounter, and in good spirits they set out on their expedition. They had not got far when Alice, touching Walter's arm, whispered, "Do not speak, or we shall frighten them. Look at those beautiful birds; what can they be?" She pointed to a tree a short distance off, on which were perched a number of birds of the most magnificent plumage, with bodies about the size of thrushes, having a mass of feathers which extended far beyond their tails, making them look much larger than they really were. The birds did not apparently observe the intruders on their domain, and continued dancing about on the boughs, exhibiting their richly coloured feathers to each other, as if proud of their beauty. Walter and Alice had never seen any birds to be compared in beauty to them, though they differed considerably from each other. The most beautiful had a bill, slightly bent, of a greenish colour, around the base of which was a fringe of velvet-like black plumes. The head and part of the neck was of a pale golden-green, the throat being of a still richer hue, while the remaining plumage on the body and the tail was of a deep chestnut,—except on the breast, which was a rich purple. From each side of the body beneath the wings sprang a mass of long floating plumes of the most delicate texture, of a bright yellow ; and beyond the tail projected a pair of naked shafts, far longer even than the yellow plumes. Sometimes, when the bird was at rest, it allowed these plumes to hang down close together; then suddenly it would raise them, when they arched over, covering the whole of the body, which shone brightly in the sun. This was evidently a male bird; the females, though possessing much beauty, were not nearly so richly adorned. Another bird, much smaller, was seen among them, perched on a bough above the rest, and evidently considering itself of no small importance. Its colour was mostly of a beautiful red-chestnut, the base of the bill being surrounded with velvet-like plumes, while the throat and upper part of the breast were of a deep purple-red; a bright golden-green zone running across the lower part, separated from the red above by a line of yellow; the lower portion of the body being perfectly white. On each side was a bunch of feathers, tinged with the richest golden-green; and from the middle of the tail extended two very long, naked shafts, which terminated in a broad golden-green web of spiral form. So delighted were the young people with the spectacle, that they could not tear themselves from the spot, forgetting all about the object of their excursion. They were still intently watching the birds, when they were aroused by the voice of the doctor, which had also the effect of startling the beautiful creatures. Away flew the birds, the doctor, however, catching a glimpse of them.

"Oh, what a pity you did not come sooner!" exclaimed Alice.

"Had I done so, I should have deprived you of the pleasure of watching the birds," answered Mr. Lawrie. "From the glimpse I caught of them, I have no doubt that they are birds of paradise, which, I have heard, inhabit New Guinea and the surrounding islands. I have seen some dead specimens, but of course they can give but a very inadequate idea of the birds when living, which I believe are the most beautiful of the whole feathered tribe."

The doctor's arrival was most opportune, for Walter and Alice had remained so long looking at the birds, that they had forgotten the direction to take, and would very probably have lost their way. Conducted by the surgeon, they reached a spot where a bright, sparkling stream fell over a high rock, forming a small cascade, into a pool of clear water about three feet deep. A ledge enabled them to reach the cascade, where they could drink the water as it fell. How cool and refreshing it tasted! They all felt wonderfully invigorated; and the doctor owned that, under their circumstances, no tonic medicine he could have given them would have a more beneficial effect. The rock extended some way down on the opposite side of the stream, and the path they had pursued appeared to be the only one by which the pool could be approached.

"What a delightful place for a bath!" said Alice, looking at it with a longing eye.

"You shall have it all to yourself," answered Walter; "but let me sound it with my stick first. It may be deeper than we suppose."

Walter, as he suggested, went round the pool, plunging in his stick. It was fortunate he did so, for the upper side, into which the cascade fell, was, he found, much out of Alice's depth. He charged her, therefore, to keep on the lower side, where the water was less deep. He was satisfied, too, that no creature lurked within, for the bottom was everywhere visible, though, from the clearness of the water, it was difficult to judge the depth by the eye.

"It's a mercy that you thought of trying the depth," said Alice; "for I intended to have gone under the cascade and enjoyed a shower-bath."

Leaving Alice to bathe in the retired pool, the doctor and Walter hunted about in search of game or fruits, which might serve as an addition to their breakfast. Birds of gorgeous plumage flew about overhead, or flitted among the branches of the trees; and high up, far beyond their reach, they observed some tempting-looking fruit, on which numerous birds were feeding. They gazed at them with envious eyes.

"Our only chance of getting any will be if those feathered gentlemen should be kind enough to let some fall," observed the doctor. "We must not be too proud to take advantage of their negligence."

While he was speaking, a large bird of black plumage, with an enormous beak, and a horn-shaped ornament on the top of it, flew at one of the fruits, and nipping it off, down it came to the ground; while the bird, perching on a bough, attacked another, with more benefit to himself. Walter picked up the fallen fruit, which, though it had a somewhat hard skin, was full of a delicious juicy pulp. While he was examining

the fruit, the doctor watched the bird, which, picking off fruit after fruit, appeared to throw them up
and catch them in its mouth as they fell.   The bird
having apparently satisfied itself, then flew off to the
trunk of a tree of enormous size and height.   The doctor followed it, and found that it made use of its beak
to carry food, with which it was supplying another of
its species—poking its head out of a hole in the trunk.

"We must have those birds if we are hard pressed,
as I am afraid we shall be unless our traps succeed, or
we can manage some serviceable bows and arrows for
shooting game," said the doctor to Walter, who had
followed him.

On their way back to the pool they picked up
several more fruits which had dropped.   They met
Alice, who had not only bathed herself, but had washed
her clothes, and dried them in the hot sun, which
struck with great force against the side of the rock, so
that in a few minutes they were again fit to be put on.

"We must follow your wise example by-and-by,"
said the doctor; "but we will now go back to breakfast, or Mr. Shobbrok will wonder what has become
of us."

CHAPTER XII.

THE doctor, with Alice and Walter, had just left the side of the stream to return to the camp, when they met Dan and Nub carrying the cask, slung on a pole between them.

"We go to get fresh water, and be back soon wid it," said Nub as they passed. "Mr. Shobbrok, him roast de duck ready for breakfast."

The doctor and his young companions hurried on, for their morning's walk had made them very hungry. They found the mate employed in roasting the duck in the usual camp fashion, on a spit supported by two forked sticks. Near it was the large shell of the mollusc on another fire, where Nub had placed it to warm up its contents.

"We have fish and fowl; but I wish that we had some farinaceous or other vegetable diet in addition—for the sake of our young lady, especially," observed the mate.

"We have, at all events, brought something of the

sort," said Walter, producing his handkerchief, full of the fruits he had picked up.

" I am indeed thankful to see them," said the mate ; " for I began to fear that we should all suffer from living so entirely on animal food."

" I have little doubt that we shall find more fruits and probably various vegetables," said the doctor ; " and I will undertake to go in search of them after breakfast."

"I should like to accompany you," said Walter ; " though, if the fruit in these regions only grows high up on the trees such as these do, we shall be puzzled to get them."

" We must climb the trees, then, or find some other means of bringing it down," said the mate. " My idea is, that, before we do anything else, we should set about making some bows and arrows, as well as some spears, to defend ourselves against any savage animals, or to kill any we may be able to chase."

The doctor agreed to the mate's proposal, though he believed, he said, that there were no savage animals of any size in the Pacific islands likely to annoy them. As the duck was not quite cooked, they sat themselves down under the shade of a lofty tree, to await the return of Nub and Dan. They very soon appeared ; and while Nub went to have a look at the mollusc which he and Dan were to have for breakfast, the seaman came and threw himself down at the mate's

THE CAMP ON THE ISLAND.

side with a small branch of tree in his hand, which he was examining attentively.

"What is that you have got there?" asked the mate, turning round to him.

"Faith, your honour, it's something, I suppose; for Nub says that if we can cut enough of it, and can get a ship to carry it away, we shall all make our fortunes." Dan as he spoke handed the branch to the mate, who turned it about, evidently puzzled to know what it was.

"Let us look at it," said the doctor, who then examined the branch carefully. After biting the thick end, he observed: "This is undoubtedly santulum, of the natural order *Santalaceæ*. From it is produced santalin, with which certain tinctures are made. It is also used in India for colouring silk and cotton. Yes, this is indeed the valuable sandal-wood, which the Chinese burn as incense, and employ largely in the manufacture of fans, and of which in England the cases for lead pencils are formed. Nub is right; and as it is of great commercial value, if, as he suggests, we can cut down a quantity, and find a ship to carry it away, we may make enough to pay our expenses home and have something in our pockets at the end of the voyage. From what sort of a tree did you break this off?" inquired the doctor, turning to Dan.

"A big shrub, or what they would call a goodsized tree in other parts; but those near it were so much larger that I suppose they would be offended if we called it a shrub," answered Dan. "It is not far off, and we saw a good many like it in that part of the forest."

"We will go and examine it presently," said the doctor, who was an enthusiastic naturalist.

"We must see about getting food first," observed the mate. "We have many things to do before we can think of cutting down sandal-wood."

"Yes; we must eat our duck first," said the doctor.

"I tink de duck done now," observed Nub, who had been employed during the discussion in giving the roast a few more turns. Plucking some large leaves, he arranged them on the ground before the party, to serve the double purpose of table-cloth and plates; then taking the duck up by the end of the spit, he placed it before the doctor, remarking, "You carve better dan any one of us, sir."

The doctor scientifically cut up the bird, a portion of which Nub presented to Alice and Walter. When the doctor offered some to him and Dan, they both declared that the stewed mollusc was quite enough for them. The voyagers' first breakfast on the island would have been more satisfying had they possessed some bread or biscuit, and, above all, some tea or coffee; but as they could finish it with a good supply of fruit and fresh water, they acknowledged that they had ample reason to be thankful.

Their plans for the future were naturally brought

under discussion. "Don't you think, Mr. Shobbrok, that we could manage to enlarge our boat so that we might reach some civilized place?" asked Walter.

"We might certainly improve her," answered the mate; "and if we could obtain a sufficient amount of provisions and water, we might make a long voyage in her, provided we were favoured with fine weather. But the risk, I warn you, would be very great. Occasionally the seas in these latitudes are excessively heavy and dangerous, and no improvement we could make would enable her to stand them. We should also, as I observed, have to carry a large supply of provisions and water, or we might be compelled to land on a part of the coast where we should have to encounter savages, who would probably attack and destroy us before we had time to convince them that we came upon a peaceable errand. Or, even should they be friendly, we have no goods with which to purchase provisions; and from what I have heard of them, they are not likely to supply us without payment. However, we will examine the boat, and consider how we can enlarge her. We must first ascertain if we can manage to cut out a sufficient number of planks and ribs; and then, if we enlarge the boat, we shall want more sails and spars and rigging. We shall also require casks to carry the water, and a stove for cooking; and as we have no compass or quadrant or chart, we can only make a coasting voyage. We are

also many hundred miles from Sydney in New South
Wales, which is the nearest port where we can obtain
assistance.   It is my belief that we are now off the
north-eastern end of New Guinea, either on the mainland or on an island; though I suspect the latter, or
we should probably have fallen in with natives.   This
point we must ascertain as soon as possible, for we
should do well to avoid them, as at the best they are
a savage race, who are more likely to prove foes than
friends.   Now, the first thing we have to do is to
provide food for ourselves.   See, I was not idle during your absence."

The mate on this showed several contrivances for
catching game.   The question was where to place
them.   It was first necessary to ascertain the places
frequented by the birds or beasts in the neighbourhood.   Dan had formed some traps composed of stones
collected on the sea-shore, such as boys in England
are accustomed to set for sparrows and robins; but
the doctor very much doubted whether the birds of
those regions were likely to hop into them, as they
appeared, he observed, to take their food from the
tops of the trees, and seldom descended to the ground.

"Arrah, I hope they will be after changing their
custom when they see the traps, and just come down
to have a look into them," said Dan.   "I will place
them under the trees and give them the chance, at all
events."

" I would rather trust to bows and arrows," said Walter. " We must look out for the proper sort of trees to make the bows. Perhaps we may find some wood similar to the yew-tree of old England."

The doctor and Nub set off with Walter for the object he had in view, while Alice remained with the mate and Dan, who were finishing their traps. They first proceeded towards the stream. On their way Nub showed them the sandal-wood trees which he had discovered. The doctor was satisfied that he was right. Many of them were of considerable size, really deserving the name of trees, though some could only be called large bushes. In general appearance they were something like myrtles, the trunk being about nine inches in diameter, the leaves very small, alternate or nearly opposite. The doctor, who had carried the axe, cut into the trunk of one of them, which was of a deep red colour. "At all events, though we cannot carry a cargo away with us, we may return here some day and obtain one," he said. "If there are no inhabitants, the trees cannot be claimed as the property of any one ; and we may load a vessel with great ease in the harbour."

" I tink, Mr. Lawrie, dat we better look out for food just now," said Nub, who thought the doctor was spending more time than necessary in speculating on the future.

" You are right, Nub," answered the surgeon, leading the way. They examined numerous saplings of small size, but none seemed likely to suit their purpose. On the banks of the stream they came to a magnificent grove of bamboos of all sizes, some being as thick as a man's leg.

"Here we have the means of building a house ready to our hands," said the doctor. "Perhaps they will assist also in decking over the boat."

"But I doubt if they would keep out the water," observed Walter. "I think, however, that the fine ends or some of the very small canes may serve for arrows."

"Dey make very good cups for drinking out of," said Nub; and asking for the axe, he cut down a large bamboo cane, though not one of the thickest, and showed Walter that numerous divisions or knots filled up the centre of the cane, and that thus each knot would make the bottom of a cup.

On passing near the tree where the doctor had seen the hornbills, they observed one of the birds poking its long beak out of its hole.

"We pay you visit before long," said Nub, nodding his head. "Me tink I know how."

Going up the stream, they found a tree which had fallen over it, by which they crossed to the opposite bank. Nub begged to go first. "I go to see de way. We no want to pop into de middle of a village; if we do, de women begin to shriek, and de babies cry

out, and tink dat white debils come among dem, and
den de men come out and kill us."

The doctor agreed to Nub's proposal, and they proceeded more cautiously than before. Walter pulled
away at every young tree they met, and at last
he found one which the doctor thought would suit
their purpose. Nub, who came to examine it, was
of the same opinion; and they quickly cut down
several which grew near to the proper length, and
returned with them the way they had come. As
they passed under the tree in which they had seen
the hornbills, Nub exclaimed, "I tink we come and
get dese fellows at once, if de mate will please to accompany us."

On passing under the tree where the fruit had been
found, Walter looked about for some more; but the birds
were not feeding, and none had fallen since they had
been there. On their arrival at the camp, the mate
and Dan had to confess that their traps had not as
yet been successful; Nub then told them his plan
for reaching the hornbills, which could not fail with
regard to the hen, who was certain not to leave her
nest, and might possibly either be sitting on her eggs
or have some young ones.

"How is that?" asked Walter. "When she sees
you, if you succeed in reaching her, she will surely
fly away."

"No, Massa Walter," said Nub, "she not do dat;

for de hole is shut up with clay, and she only got room to poke her head out."

Nub's plan was to form a ladder up the tree with the bamboos they had seen. With a little patience, he assured them, the feat could be accomplished; so they all eagerly set out to commence operations, Alice accompanying them; while the doctor continued his search for the vegetable food they so much required. He first, however, cut a stick from the thick end of a bamboo, for the purpose of digging edible roots, which he thought it probable he might discover.

Nub also suggested that they should forthwith set to work to build a house large enough to contain the whole party. A house would be far better for Alice than the tent, in which she had to lie close to the ground, with some risk of the intrusion of snakes or noxious insects; besides which, bad weather might come on, when they would all require shelter.

" Nothing like bamboo-house," observed Nub. " If earthquake come, it no shake down ; if storm come on, it no blow away."

The mate assented to the black's proposal, and agreed at once to cut down a sufficient number of bamboos, not only for the ladder, but for the house. This was not quite so easy a task as it at first appeared, for though the canes were hollow they were excessively hard, and it was only by chopping downwards all round that they could be broken off. At length, however, a sufficient

IN SEARCH OF HORNBILLS

number for the proposed ladder were cut down and carried to the foot of the tree.

Nub was not going to make a ladder of double poles; the tree being of soft wood, he intended to stick in the rounds horizontally, and to support them with a single pole. They had also to collect a quantity of tough and lithe vines, which would serve to bind the rounds to the outer pole, the thickest end of which was stuck deep into the ground. This done, the work went on rapidly, round after round being driven into the tree, about three feet apart. Nub, continuing his work, went on ascending step after step, Dan following him when he got too high up to reach the long poles from the ground. The height looked perilous in the extreme, and Alice, as she watched him, could not help dreading that he might miss his footing and fall down; but Nub was highly delighted with the success of his undertaking, and seemed to have no fears on the subject.

"Nub puts me in mind of 'Jack and the Bean Stalk,'" said Walter, laughing. "I only hope that he won't find an ogre at the top of the tree."

"No fear about Nub," observed the mate. "I hope that he may soon wring the necks of the hornbills and send them down to us."

Nub was now near the hole where the female hornbill had been seen. She had drawn in her head; and her mate was either absent from home or was concealed among the thick foliage at the top of the tree. The last round was in, and Nub was seen preparing to mount on it, that he might put in his hand and haul out Madam Hornbill. He was just about to do so, when she put out her long beak, and began pecking away furiously at his hand; while, at the same moment, down flew Mr. Hornbill from a bough on which he had been snugly ensconced till a favourable opportunity arose of making an attack on the assailant of his fortress. That every man's home is his castle, is rightly held in England as an established law, and the hornbills naturally considered their nest their castle. With loud screams of rage the male bird attacked poor Nub, who slipped down to the next round, where he held on with might and main, trying to defend his head from the furious onslaught of his feathered foe. Fortunately, his curly head of hair was a good thick one, and prevented the bird from inflicting the injury it might otherwise have done. Keeping his head down, so as to defend his eyes, he rapidly descended the ladder, the hornbills cawing and screaming all the time. The male bird, however, did not attempt to descend beyond the upper rounds of the ladder.

"I no tink we lose our dinner, though," said Nub, as he got to the bottom. "What say you, Massa Shobbrok ?"

"Certainly not, Nub," answered the mate. "I have got a notion which I am pretty sure will succeed."

ATTACK AND DEFENCE.

"Den, if you show me what it is, I go up again, pretty quick," said Nub, who was afraid that the mate would deprive him of the honour of catching the bird. The mate took a line from his pocket, forming a noose, which he secured to a light bamboo. "I see it," cried Nub, "I see it. I soon catch both of dem, one after de oder."

Taking the bamboo, he quickly ascended the ladder till he got near enough to reach the hornbill, which was still standing screaming defiantly on the upper round; and before it was aware of what the black was about, the latter slipped the noose over the bird's head and drew it tight, and then with a violent jerk pulling it off its perch, down it came, with its huge bill first and its wings fluttering, to the ground, where Dan quickly despatched it. Nub immediately descended for the bamboo; and mounting again, slipped the noose over the head of the hen hornbill, which she had poked out to see what had become of her partner. He held her fast enough, but could not drag her out of her hole. By standing on the upper round, however, he was able to batter in her fortress with his fist, after which he speedily sent her to the ground. Then putting in his hand, he drew out a curious creature like a ball of down, bearing no resemblance whatever to its parents. Though scarcely fledged, it was not to be despised, being very fat, and about the size of a young chicken. So Nub threw it down to join its parents, shouting out, "Dere, dat make a fine dinner for Missie Alice." Poor Alice was grieved when she saw the little creature come tumbling to the earth, and declared she could not touch it.

"Bery sorry, Missie Alice," said Nub, when he came down again, putting on a penitent look. Then turning aside to Dan, he whispered, "She talk bery differently when she see it nicely roasted by-and-by."

Their success in obtaining food encouraged the voyagers to hope that they were not doomed to starve on an inhospitable shore, but that with diligence and a due exertion of their wits they might obtain sufficient food to support life. The hornbills would, at all events, afford them an ample meal for that day, and they might reasonably expect to obtain a further supply of shell-fish from the sea-shore; though Nub might not succeed in finding another huge mollusc.

"Shall we remove the ladder?" asked Walter. "It might help to build the house."

"I tink not," answered Nub, looking up. "Perhaps anoder hornbill come and make her nest dere, den we catch her and her husband. Bery good chance of dat, I tink."

As it was important to get their house built without delay, they all returned laden with as many bamboos as they could carry,—Alice taking charge of the birds, slung, Chinese fashion, at the end of a bamboo, which she balanced on her shoulder; the little one being hung behind her, that her tender heart might not be grieved at seeing it.

" Shall we all assist in putting up the house, Mr. Shobbrok, or might it not be as well to try and get one or two bows made first ?" asked Walter.

" We canuot obtain food without them, so, by all means, make two or three," answered the mate. " You and Nub can work at them, while Dan and I arrange the plan for the house, and begin to put in the uprights."

Alice assisted the mate in holding the line.

" We must try to get the opposite sides even, and the walls at right angles with each other, and the corner-posts perpendicular," he observed. " The sides of our house must depend very much, in the first instance, on the length of the bamboos ; and we can so arrange it that we may increase it without difficulty."

As it was not time to begin cooking, all hands set to work at the occupations they had settled to follow. While Walter and Nub were shaping the bows with their knives, the mate, with his two assistants, having selected a flat spot a considerable height above the water, marked out the plan for the house—in front of which they intended to add a broad verandah, facing the sea-shore. The ground-floor they divided into two rooms, with space for a staircase to lead to the upper floor. This floor was to be divided into three rooms,— one for Alice, another for Walter, and the third for the surgeon; while the mate and the two men were to occupy one of the lower rooms, the other being intended for a parlour. The kitchen, they agreed, it would be best to form at a little distance from the house, lest it might by any accident catch fire.

While they were thus busily employed, the doctor came back with a large supply of two different kinds of fruit—one like a plum, the other having a hard rind but a delicious pulp—while his pockets were filled with some roots, which he considered were of even more value. He also reported that he had found a palm which he had no doubt would yield an abundance of sago ; but it would take some time and labour to prepare it. He proposed forming a manufactory near the stream, as an abundant supply of water was required for the necessary operations : also that they should commence the work next morning ; for he considered that no time should be lost, as it would afford them an abundant supply of nutritious food, on which they could depend under all circumstances. He would, however, require one hand to assist him. Nub at once volunteered his services. " I hope by that time to have one of the bows finished," said Walter, " and I will go and shoot game, while Mr. Shobbrok, Dan, and Alice continue working away at the house." The mate agreed to this proposal, though he observed that he thought it would be advisable, as soon as a sufficient supply of sago was got, for all hands to set to work at the house, so that they might have shelter should bad weather come on.

Nub had not forgotten to spit and put the hornbills before the fire in good time; and when evening came on, and they could no longer see to work, they sat down to the most ample meal they had yet enjoyed, aided by the roots and fruits the doctor had collected.

"In a couple of days more, Miss Alice, I hope you will have a good roof over your head, and a room to yourself," observed the mate. "I shall not rest satisfied till I see you comfortably lodged."

Alice declared that she was perfectly satisfied with her tent.

"That's very well while the weather is calm and dry; but should the rain begin to fall, which, from the look of the foliage, I have no doubt is very heavy hereabouts, it would be a very different matter," he answered.

"I was, selfishly, only thinking of myself," said Alice, "and forgetting that you, at all events, would be exposed to the rain; so I hope that you will set to work and get the house up as soon as possible. I only wish that I was a man, to be able to help you more than I have done."

"You do help us, Miss Alice," said the mate; "and you encourage us by your patience and uncomplaining spirit, and your cheerful temper. Do not think that you are of little use, for I don't think that we could do without you." Alice, being assured that the mate spoke the truth, was well pleased to think that, young as she was, she was of use to her companions.

Not only on a desolate island, but in the quiet homes of England, many little girls like Alice have the power, by their cheerfulness and good spirits, and, we may add, by their piety and kindness, to be of inestimable use to all around them.

CHAPTER XIII.

THE house was nearly finished. The whole of it was constructed of bamboos. The uprights were the thickest canes; the next in size formed the horizontal beams, lashed together tightly with the long trailing vines which abounded in the forest. The rafters of the flooring and the roof were of a third size; while the flooring itself and the walls were composed of the larger canes split in two, and, after being well wetted, pressed down by heavy stones till they were perfectly flat. The roof was thickly thatched with palm leaves, which served also to cover the outside walls of Alice's room. There was a broad verandah in front, in which the occupants could sit and work during the heat of the day. The common sitting-room was intended to serve them chiefly at night, when the weather proved bad. There was no fear of cold in that climate, and they had, consequently, only to guard against wet and an inconvenient amount of wind.   The lower rooms were not more than seven feet in height, and the upper scarcely so high ; so that the whole building, independent of the roof, which had a steep pitch, did not reach more than fourteen feet from the ground.   A ladder with numerous rounds, which would allow Alice to climb up and down with ease, led from the sitting-room to the upper story.   As, of course, they had no glass, window-shutters were formed of the same material as the house, and served well to exclude either the sun or rain.

" Why, we have forgotten a store-room !" exclaimed Walter, just as the house was finished.   " If we have no larder, how are we to keep our game, and the sago which the doctor is going to make, and the roots and fruits, and anything else we may obtain ? "

" It was indeed an omission, and I wonder none of us thought of it before," said the mate.   " However, a few more hours' labour will enable us to set up a building which will answer the purpose better than had we put it inside the house."

Another journey to the bamboo brake supplied them with the necessary amount of canes, and a small building was erected at one end of the house—which served for one of its walls.   It had three stories, each about three feet in height, with a ladder reaching to them, so that no marauders, unless they were climbers, could get in.   This could not have prevented either monkeys or snakes, or such active creatures as tiger-cats, from robbing their stores. Well-fitting shutters were therefore fixed on in front of the building, which was completed before dark, and was considered strong enough for the purpose they had in view. It was, indeed, a gigantic safe standing on four legs, the lower part being quite open.

"Now we must set to work to kill game, and obtain other provisions, to put in it," observed the mate.

"I shall be able to manufacture more bows for the rest of the party; for though I am improving, I can scarcely expect, as yet, to kill game enough for all hands, or to obtain a sufficient supply to lay by for the voyage," said Walter.

"We will devote the remainder of this evening, then, to manufacturing bows and arrows," said the mate.

"To-morrow I must beg you all to come and assist me in manufacturing sago," observed the doctor. "I can employ all hands. We must first cut down a tree, and then divide it into lengths, and drag them to the water, where we must erect our machinery, which need only be of a very rough character,—and probably the bamboo canes will help us to form it."

"Mr. Shobbrok, when do you propose to begin enlarging the boat? I do so long to set sail in search of papa," said Alice.

"I have been considering the subject, young lady,

and I am as anxious as you can be, but there is a great deal to be done first. We must collect provisions, and also ascertain that they will keep good during a long voyage. One difficulty can be got over more easily than I at first supposed; for the thick ends of the large bamboos will, I have no doubt, carry a quantity of water, though I am afraid they will take more space in stowing than I would wish. If the doctor succeeds in producing sago, we shall have a substitute for bread; and it also may be preserved in bamboo casks. I think, too, that we may manage to salt and smoke the birds and fish we may catch; though, without hooks and lines, we can only hope occasionally to kill some larger fish with our harpoons."

"I have been thinking, Mr. Shobbrok," observed Walter, "that I could make some fish-hooks from nails, with the help of a small file which I have in my knife; and as we have plenty of rope, we may unpick some of it, and twist some strong line."

"Pray set about it then, Walter," said the mate; "for time will be lost if we go out in the boat in search of large fish to harpoon, when small ones may be caught from the rocks on the sea-shore."

The next day the whole party started, under the guidance of the doctor, to the spot where he had seen the sago palm. He observed that it was the best time to cut down the tree, as the leaves were covered with a whitish dust, which was a sign that the flower-bud was about to appear, and that the sago, or pith within the stem, was then most abundant—it being intended by nature for the support of the flowers and fruit. Nub having climbed to the top of a tree, secured a rope, at which the whole of the party hauling together, hoped to bring it down in the right direction. The mate, axe in hand, then commenced chopping away. The wood was tolerably soft, and as the weapon was sharp and he was a good axe-man, the tree was soon cut through, and came crashing down to the ground. He then, by the doctor's directions, divided the trunk into pieces five feet in length. While he was thus occupied, the doctor got his other companions to pull off the leaves, and to manufacture a number of cylindrical baskets—in which, he told them, he intended to put the pulp produced from the pith. The tree being cut up, ropes were fastened to each piece, to enable them to be dragged to the side of the river. Two men were required for each. Walter and Alice tried to drag one of the smallest, but could not move it over the rough ground ; they therefore carried the baskets, and remained by the river to assist the doctor and Nub, while the mate and Dan went back to bring up the other logs. The first operation was to slice off a part of the outer hard wood till the pith appeared. The log was then rested on bamboo trestles a couple of feet from the ground. The two workmen now cut across the longitudinal fibres and the pith together, leaving,

however, a part at each end untouched, so that the log
formed a rough trough.   The pulp thus cut into small
pieces, and mixed with water, was beaten by a piece of
wood, by which means the fibres were separated from
it, they floating on the top, while the flour sank to the
bottom.   A number of bamboo buckets, manufactured
by Nub, enabled Walter and Alice to bring the water
required for the operation.   The coarser fibres floating
on the top being thrown away, the water was drained
off, and the remaining pulp was again cleared by more
water.   This operation was repeated several times, till
a pure white powder alone remained.

"There, Miss Alice," said the doctor, showing it to
her, "I beg to offer you some, with which you can
make cakes or puddings,—though I confess that it is
not equal to wheaten flour, as this is in reality starch :
but it will afford nourishment to us, as it would have
done to the flowers and roots of the tree had we not
cut it down."

"I thought sago was like little white seeds," re-
marked Alice.

"What is imported is so in appearance," answered
the doctor.   "In order that it may keep, it is prepared by being first moistened, and then passed through
a sieve into a shallow dish, and placed over a fire,
which causes it to assume a globular form.   The sago,
when properly packed, will keep a long time ; but the
flour we have here would quickly turn sour, if exposed

to the air. I propose filling the baskets we have made with what sago we do not require for immediate use, and sinking them in fresh water, when it will thus keep for a long time. Had we but an iron pot, we might easily prepare it for a voyage; but we must, of necessity, find some other means of doing so."

"Don't you think the large mollusc-shell will answer the purpose?" observed Walter. "If it will cook meat, it will surely bake the sago."

"In that instance it had water in it," observed the doctor. "I am afraid that with dry sago in it the shell will take fire. However, we will try. Perhaps we may find a large flat stone which we can surround with a rim of wood; and by applying heat under the centre our object may be attained."

"Oh, that will do capitally," said Walter; "and I am sure that we can easily manufacture a sieve."

The mate and Dan had now brought up all the logs; and seeing how well the doctor had succeeded, they heartily congratulated him.

In a short time the pith of the whole tree was turned into sago powder, amounting, they calculated, to about one hundred pounds. The doctor told them that this was but a small quantity compared with that which a large tree produces, as frequently one tree alone yields five to six hundred pounds' weight of sago. The greater part of the sago having been buried in a quiet pool, where there was little fear of its being disturbed, the party returned with the remainder late in the evening to their house.

Walter was up next morning at daybreak, searching along the shore for a flat stone to serve for the bottom of the pan he wished to make for granulating the sago. To his great delight, he found one of considerable size, almost circular, and with the edges washed smooth by the action of the waves. He had brought some strips of the palm which had been chopped off the sago tree on the previous day. One of these was of sufficient length to bind round the stone; another served for the rim of the sieve, and a number of large leaves cut into strips made the bottom. Both contrivances had a rough look, but he hoped they would answer the purpose. He placed the pan between two stones in the way the mollusc had been fixed; and then hurrying to the doctor, brought him to see what he had done. The fire was soon lighted under the stone, which was heated without cracking; and the doctor then shook some flour from the sieve on to the pan, and, greatly to his and Walter's delight, it granulated perfectly.

"You have rendered our community a great service, Walter!" exclaimed the doctor. "We may perhaps improve upon your contrivance, or, at all events, make a number of pans and sieves, as the process at present is a slow one, and it would take a long time to manufacture as much sago as we shall require for the voyage."

Walter, however, begged that he might continue the manufacture, so that he might be able to judge how much could be produced. Though he laboured all day, he had only two or three pounds' weight to show; still that was something, and no doubt remained that a supply of sago could be obtained for the voyage. Alice, who had watched him at work, felt sure that she could carry it on as well as he could; so the next day she took his place, while he accompanied the doctor on a shooting expedition. Nub was to attend them. Each carried a bow, with a quiver full of arrows, and a long spear. They were neither of them as yet very expert marksmen. The doctor was the best, while Walter was improving. Dan always declared that his bow had a twist in it, and shot crooked; but he was more successful than any of the party in catching birds in other ways.

They had been waiting for Nub, who had gone out early in the morning; but just as they were starting, they met him coming back with a couple of hornbills, which had taken refuge in the hole occupied by the birds before captured.

"I thought oders would come," he observed, holding them up; "and I got one egg, too, which do nicely for Missie Alice's breakfast."

The doctor told him to take the birds home, and then to follow them. They several times caught sight, as they went along, of some beautiful birds of paradise, which, however, kept too high up in the trees to be shot by arrows.

"We are out of luck this morning," said the doctor, when they had gone some way without killing a bird.

"Don't you think that if we could make some bird-lime we might have a better chance of catching the smaller birds?" asked Walter.

"No doubt about it, if we could get the ingredients, and a bait to attract the birds," answered the doctor. "The idea is worth considering. Keep your mind at work, my lad; you may be, at all events, of great use in our present circumstances. I have known instances where shipwrecked crews have starved when they might have supported their lives, simply because they were too ignorant or too dull to exert themselves and search diligently for food. An Australian savage will live in the wilds where the white man will perish. But then the savage knows the habits of all the living creatures in the neighbourhood, and the roots and herbs, and indeed every vegetable substance which will afford him nourishment. Had we more skill as marksmen, and did we know the haunts of the animals frequenting these woods, I have no doubt that we should have before this abundantly supplied ourselves with food of all sorts. We are, however, improving, and I have no longer any anxiety on the subject."

While the doctor was speaking, Walter had been intently looking towards the branch of a large tree seven or eight feet above the ground.

"Oh, Mr. Lawrie," he exclaimed, "what is that terrific monster? If it should run at us it will kill us. The head looks to me like that of a crocodile; but do such creatures exist on land? Shall we attack it, or will it be better to get out of its way?" he asked, quickly recovering his courage, and bringing his spear ready for battle. Walter's sharp eyes had detected what Mr. Lawrie had before failed to see in the gloom of the forest.

"If we are not cautious, it will be getting out of our way, which I should be sorry for," answered the surgeon with a calmness which surprised his companion. "That creature is a species of iguana, some few of which inhabit the East, though the larger number are found in South America and the West India Islands. They are not very formidable antagonists, and are more likely to run away than attack us. If we had a good strong noose, we might throw it over the head of the animal, and soon haul it down from its perch, where it at present seems to be sleeping."

While they were speaking, Nub overtook them, and was highly pleased when they pointed out to him the hideous-looking lizard.

"Look, I brought dis," he said, producing a piece of rope. "Now I go and slip it ober de head of de iguana ; and when I pull him down, you pin him to de ground with your spears."

The doctor and Walter agreed to follow Nub's advice, and cautiously approached the sleeping brachylophus, as the doctor called the creature. It looked still more formidable as they approached ; for it had a long pointed tail, large claws, a row of spines down its back, and numerous teeth in its long jaws. Lumps and excrescences of various sizes added to the hideous appearance of its head.

Nub got the noose ready to throw, while the doctor and Walter held their spears prepared for action. Nub drew nearer and nearer ; the reptile opened one of its eyes, and then the other, and moved its tail slightly. In a moment the noose was dexterously thrown over its head, when Nub gave a violent pull before it had time to grasp the branch with its claws, and hauled it to the ground. "Now, Massa Walter," he shouted out ; "hold on to him tail." But though both Walter and the doctor attempted to catch the creature's tail, it whisked it about so violently that the task was no easy one. Nub meantime kept jumping round and round, as it made attempts to bite his legs. The doctor at length getting in front, ran his spear into its open mouth ; while Walter, with the point of his, pressed its neck down to the ground. The creature had, however, still an abundance of life, and made desperate efforts to escape. When it advanced, the doctor drove his spear further down its throat; and when it retreated, finding the point unpleasant, Nub hauled away on the rope, which grew tighter and tighter round its neck.

"Hit it on the tail with your spear, Walter; a few heavy blows will soon render it helpless," said the doctor; and Walter, as directed, belaboured the unfortunate creature, till at length its struggles ceased.

"Hurrah! we got him now,—and plenty of dinner to last us for many days," shouted Nub. "I tink what we now got to do is to make ropes fast round him neck and drag him home."

Nub's suggestion was acted on; and having cut some vines and fastened them round the creature's neck, they harnessed themselves and began hauling it along. The operation was somewhat fatiguing, owing to the roughness of the ground and the numerous roots which projected in all directions. Their arrival was welcomed cordially by the mate and Dan; Alice, however, could not believe that they intended to eat so hideous a creature. It was forthwith hoisted up to the branch of a tree; and while Nub and Dan prepared the fire for cooking it, the doctor cut open its inside, which was found full of tree-frogs, small lizards, and other creatures. Walter stood by watching him, as with scientific skill he dissected the huge lizard, discoursing as he did so in technical language, which was perfectly incomprehensible to his young hearer, on the curious formation of the creature,—on its bones, muscles, and other internal parts.

"I tink one ting," observed Nub, who, after he had deposited a bundle of faggots near the fire, had come back to watch the proceedings. "I tink that he make bery good roast, and remarkably fine stew, if we had salt and pepper, and a few oder tings to eat wid him. I bery glad if we catch one of dese beasts ebery oder day."

As soon as the doctor had satisfied his curiosity, Nub begged that he might have the joints, as it was time to begin cooking them for dinner. The remainder of the carcass was now hung up in the larder, which had been finished in time for its reception.

"We must see about preserving our meat, however," observed the doctor, " or we shall always be liable to starvation; and the sooner we begin the better."

"What do you propose doing?" asked Walter. "I was thinking of searching for salt on the sea-shore."

"A still more effectual way of preserving the meat will be to smoke it, I suspect," said the doctor. "We have an abundance of stones, and we can easily build a 'smoking-house,' with the ever-useful bamboos for rafters. We shall have time to do something before dinner."

"At all events, we can make a beginning. There's nothing like setting at once about a thing which has to be done," observed Walter.

DISSECTING THE LIZARD

" You are right, my boy ; and we will get the mate and Dan to help us, as Nub, I see, is busy attending to our roast," said the doctor.

They immediately set to work to erect a circular wall about six feet in diameter. They did not stop to procure cement, as even should the structure tumble down no great damage would be done, and it might easily be built up again. They had already raised it two or three feet in height before Nub had finished his culinary operations. Dinner was laid out, not, as hitherto, on the ground, but on a rustic-looking table, with benches on one side, and a large arm-chair at one end for Mr. Shobbrok. Alice superintended the arrangements. They had leaves for plates, sticks for forks, and their clasp-knives enabled them to cut up their meat ; and a neat bamboo cup stood by the side of each person, while one of larger dimensions served to hold their only beverage, pure water. At length Nub shouted " Dinner is ready ; " and he and Dan entered the house, each bearing a large shell which they had picked up on the shore,—one containing a piece of roast lizard, and the other one of the hornbills captured in the morning. Nub then hurried out again, and returned with a third shell full of sago ; while a fourth was filled with some roots which the doctor had dug up. The latter assured his friends that they were perfectly wholesome, as he knew the nature of the plants. They complimented Nub on his cooking, and all sat down with excellent appetites, and hearts thankful for the substantial meal which had been supplied them.   Little had they expected to find so large a supply of wholesome food when they first landed.

The next day the doctor and Nub went on with the erection of the smoking-house ; while the mate, assisted by Dan, made preparations for the proposed alterations in the boat.   He looked somewhat grave, however, over the business ; and Dan heard him saying to himself, " I wish that I thought it would do.   But it's a fearful risk for those young people to run."

The doctor having at length finished the smoking-house, which was covered over thickly with palm-leaves, he observed,—" And now we have finished our house, we must get some game to put in it.   Your bow and arrows, Walter, will, I hope, give us a good supply."

" But are we not to try and catch some fish ?" asked Walter.   " They can be more effectually smoked than birds, and will keep better, I fancy.   I have begun a hook, and I think that I may be able to finish two or three more before night."

" By all means.   If Mr. Shobbrok does not intend to commence immediately on the boat, we might take her into the middle of the harbour, or out to sea, and try what we can catch."

The mate agreed to the doctor's proposal ; so the next day they and Walter went off, taking Alice, who wished to accompany them. Nub and Dan remained on shore to attend to the traps, and shoot some birds, if they could, for dinner. The fishing-party first threw their lines overboard in the harbour, but after trying for some time they caught only two small fish; they therefore pulled some way out to sea, where the water was sufficiently shallow to allow them to anchor by means of a large stone which they had brought for the purpose. They quickly got bites, and began rapidly to pull up some large fish, which the doctor believed, from their appearance, were likely to prove wholesome, though he could not tell their names. They were so busily employed that the time passed rapidly away, and evening was approaching before they thought how late it was. They did not fail, as may be supposed, to keep a bright look-out for any passing sail; but none appeared. With nearly four dozen fine large fish, they returned to the harbour. Nub's eyes glistened, as he came down to assist in hauling up the boat, on seeing the number of fish.

"No fear now of starving, I tink," he observed. "I neber thought we get so much as dat. God gives us all good tings, and we tank Him."

The rest of the day was employed in preparing the fish and hanging them up to dry, after which a fire of green wood was placed under them; and the doctor expressed his confidence that his plan for curing both fish and fowl would succeed.

The mate had for some time wished to explore the island, and at supper he proposed that they should set out the next day.   Being unwilling to expose Alice to the dangers they might have to encounter, he suggested that she and Walter, with Nub, should remain behind at the house; for, as they had now an ample supply of provisions, they might safely do so without fear of starving.   They both, however, begged so hard to go, that he at length yielded to their wishes; and it was agreed that the whole party should set off directly after breakfast the next morning.

CHAPTER XIV.

ALICE and Walter were up betimes, eager for the intended expedition. As it was uncertain whether fresh water would be met with, they all carried bamboo casks slung over their backs, with a small quantity of smoked fish,—the doctor's plan having been found to answer admirably. Each one of the party also carried a supply of sago flour packed in cases of the invaluable bamboo. Walter had one evening, for his amusement, cut out a fork of bamboo for Alice, and his example had been followed by the rest of the party. The bamboo likewise made very fair dinner-knives; and he had contrived some spoons by putting a piece of wood at one end—though, seeing they had as yet no soup for dinner, they were not of much use.

"So we must leave all these luxuries and conveniences of life for the wild bush," said Walter, with a pretended sigh.   " Well, well, we shall enjoy them so much the more when we come back again."

 " We are not likely to be long absent from home," observed Mr. Shobbrok.   " If we find that we are on the mainland, we will certainly not venture further into the interior.   As far as my recollection serves me, there are only small islands off the coast; and I am inclined to the opinion that we are on one of these, —in which case we shall speedily return."

" I trust so, for I have no wish to fall in with the inhabitants, who are sure to be savages, and will probably treat us as enemies," observed the doctor.

" But, Mr. Shobbrok," said Walter, " suppose we get back safely, when do you propose altering the boat, so that we may commence our voyage to Sydney ?"

" Immediately on our return,—if, as I expect, we shall be able on our expedition to discover spots where we can obtain a more ample supply of game than we have found in this neighbourhood."

" I shall indeed be very thankful," said Alice, with a sigh ; " for though I am very happy here, I long to see papa again ; and I cannot help thinking that he is safe at Sydney by this time."

This conversation took place at breakfast.   As soon as it was over the whole of the party got into marching order.   The doctor and Dan went first to explore; the mate, with Alice and Walter, followed next; and Nub brought up the rear.   It was agreed that, should any Indians or human habitations be seen, the doctor and Dan were to fall back on the rest of the party; when, as the safest course, they would all quickly retreat rather than run the risk of a collision. Dan was well adapted for the task he had undertaken. Active as a monkey, lithe as a snake, and possessed of a keen pair of eyes, he made his way among the bushes, looking carefully ahead before he exposed himself in any open space. The doctor kept at a short distance behind him, generally in sight of the rest of the party, so that he could make a sign to them should he receive a warning signal from Dan.

They took the way to the stream, over which the mate carried Alice on his shoulders. They then continued along its banks, till the dense foliage compelled them to turn aside and proceed towards the sea-shore. Dan carried an axe, which he had to use occasionally in cutting his way through the underwood; but the mate had charged him to avoid doing so as much as possible, as, should there be natives in the neighbourhood, they would be more likely to discover their traces and follow them up. Fortunately the underwood was perfectly free from thorns, or they would have had their clothes torn to shreds, even had they been able to penetrate it. It was generally of a reed or grass-like nature, so that they could push it aside or trample it down; and under the more lofty trees the ground was often for a considerable distance completely open, when they made more rapid progress. They seldom, however, went far from the sea-shore ; but in many places they found walking on it very difficult, from the softness of the sand, or from its rugged and rocky nature. Besides this, they were there exposed to the full heat of the sun; while by keeping inland they were sheltered from its scorching rays by the wide-spreading tops of the lofty trees. Now and then, when the beach presented a long stretch of hard sand, they were tempted to go down to it, but were soon glad to return to the shelter of the woods.

As they advanced, the beach trended more and more to the west, and the mate's opinion that they were on an island became fully confirmed. At noon they sat down to rest and dine in a shady spot with the sea in view, Dan having first gone out some distance ahead to ascertain whether any native village was in sight.

"All right!" he exclaimed as he returned, flourishing his stick. "As far as my eyes can see, there is no other living being anywhere on the island ; and we would be after adding a fine counthry to the possessions of England, if we had but the British flag to hoist to the top of a tall pole, and take possession of it in the name of King George." Dan was a loyal Irishman, and there were many such in his day.

"We may take possession of the island, though we should find it a different matter to keep it should any one choose to dispute our right," said the mate.

EXPLORING THE ISLAND.

"However, when we have finished our survey, we
will think about the matter; and if we get to Sydney,
we will petition the governor to follow up your suggestion, Dan. At present, we must get our dinner
ready."

Till Dan's return they had refrained from lighting
a fire; but wood having been collected, a light was set
to it, and their smoked fish and iguana flesh were put
before it to cook. They were thankful that they had
brought water, as not a rivulet or pool had they come
to, and they would otherwise have suffered greatly.

They had just finished their meal, and were still
sitting, no one speaking, as they all felt somewhat
tired, when Walter, hearing a whistle or chirp close
behind him, turned his head and saw standing not far
off a large bird of dark plumage,—or rather with
feathers, for he saw no wings,—with a helmet-like protuberance at the top of its head resembling mother-
of-pearl darkened with black-lead. It had enormous
feet and legs of a pale ash colour; the loose skin of
its neck was coloured with an iridescent hue of bluish-
purple, pink, and green; the body being of a rufous
tinge, but of a purple-black about the neck and breast.
The bird stood its ground boldly, not in the slightest
degree alarmed at the appearance of the strangers, as
it eyed them with a look of intense curiosity. Now
it poked forward its head, and advanced a little;
now it stood up, raising its head to the ordinary

height of a man; now it sank down again, till its back did not appear more than three feet from the ground. Though strange-looking, there was nothing ferocious in its aspect; on the contrary, it appeared to have come simply to have a look at the intruders on its domain.

"Well, you are an extraordinary creature!" exclaimed Walter. His remark made the rest of the party turn their heads, when Nub and Dan started up with the intention of catching the bird.

"Ho! ho! is that your game, my lads?" the strange creature seemed to say, as it struck out alternately in front with both its feet, sending the black and the Irishman sprawling on their backs to a considerable distance—happily not breaking their limbs, which, from the apparent strength of its legs, it might very easily have done. It then whisked round, and rushed off with a curious action at a great rate through the forest, leaping over fallen trees and all other impediments in its way in a manner which would have made it a hard matter for the best steeple-chase rider in all Ireland to follow it. Dan and Nub, picking themselves up again, attempted, along with the doctor, to catch it, but they were soon left far behind. At length returning, they threw themselves on the ground panting and blowing.

"I would have given fifty pounds to have got hold of that creature!" exclaimed the doctor. "I have never seen anything like it before.   I have heard that there are similar wingless birds in New Zealand; but as no Englishman has ever caught sight of one, I was inclined to doubt the fact."

The bird seen by the party was a species of cassowary, which is found in Java and other East India islands.   Several specimens have long since been brought to England from the island of New Britain, the natives of which call it the "mooruk," and hold it in some degree sacred.   When they are found very young, they are brought up as pets, and become thoroughly domesticated, exhibiting the most perfect confidence and a wonderfully curious disposition.

Dan and the doctor had both started up with their bows; Nub had taken his, but when the mooruk kicked him it had been sent flying out of his hand, and before he could recover it the bird had got to such a distance that his arrow would have glanced harmlessly off its thick feathers, had he attempted to shoot.   Dan was excessively vexed at having let the bird escape.

"Shure, now, if we had thought of throwing a noose over its head, we might have caught the baste; and it would have given us as many dinners as a good-sized sheep!" he exclaimed.

"Not for five hundred pounds would I have allowed it to have been killed!" cried the doctor.   "If we could have taken it to England, it would have been of inestimable value, and would have made ample amends for all the dangers and hardships we have gone through."

"Well, well, doctor, I don't know that the owners of the *Champion* would be exactly of your opinion, any more than the rest of us," observed the mate, laughing; "but perhaps we may find some other curious creature before long to recompense you for your loss. It's time, however, to be on the tramp. I should like to ascertain before dark how far we are from the mainland; for that we are on an island I feel confident."

The explorers accordingly once more got into motion. As they advanced, they found the sun still shining down on the shore, a proof that they were making a westerly course, and as it sank in the sky they saw that it almost faced them.

"I have no longer any doubt about the matter," observed the mate. "See yonder distant line of blue land which runs nearly due north and south. We have evidently almost reached the extreme western end of the island; and I believe that we shall have no difficulty in getting back along the southern shore by to-morrow evening. We will go on a mile or two further, and then make preparations for encamping. We must provide proper accommodation for our little lady here; and we shall want daylight in which to build our hut, and to collect firewood."

The party continued on much as before, and though,

as a precautionary measure, Dan still went ahead to scout, on the possibility of meeting with Indians, they had no longer much apprehension on the subject. At length they reached an open spot close to the sea-shore, though somewhat raised above it, well suited for an encampment. They accordingly resolved to remain there for the night. Tall trees rose on either side and behind them, with a sandy beach in front; beneath was a line of low rocky cliffs, which formed a bulwark to the land. A wide channel ran between them and the mainland, which could be dimly seen in the distance.

All hands immediately set to work : the mate, doctor, and Walter to build a substantial hut for Alice; and Nub and Dan to collect firewood for cooking their evening meal. Alice was not idle. She employed herself in gathering leaves and dry grass to form her bed, which, at the doctor's suggestion, was made with a layer of twigs and small branches, the leaves being thickly strewed on the top of them.

"I wish that, instead of taking so much pains about me, you would arrange some better accommodation for yourselves than you seem to think of doing," she said. "I feel as if I was very selfish, in allowing you to take all this trouble about me."

"You require to be more carefully attended to than we do," answered the doctor. "You are more delicately constituted than we are, and though your spirit might sustain you, you would suffer more from exposure than we should."

The doctor's arguments quieted Alice's scruples; so a small hut was formed for her, with a thick roof of palm leaves tied down with the vines they had before found so useful. The rest of the party formed their sleeping-places of twigs and small boughs, which Walter declared made as good beds as any sailors need require. By the time these arrangements were finished supper was ready, and they sat down to their repast with thoroughly good appetites.

"I am thankful that we came, though I was rather doubtful at first about making the journey," observed the mate. "It has shown us that we are on a small island; and also that, to a certainty, it is uninhabited, so that we need not be compelled to proceed on our voyage till the favourable season comes round. If we were to go to sea now we should very likely encounter heavy gales, which would sorely try our little craft, even though she might be enlarged and strengthened to the utmost of our power. In the meantime, we shall have enough to do in preparing provisions for the voyage, and we need have no fear of starving while we remain."

"I thought that we were going to sail as soon as the boat could be got ready," observed Alice in a tone of disappointment.

"So we will, Miss Alice," said the mate; "but it

will take us many weeks to get her ready, with the limited number of tools and the scanty materials we possess. As we have no saw, we must split the planks; and every plank will have to be brought down to the required thickness with our single axe or our knives; and we shall have to cut out the ribs in the same way. Patience and perseverance can alone enable us to overcome the difficulties before us."

"Well, I am ready to do my best," said Walter; "and perhaps our raft may be cast on shore, and that will help us."

While they were talking, the gloom of night was coming on; but the fire cast a cheerful blaze, lighting up the trunks of the tall trees around them, shedding a glare over the yellow sand, and tinging the thin white line of foam which rolled over it, now running up some way, now receding with a measured, hissing sound, scarcely amounting to a roar.

Nub, who was sitting nearest the sea, had been looking out across the sand. Suddenly he exclaimed, "I see someting. Hist! hist! I know what it is. Come along, Dan; we will catch it." Saying this, he started up, followed by Dan. "You go on one side, I go on de oder, and den we run as fast as our legs can carry us," he cried to his companion.

They were soon scampering along over the sand, at some distance apart from each other. Not far from the water they again united, by which time the rest of the party had got up, and were proceeding in the same direction. They could just make them out engaged apparently in a desperate struggle with a dark object; and shortly afterwards they heard Dan's Irish shouts of "Hurrah! hurrah! Erin go bragh!" and Nub exclaiming, "We got one big turtle. Come, Massa Shobbrok,—come, Massa Lawrie, and drag him up. We get fine food for supper."

The mate had brought several pieces of rope, which were fastened round the fins of the turtle, and the poor creature was dragged on its back up to the encampment. The doctor was eager to cut it up; but the mate suggested that it would be better to let it remain alive till the morning, that they might be able to carry some of the meat home with them. "At all events, we may hope, as this turtle has come to the shore, that others may also visit it, and afford us an abundant supply of wholesome food," he observed.

The turtle cannot move when turned on its back, but as a further security it was tethered by the two fore paws to a stick stuck in the ground near the fire.

As all the party were tired, they did not sit up late; but soon lay down in their respective bed-places, with a few boughs stuck in the ground to shelter their heads. They had not been long asleep when they were all aroused by a terrific peal of thunder, and looking up, they saw that the sky, which had been glittering with countless stars when they went to sleep, was now obscured by dark masses of clouds rushing across it. Vivid flashes of lightning illumined the air, now darting across the ocean, now playing round the topmost boughs of the trees; while the wind began to blow with great violence, increasing every instant, and sending the leaves and twigs flying around them, sometimes tearing off huge branches, and even breaking the stout stems in two, or hurling whole trees to the ground. Alice was sheltered in her hut; the mate did not at first like to propose that she should leave it, but he watched with great anxiety the tree-tops bending. At last he felt that it would be wrong for them any longer to run the risk of being crushed by a falling tree, or being injured by the lightning which ever and anon played around the trees near them.

"We shall be safer under yonder rocks than here," he said; "although our little lady will, I fear, soon be drenched to the skin."

The doctor agreed with him. "And the sooner we are off the better," he added. The mate, therefore, called to Alice, and, accompanied by Walter and the rest of the party, hurried down to a high rock which overhung the beach, where a hollow at the bottom of it afforded some protection from the storm. Scarcely had they left their encampment when a tremendous crash was heard; and Walter, looking back, saw that a tall tree had fallen nearly over the spot where they had been sitting, and directly on Alice's hut. Most mercifully had they been preserved; a moment later, and his dear little sister must have been crushed to death. They all sat down in the cave, with Alice in the midst of them—by which means they managed to shield her from the rain, which came pouring down in torrents—and they could hear the water rushing over the ground like a mill-sluice. Looking out sea-ward, they saw the waves, foam-crested, rolling in large billows across the channel; but, happily, as they were on the lee side of the island, the surf did not reach them, though it sometimes came hissing up to within twenty feet of where they were sitting. The question was, whether the tide was rising. If it was, too probably they might be driven from their retreat, and be compelled to retire back to the high ground, where they would be again exposed to the danger of falling trees. They anxiously watched the foaming waters which thundered and dashed on the projecting rocks, and, as the seas came rolling round from the weather side, sent the white foam high into the air, glittering brightly amid the darkness during the repeated flashes of vivid lightning which darted from the clouds.

"What should we have done had we been at sea!" exclaimed Alice.

"I tink we all go to de bottom," observed Nub. "Bery glad we here."

"We may all be very thankful that we are here," said the mate. "I dreaded bad weather when I first thought of continuing our voyage in the boat, but I hope that we may not be exposed to such a gale as is now raging. As far as I can judge from the look of things, the present gale is as heavy as any we are likely to encounter."

They sat watching the surf as it rolled up over the smooth sand. Nearer and nearer it came. The mate had ascertained that there was a secure retreat to the high ground, or he would not have ventured to remain so long. He held Alice securely in his arms, as, should the surf come higher up than before,—not unfrequently the case during a storm,—she would be safe from the risk of being swept away, or from the lesser danger of being wetted through. Alice had witnessed two or three thunderstorms at sea, but this surpassed them all. Crash succeeded crash with fearful rapidity. The lightning often showed objects around as clearly as at noonday, and the next moment all was inky darkness. But few words were exchanged among the party, for who could speak at such a fearful time?

"De sea come nearer still, Massa Shobbrok," said Nub at length, as he darted forward a few paces to ascertain how far the surf had reached.

"Shove in your stick, Nub; and if the water comes a foot beyond it, we must lift our anchor and risk the falling trees," said the mate.

Nub did as he was bid, and then springing back, crouched down again under the rock, with his eyes intently fixed on the stick. Sea after sea came roaring up, but the surf did not get so far as the stick. Another came with a roar very much louder than its predecessors, and Alice felt the mate half rise with her in his arms, while the doctor seized Walter's hand. On came the surf with a roaring hiss, high enough apparently to sweep a strong man off his legs; but it barely reached the stick, and went rushing back again as rapidly as it had advanced.

The mate sank down once more into his seat. "Unless the tide rises higher, we are safer where we are than we should be anywhere else," he observed.

The tide apparently was not rising, for though the surf rolled over the sand, the fiat had gone forth, "Thus far shalt thou come, and no further." Still the occasional sound of falling trees, and the crashing of boughs rudely rent off, showed that the storm continued with unabated fury.

Daylight came stealing silently over the tumultuous ocean, still tossing and foaming before them; but there the explorers sat safe from harm, sheltered beneath a rock which no tempest could move. They did not forget to kneel and offer up a morning prayer, returning thanks for their preservation.

"I tink Missie Alice hungry," said Nub at last. "I go and get de fish and de oder tings we leave at de camp."

The mate, though anxious to obtain food and water

especially for Alice, was unwilling to let the black risk his life. But Nub promised that he would keep his eyes open, and rush out of the way should he see any branches likely to fall.

He soon came back, carrying a single small cask of water and one bundle of dried fish.

"All de rest washed away," he exclaimed in a disappointed tone. "De turtle still dere, too, but de tree fall down and crush him. Still I tink I get meat enough for dinner."

This was not satisfactory news; for though they might obtain water after all the rain that had fallen, they could not replace the sago flour; nor would it be satisfactory to eat the raw turtle, and it would be impossible to light a fire unless the sun should shine forth and dry the wood.

"But I brought my case of sago with me. I snatched it up when you called me out of the hut. Here it is," said Alice.

"Then you shall benefit by it," said the mate; "though I am afraid that we have nothing to mix it in at present."

"I find someting," cried Nub; and darting out, he soon returned with a big shell, in which some sago flour was quickly stirred up with water. Though not very palatable, Alice was very glad of it; and the rest of the party satisfied their hunger with the smoked fish.

While the storm lasted they remained under shelter

of the rock, where they were perfectly dry ; and they congratulated themselves that they had no friends waiting for them at home.   As the day drew on, though the wind continued blowing, the clouds broke away ; and the sun coming out, quickly dried the lighter wood, which Nub and Dan soon collected.   A fire was lighted under the rock by the side of the cave.   They then brought down a portion of the turtle and roasted it. Though not particularly well done, it was wholesome food, and Alice was glad to take some of it.   The tempest now somewhat abated, and she and Walter were able to take some exercise under shelter of the rock.

Another night was spent in the cave, one of the party being on the watch lest the tide should unexpectedly rise and sweep over them.   However, the water did not reach even so far as on the previous night ; and they all awoke much refreshed, and ready to continue their journey.   More of the turtle was first cooked, to serve them for breakfast, and to afford them another meal should they not meet with any game on their way.   They determined rather to continue their journey round the island than to go back the road they had come.   Just before starting, Nub and Dan made another search near the encampment, and were fortunate enough to find a second cask of water and a case of flour, so that they had now no fear of starvation.

As they proceeded along the western coast, they found the country generally much flatter than on the other side. In some parts near the coast it consisted of a sandy plain free from trees, partly barren and partly covered with long wavy grass. By keeping close to the higher ground, they were able to cut off a considerable point, and soon found themselves with their faces eastward. They were also fortunate enough to come upon a stream, which, flowing down from the central hill, lost itself in the plain. It enabled them fully to quench the thirst from which they were suffering.

Soon after they had crossed the stream, Dan, who had gone ahead, came hurrying back. "Advance aisy now," he exclaimed in a low voice. "There's something worth seeing, and maybe worth getting too. Just as I was creeping along, not two hundred yards ahead, what should I see before me but a score of big birds all dancing and jigging away together, for all the world as if they were at a wake or some sort of merrymaking. They were all so busy that none of them saw me, and I hurried back, lest you should come upon them suddenly and frighten them away."

Warned by Dan, the party advanced cautiously, hiding themselves among the tall grass. He led them to a spot slightly elevated above the plain; and peering forth from their hiding-place, they caught sight of a number of large birds, apparently employed as Dan had described. They soon saw, however, that the birds had some object in their movements. They formed a circle, with a mound in the centre, towards which they were busily removing the earth with their feet, throwing it up behind them towards the centre. When they reached a certain point, they turned round, and walked away with a steady pace to recommence the same process.

Nub, without saying anything, had stolen away, carrying a long pole with a noose fixed at the end of it. No one noticed his absence till he was seen creeping along the ground, with his head scarcely raised above it, and his stick in advance. The birds (which were about the size of turkeys, their heads bare, and their necks ornamented with large frills of feathers), not descrying the approach of an enemy, continued their labours, and had already produced a mound two feet in height and a dozen or more yards in circumference. It was evident, from the way they worked, and the quantity of earth thrown up at each movement, that they had remarkably strong legs and claws. Walter doubted much whether Nub would succeed in catching one; and so got ready an arrow to shoot, in case they should, on discovering the black, take to flight, and pass near them, as he thought it probable they would do.

Sometimes Nub lay perfectly still; then again he crept forward, shoving his noose carefully along the ground till it got very near the outer circle, to which the birds advanced before beginning to kick up the soil. At length reaching the last tuft of grass which

MOUND·MAKERS AT WORK

would assist in concealing him, he shoved forward his pole to its utmost extent. Back came one of the birds, and Walter saw that it had actually passed the noose; then round it turned and began energetically kicking away, not noticing the trap laid in its path. Presently it stepped into the very middle of the noose, when Nub by a violent jerk drew it tight, and starting up, rushed away, dragging the astonished bird after him. The rest looked about for a moment, very much surprised at the unusual movements of their companion; but its cries and the appearance of the black soon told them what had happened, when with loud, croaking sounds they set off, and rushed towards the very spot where the party lay hid, evidently intending to fly into the neighbouring trees for shelter. As they came close, Walter started up, bow in hand, and instantly shot at the nearest bird; but, to his great disappointment, he missed. The doctor was equally well prepared; and shooting with steady aim, down came a bird close to his feet, when, in spite of its struggles and the fierce way it defended itself with its beak, it was quickly captured. Dan managed to let fly an arrow; but missing, he immediately gave chase to the rest, several of which, trusting to their feet rather than to their wings, rushed by him, and went scuttling away at a rapid rate amid the brushwood.

"Arrah, now," he exclaimed, as he came back, "they all vanished like imps just in one moment, before I could get hold even of the tail of one of them."

However, the two birds which had been killed by Nub and the doctor were of great value. The latter said that he believed they were a species of "brush-turkey," often found in New South Wales, and that their flesh was excellent.

On examining the mound, they discovered several eggs buried deep down in it, leaving them in no doubt as to the purpose for which it was made by the birds, —namely, that of hatching their young. Half-a-dozen fine eggs were secured, and Dan and Nub, hanging the turkeys on a pole, carried them along in triumph between them.

As the party had still a long day's march before them, they pushed on without stopping, the doctor and the mate insisting on carrying Alice between them. She declared that she did not feel at all tired ; however, as they were anxious to reach home if possible that night, they would not listen to her expostulations. In reality, she was very thankful to be conveyed in so comfortable a manner.

Just before dark they caught sight of their harbour. The house was standing,—a proof of the sailor-like way in which it had been constructed ; but when they looked for the boat, which had been hauled up on shore, out of reach of the sea, as they conceived, she was nowhere to be seen.

CHAPTER XV.

THE first impulse of all the party was to rush along the shore of the harbour in search of the boat. Their worst fears were quickly realized. Fragments of the wreck lay scattered along the beach, giving certain evidence of her fate. The sea, aroused by the gale, which struck directly on the coast, had rushed up the harbour; and the water rising much above its usual height, had floated the boat and then dashed her to pieces on the rocks.

Alice, giving way to despair, wrung her hands. "Oh, poor papa!" she exclaimed; "we shall never be able to go in search of him, and he will think that we are all lost."

Walter felt very much as Alice did, but after being silent for some time, he took her arm and said, " Remember, our father always told us to trust in God; and I am sure we ought to do so, and must do so, if we would not live in constant anxiety and fear. He will guide us and direct us, and find a way for us to escape."

"I know that. I was very weak and wrong to say what I did; but it seems so impossible now that we shall ever get home, that I cannot help it," answered Alice.

"Perhaps it is the very best thing that could have happened to us," said Walter; "and I am sure of it, as God ordered that it should be so," he added.

In the meantime the rest of the party were giving vent to feelings of dismay and sorrow at what had happened, till Nub made a remark very similar to Walter's.

"You are right, Nub," said the mate. "I always doubted the prudence of putting to sea in that boat. I know well that God could, if He chose, have enabled us to reach Sydney in her; but we have no business to run risks which our sense and experience tell us are very great: and it's my belief that had a storm of half the violence of that which has passed over this island overtaken us, we should have foundered. We must now, like wise men, make the best of our position. The first thing we have to do is to see what damage our house has suffered, and to repair it. We must then set to work to collect provisions. After that, I tell you what we must do: we must establish a look-out place on the high point at the south side of our harbour, from whence we can obtain a wide range over the ocean, and signal to any vessel which may heave in sight. There is every reason to hope that one may come near us some day or other; and we have a much better chance of getting off from an outlying island, like this one, than we should have enjoyed had we landed on the mainland, or on any dangerous cluster surrounded by reefs. So, my friends, you see we have plenty to do to keep our minds from dwelling on our misfortune; and I have good reason to believe that help will come in time."

The mate's remarks restored cheerfulness to all the party, who no longer spoke of the loss of the boat as an unmitigated misfortune.

"We must depend on the land, however, for supplying us with provisions, as we cannot go out fishing," observed the doctor.

"Not so sure of dat, sir," said Nub. "We build a canoe, which go out quite far enough to catch fish. No bery difficult job, I tink."

"You are right, Nub," said the mate; "and we will put her in hand as soon as our look-out station is established."

"Capital!" exclaimed Walter. "That is the very thing I thought of doing, for I have very often fancied how delightful it would be to 'paddle my own canoe.'"

On visiting the house, the settlers found that the water had penetrated in all directions, and that the wind had torn away part of the verandah, as well as the roof, and blown down their safe. Bamboo canes had therefore to be cut and palm leaves collected; and by the evening of the next day all was set to rights, and Alice and Walter took possession of their snug little cabins.

A tall tree, suitable for a flagstaff, was found and cut down. It took some time to fit the rigging to it; and as it was formed of creeping vines, the mate acknowledged that it had not a very ship-shape appearance. It was set up on the highest part of the point, and a flag manufactured with the mate and Nub's red handkerchiefs and the linings of the jackets of all the party. (Alice wanted to contribute a portion of her dress, but this was not accepted.) The flag even then was not of sufficient size to be seen at any great distance.

"We ought to be able to manufacture a material to answer instead of bunting," observed the doctor; "I cannot help thinking that it can be done."

"Of course it can," said the mate. "We should deserve to be left here for ever if we cannot do that."

After considering the matter for a short time, the doctor constructed a large frame, the size of the intended flag. Then procuring an ample supply of fine fibre, it was soon woven into material scarcely inferior to bunting. It had, however, to be coloured.

Here, again, the doctor's science was of use. From the trunk of the sandal-wood he produced a fine red dye.

The flag, when finished, presented a large red cross on a white ground. It was hoisted with loud acclamations, and was soon floating in the breeze. At the foot of the flagstaff a substantial hut was next erected, so that one of the party might be there from daybreak to dark—and also at night, when the moon shone brightly; a quantity of faggots was next collected, and a pile got ready at a little distance from the flagstaff, that fire might be set to it should a ship appear during the evening.

The doctor and Dan went out hunting the greater part of each day. They found an ample supply of fruit, which the storm had shaken down; and though some had been attacked by insects or birds, enough remained to supply their wants. They managed generally on each excursion to bring down three or four birds, Dan having by degrees found how to make his bow shoot straight. He one day killed what he took to be a large bat, but on showing it to the doctor, he was highly delighted to find that it was in reality a flying lemur. It had a largely developed membrane, connecting the fore limbs with the others, and the hind limbs with the tail. With this apparatus the animal can fly from one bough to another separated by a wide distance, which it could not possibly reach by a mere leap. Dan caught sight of it as it was making its way through the forest ; but at each flight it reached a bough somewhat lower than the one it had left, till it pitched very near the ground, when, closing the membrane round its body, it ran nimbly up the trunk, its sharp claws enabling it to do so with great ease and speed.   After this Dan killed several smaller animals, the flesh of which was found to be palatable.   Nub, also, who had an especial fondness for turtle, made an excursion in the hope of finding some along the sea-shore.   He brought back the satisfactory report that he had turned a couple, which were waiting to be brought home and eaten ; while he exhibited a dozen eggs which he had discovered in the sand.   He then, accompanied by the doctor and Dan, returned and dragged home the two turtles ; one of which being placed in the shade, and kept constantly covered with wet grass, was preserved alive till required for food.

The sago bags left in the pool had remained undisturbed, with the contents perfectly good.   The doctor, however, made a further supply, as the consumption of it, from the want of farinaceous food, was considerable.

A proper tree having been found for the canoe, it was cut down, and the mate, with Nub and Walter, began to shape it.   They afterwards hollowed it out with fire.   It was somewhat heavy ; but when a weather-board was placed round it, the mate considered that the craft was fit not only to paddle about in their harbour, but to go out to sea in fine weather. Walter having manufactured some more hooks and fish-lines during the evenings, an ample supply of fish was procured.

Thus day after day and week after week went rapidly by, and had not the mate kept careful note of the time, in Robinson Crusoe fashion, by cutting notches on a stick, the settlers would soon have forgotten how long they had been on the island. The Sabbath was duly observed, as far as they had the means. Although they had no Bible, the mate recollected large portions of Scripture which he had learned in his youth; while Walter and Alice knew the Sermon on the Mount and several psalms by heart. The mate was also well acquainted with the subjects of many other parts of Scripture, which every Sunday he explained in simple language to his hearers, while one or more psalms were repeated; and thus they were able to keep, if not to the form, at all events to the spirit of a Sabbath service.

They had many causes for thankfulness. Notwithstanding the hardships they had gone through, their health was excellent—even Alice never had an hour's illness—while the products of the island and the ocean supplied them with an abundance of wholesome food. Besides, they had plenty of work to keep their minds occupied. Alice, taking a hint from the doctor's frame for forming a flag, contrived a loom, with the assistance of Walter, with which she set diligently to work to manufacture material which would serve as clothing when her own garments were worn out. The doctor also took into consideration various means for replacing their shoes when these should come to pieces,—which his and Dan's already gave signs of doing.

By the mate's calculation they had already been three months on the island; and though a good look-out had been kept from their watch-house during that time, not a sail had appeared in sight. One evening Dan had been keeping the afternoon watch, when Nub, whose turn it was to keep the first watch, went to relieve him. He soon came running back, however, dancing, leaping, and clapping his hands, as if he had gone mad, while he shouted at the top of his voice—

"A sail! a sail! She come dis way."

The doctor was away shooting and botanizing; but the mate and Walter immediately hurried towards the point; while Alice, who had heard Nub's shouts, dropped her work and quickly followed them. They all looked out eagerly in the direction Dan pointed, where, in the north, just rising above the horizon, was seen the white sail of a vessel, lighted up by the rays of the setting sun. The wind came from the point where she was seen, and it was evident that she was standing towards the south; but whether or not she would pass near enough to observe their signal was extremely uncertain. The wind being fresh, sent the stranger rapidly along; and though she was still too far off to see the flag, it was at once hoisted. How the hearts of all the party throbbed with anxiety! Darkness was coming on, and would soon shroud her from sight, and also prevent those on board from seeing the flag.

"We must make our fire blaze up brightly as soon as night falls," said the mate.

"Yes, Massa Shobbrok, we make it blaze, neber fear," said Nub, readjusting the faggots, and shoving in a few handfuls of dry leaves under them.

"If the wind holds, she will be down in time to see our signal," observed the mate.

"Oh, I do hope so," exclaimed Alice. "Is the ship standing towards the shore, do you think?"

"She is certainly not standing away from it," answered the mate; "but I doubt whether the wind will keep up. It has dropped since I came here."

They stood intently watching the sail, too anxious to talk. Already the shades of night were stealing over the ocean. The sun went down, and the vessel's white canvas changed to an inky hue. Still the mate could discern her, and he declared that she was a brigantine or a square-topsail schooner. Gradually, however, the wind dropped, and the ocean assumed a glass-like appearance. There could be little doubt that by this time the stranger was becalmed. But darkness now came on, and completely shut her out from sight.

The mate having struck a light, the fire soon blazed up brightly. "Put on more faggots, Nub," he cried. "She may stand nearer the shore if the breeze gets up again; but she is as likely to stand away from us, and we may not have so good an opportunity of being seen as now."

Walter ran off to a distance, so as to be out of the glare of the fire, and peered with all his might into the darkness; but no vessel could he see, and he began to fear that she must, as the mate had thought probable, have stood away from the land. His heart fell, but he did not like to tell Alice.

All of them were still too anxious to leave the spot. They were at length joined by the doctor, who surmised where they had gone from seeing the glare of the fire in the distance. The mate advised Alice and Walter to go back to the house; but they both declared that they should not sleep a wink, and would much rather remain where they were. "Perhaps the fire may be seen, and a boat sent on shore from the vessel to ascertain the cause of it," said Walter.

"She is too far off, I suspect, for the fire to be seen," answered the mate. "We must have patience. Daylight will come at last, and the matter will then be settled."

"But suppose she has sailed away," said Walter.

"Oh, don't think of such a dreadful thing," cried Alice.

"If she has, we must have patience still," said the mate. "We talk a good deal about putting our trust in God; this is an occasion which will show whether our trust is real. We are *always* to trust Him."

"So I try to do," said Alice. "I will not doubt again that He will order all things for the best."

"Well, my little girl, you must take my advice, and go back to the house with your brother. Your staying here won't bring the vessel nearer; and I will send for you at daybreak should she be seen."

The doctor, approving of the mate's advice, accompanied Walter and Alice, and promised to stay in the house with them; while the mate, Nub, and Dan remained at the station to keep the fire burning. Alice thought that she should not go to sleep; but she did, notwithstanding, and afterwards confessed that she dreamed all sorts of delightful dreams—and, what was not altogether wonderful, some of them came perfectly true.

The light was streaming through the chinks in her shutters, when she was awakened by Nub shouting out, "De vessel in sight! de vessel in sight!" Walter was so fast asleep that she had to call him, and she was ready to leave her room as soon as he was. The doctor had waited for them, and all three followed Nub, who had run back to the flagstaff.

A light breeze was floating out the flag, and filling the sails of a small schooner, which came gliding on towards the mouth of their harbour. When at about a mile distant she hove-to, and a boat was launched from her deck, and, impelled by four lusty rowers, rapidly approached the shore.

The mate watched her eagerly. "She is a whale-boat," he exclaimed; "and I cannot help thinking that I have seen her and her crew before, as well as the man standing up and steering with an oar. Alice, —Walter, can you guess who that man is?"

"Yes! yes!" exclaimed Walter; "I know his attitude. Alice, it is our father!"

Alice did not faint, but she cried for joy. The mate waved with his hand, pointing to the entrance of the harbour; and then they all hurried down, and along the shore to the nearest spot where the boat could safely put in. The doctor and Walter had to support Alice; while Nub, frantic with joy, eagerly rushed on ahead.

The boat had hardly reached the rocks when the father recognized his children, and in a few minutes he had sprung on shore and clasped them in his arms. Neither could speak for some minutes. He then shook the mate and the doctor warmly by the hand; while Nub and Dan were exchanging greetings with the crew, and learning something about each other's adventures. The captain then accompanied the party to the house, and on the way they briefly told him what they had gone through. He also had a long story to tell. He was much pleased with the appearance of their house, and expressed his deep gratitude to the faithful men who had so carefully watched over his children. On seeing the pile of sandal-wood, with the nature of which he was well acquainted, he remarked that it was of considerable value, and although he could carry but a small portion of it at present, it would be well worth while to send a vessel back for a cargo. As he had several people on board the small schooner, he was anxious to continue the voyage to Sydney—to which port he was bound—without delay. He therefore took off his children, with the doctor, Nub, and Dan; while the mate remained to ship the provisions they had in store,—which the captain said would be very welcome,—as well as a small quantity of sandal-wood.

By noon the whole party had embarked, and the little schooner, under all sail, was standing on her course for Sydney.

"She's a strange-looking craft this of yours, captain," observed the mate, as he stepped on board.

"Not more strange than the way in which she was built," answered Captain Tredeagle.

"O father, that's what Alice and I want so much to hear about!" exclaimed Walter.

The captain, however, had no leisure to satisfy his

children's curiosity till they were seated at tea in the cabin. They had in the meantime recognized many of their old shipmates, besides whom there were several strangers on board.

Alice having resumed her old place at the table, and poured out tea for those assembled, the captain began the narrative of his adventures :—

" You may imagine my agony of mind, when I reached the neighbourhood of the spot where I had left the ship, and found only a few blackened pieces of wreck, which too surely told me what had happened. Still I hoped that some, if not all, had escaped, and that I should be picked up ; so I searched all round. But the necessity of making land where we could obtain some provisions and water, compelled me to direct our course towards the nearest island I knew of. A heavy gale coming on, severely tried the boat, and we were almost despairing of reaching a place of shelter, when we caught sight of a small island, and steered towards it. We were going round to the side on which I expected to land with least danger, when I made out a vessel on a reef at some distance from the shore. I was able to approach her. As I did so I was hailed by a voice I knew, and I discovered that she was the prize we had taken, and which had afterwards been driven on shore. The masts were gone, and the vessel was evidently a complete wreck. Some of the people were clinging to the bowsprit, and waving frantically to me. In a short

time, the wind having fallen still more, I was able to
board her; when I found that many of the French crew
had attempted to escape and had been lost, and that
those on the bowsprit were the only survivors. Happily,
the hull of the vessel had not suffered so much as I
had feared, for though she was bilged, and her bulwarks
and boats had been washed away, the greater part of
her cargo and stores were uninjured. I therefore at
once set all hands to work to build a raft, on which we
might land them. The weather holding fine, we got
everything of value on shore; but as the island was
utterly barren, I saw that before long we should be
reduced to starvation. I therefore at once determined
to build a vessel from the wreck. Fortunately, the brig
had a fresh suit of sails, and a good deal of the rigging
was still clinging to her. The French carpenter and one
of his crew had been among the saved, and I had two
of my carpenters; so, without loss of time, we pulled
the wreck to pieces, and set up a new vessel on the
stocks. She was launched but a week ago; and we
were steering a course for Sydney, when we were
driven back by a strong southerly gale. We thought
it a great misfortune, as our provisions were running
short; but it has proved to me indeed a happy occurrence."

"And *we* thought, when our boat was wrecked,
that it was a great misfortune," exclaimed Walter;
"but now we see that it was ordered for the best: for

had we sailed away, we might have been lost; or had we reached Sydney, we should very likely have gone up the country, and have been a long time before we heard of you."

"Depend upon it, my children, everything is ordered for the best in the affairs of those who trust God," said the captain solemnly.

The little schooner, notwithstanding the way she had been built, reached Sydney in safety; when Captain Tredeagle, weary of the sea, took advantage of the liberal offers made by Government to settlers, and accepted a grant of land—having determined to take up his abode there with his children. Dr. Lawrie followed his example, and settled near him. Mr. Shobbrok took command of the *Little Champion*, as the schooner was called, and made several successful voyages to " Refuge Island," bringing back on each occasion a valuable cargo of sandal-wood,—half of the profits of which belonged to Captain Tredeagle, and greatly assisted him in his new pursuits. Dan and Nub, though tempted by liberal offers from others, would not desert their old master, but remained with him, and were made his principal overseers.

Mr. Shobbrok afterwards wearying of the sea, also accepted a grant of land, and became as successful a settler as the captain.

Alice and Walter, growing up and marrying, had

estates of their own ; and often at social gatherings they would talk over with old friends their adventures at sea and their residence on " Refuge Island."   But their great delight was to narrate these to their children, and to urge them to put implicit confidence in the love and mercy of Him who guides those who trust Him through darkness and trouble, and ever orders all things for the best.